THE HONORABLE SPY

THE HONORABLE SPY

BY DOUGLAS BROWN

This book is a work of fiction. Though some characters, incidents and dialogue are based on the historical record, the work as a whole is a product of the author's imagination.

Copyright © 2022 by Douglas Brown. All rights reserved.

This book or any portion thereof may not be reproduced or used in any manner whatsoever without the express written permission of the publisher except for the use of brief quotations in a book review.

Visit the author's website at: DouglasBrown-Author.com

First Printing, July 2022
Library of Congress Control Number: 2022910503

ISBN 979-8-9863824-0-1 (paperback)
ISBN 979-8-9863824-1-8 (ebook)

Cover Design: llewellen Designs
Formatter: Dallas Hodge, dalhodge56@gmail.com
Developmental Editor: Rachel Song, Songbird Editing
Book Shepherd: Pamela Gossiaux, BestsellingBookShepherd.com

Published in the United States by Cheetah Publishing, LLC©.
Texas

DEDICATION

To Rachel, my "official" developmental editor,
and Will, my "unofficial" editor.

TABLE OF CONTENTS

Chapter 1: That Day — 1

Chapter 2: The Secret at St. James's Square — 10

Chapter 3: The Tsar's Telegram — 27

Chapter 4: The Reich's Best Interrogator — 31

Chapter 5: Agent Field — 40

Chapter 6: Ruthless Beauty — 47

Chapter 7: Fareweel to England — 55

Chapter 8: A Night at the Opera — 67

Chapter 9: The Trap — 73

Chapter 10: The Agent's Secret — 78

Chapter 11: Stopped at the Border — 91

Chapter 12: Think of Ukraine — 107

Chapter 13: The Plots Thicken — 121

Chapter 14: The Secret Meeting — 142

Chapter 15: Monsieur Beletsky's Ball — 160

Chapter 16: Peter and Paul Fortress — 170

Chapter 17: Suicide or Siberia — 177

Chapter 18: Tirpitz Triumphant	188
Chapter 19: The Alaric Tower	197
Chapter 20: The Unforgiving Minute	206
Chapter 21: The Ritual	220
Epilogue	230
Glossary	232
Historical Note	235
Acknowledgments	240
About the Author	241

CHAPTER 1: THAT DAY

London
May 19, 1905

MacKenzie scarcely breathed, let alone moved. If he so much as flinched, he could expect a Dumdum bullet between his eyes. His own sister would not recognize him then. It felt like a reciprocating engine was pounding against his rib cage where his heart should have been.

He felt the ticklish footfalls of a fly as it crawled over his sunburned leg. He dared not flick it away. A jolt of pain as the pest carved out a small chunk of his flesh. He knew how a wounded gazelle felt surrounded by ravenous hyenas. He had to pray his khaki uniform would blend in with the mud.

A Mauser rifle went off with an ear-splitting crack. A far-off voice yelped—some poor chap who could not brook his thirst any longer had reached for his canteen. He had died for a sip of water, just like the unfortunate beasts who sought a drink from a river in this blistering heat and were dragged to their deaths by crocodiles. The humid air pressed on him like a steam bath, his sweat plastering his face and uniform. The sun mercilessly beamed down from on high. What MacKenzie would not give to be able to kick it down and bring on the night!

"Bless me, Captain MacKenzie. Are you all right?"

MacKenzie jolted and swiveled in his chair. Plaid skirt. It was just Audrey, the secretary. He was back in the office and could breathe again. It was all just a memory, even though the pain in his right side felt real enough. He swallowed hard.

"Aye, fairly."

"You look like you've heard a banshee."

"It's nothing, Audrey."

"Thoughts of that day, sir?"

"Mind your own business!"

Audrey drew back a pace and held up a hand defensively. "I'm sorry, sir. I only meant..."

MacKenzie closed his eyes and clasped his hands together. He sighed, as if blowing off the exhaust of that reciprocating engine in his chest. His heart still raced.

"No, Audrey, I'm the one who should apologize. See to your duties."

"I could decode the message for you, if it's giving you too much trouble."

"I couldn't ask you to do that. It's my job, not yours."

Audrey saluted and returned to her desk. Soon, he heard the reassuring clicks of her typewriter. MacKenzie sighed again.

He had not confirmed or denied that the memories of that day had in fact gotten the better of him. He would never tell her the whole story; whatever she knew, she had gotten from the papers. Still, it was such a stupid thing to go into a panic over. What would his sister say? She had been so proud of her brother becoming an officer after graduating Sandhurst at the age of twenty—just in time for the South African War.

He glanced over the words he had just decoded from Captain Gibson's message again:

> *The castle is officially privately owned, but they have received many shipments of Mausers there...*

Shipments of Mausers. The blasted things had not even been fired. His blood ran cold when he remembered what happened when the Mausers shot Dumdums, those savage hollow-nosed bullets. A man hit by one would resemble a badly cut side of beef more than a human. He had barely recognized what was left of his own brother's face after the poor fellow had taken one through the temple.

He snuck a glance at the clock atop his oaken desk. 4:30 p.m. A little early, but this definitely required a drink.

He fished in his pocket for his flask and secretly snatched a sip of Dewar's. After glancing around, he raised the flask to his lips again and quaffed another mouthful. Almost involuntarily, he tilted the flask for another, but he thought better of it. He had seen too many other Tommies succumb to addiction after that day, and becoming a drunkard seemed about the only way things could get worse. What would his father's parishioners say? Better just to breathe deeply.

As he strove to regain control over his nerves, he fingered the bronze cross suspended from the crimson ribbon at his chest. How had his superiors thought he was worthy of the medal? He certainly did not think he had deserved it.

He could not ponder that now. As cryptographer of the special duties section of MO3 in Britain's Directorate of Military Operations, he needed to give this task his full attention. It was either this desk job or active duty with his Highland regiment, the Black Watch. Much as he loved his regiment, he felt his trauma from that day had rendered him unfit for such duty.

He reopened his pocket-sized codebook and began looking up the numbers he did not already have committed to memory and decrypting the remainder of the message.

> *I have so far been unable to ascertain the purpose of these shipments. A mist of secrecy seems to shroud the castle, and no one in Berlin is willing to mention it even by name. My anarchist contact in the Kaiser's palace flits his eyes in dread if I try to inquire of him about it. I am due to meet with him tomorrow and will send a follow-up report.*

What was the Kaiser of Germany up to? Scaring his subjects witless? Did he have secret police like the Tsar of Russia's Okhrana?

MacKenzie's heart strained as he imagined himself "on the spy" in Berlin instead of Gibson. It would be like the old days, when he had worked as intelligence officer for the Number Five Flying Column in South Africa, with their high-stakes battles of wits. Surely, he could do more out there than he could sitting behind this desk.

His mind imposed reason on him. That day had ruined him for field work forever. He had "Soldier's Heart," as his superior, Colonel Connally, called it, and with it, a propensity to panic.

The Germans carried Mausers. Could he ever face those again? Surely, it was much better for him to remain in a staff position, decoding telegrams for his service to king and country, however boring he might find it.

He finished decoding the report and rose from his chair. The main office, shaped like a square, had four doors, one for each side in orderly symmetry.

The Honorable Spy

The walls were painted in a nondescript, ghostly-gray layer of paint, and the oaken doors similarly lacked ostentation or polish. On the whole, the headquarters looked like a Spartan general's.

MacKenzie knocked on Colonel Connally's door.

"Enter."

MacKenzie stepped in and jumped to a salute with the smartness befitting a British officer. Connally returned it.

"You wish to report?" he asked.

"Aye, sir," MacKenzie said. "Captain Gibson reports some strange activity outside of Berlin. There's a castle that officially belongs to a civilian, but where the Huns are stocking up on Mausers." He stifled a shudder so the colonel could not see. "He can't obtain any information on it as everyone is too frightened to mention it. It sounds like Fontanka 16 in St. Petersburg to me."

Connally grimaced. "Yes, everyone needs secret police these days with these confounded anarchists and their bombs lurking behind every lamppost."

"I just hope those secret police didn't apprehend our anarchist contact in the Neues Palais before Captain Gibson's meeting with him. His report said he would meet with him the next day, so they've already done so, if there was no interference."

"I doubt this is much we need to concern ourselves with if it's the Germans themselves who are scared of it," Connally said. "Internal security, no doubt. Send a missive to Gibson telling him to keep his inquiries discreet and not to risk detection over some crackbrained scheme to infiltrate it. Other than that, all quiet?"

MacKenzie nodded. "So it seems, sir. None of our agents report any trouble with Russia since the Dogger Bank incident has blown over. The Baltic Fleet is almost to Port Arthur, though how much good they'll be if they mistook British fishing trawlers for Japanese torpedo boats, who can say? All indications are that His Majesty truly won the French over, so we dinna need to worry about war from that corner."

"So it all comes down to Germany, as usual." Connally frowned. "Hopefully, Captain Gibson gets good news when he meets with his contact. I'm sure the Kaiser will find a way to put all Europe on tenterhooks before long, though." He pulled out his pocket watch and clucked his tongue. "5:17. We kept you a little late today, MacKenzie."

MacKenzie forced a smile. "That's a sacrifice I'm willing to make for His Majesty, sir." He did not want Connally to know he had been delayed by another flashback.

"Dismissed," Connally said.

MacKenzie jumped to a salute and walked out of the office. Audrey's typewriter clicked like a Maxim machine gun, punctuated with rings as she reached the end of her line and had to "reload." MacKenzie's heart quickened a little as he walked over to her brown wraparound desk. She had her back to him, her attention focused solely on her pale-green typewriter.

"I say, Audrey. I dinna think there was anything so urgent today that you had to stay late over it," MacKenzie said.

Audrey jolted and swiveled her chair all the way around. She scooted her chair such that she was completely between MacKenzie and the typewriter.

"Blimey, Captain MacKenzie. I thought you'd be gone already," she said. "Punctual in, punctual out. As the Duke of Wellington said, 'My rule always was to do the business of the day in the day.' That's you!"

Her brown eyes met MacKenzie's for an instant before she darted them away.

MacKenzie smiled. "I have a feeling you've done the business of the day too and are working on extracurriculars. Let me guess: the Cause again."

She returned his smile and met his gaze. She giggled. "All right, you have me there, sir!"

MacKenzie laid his hand on his cheek as if appalled. "Really, a secretary of the special duties section using government property to print treasonous pamphlets! If the PM should find out..."

Audrey crossed her arms as if offended. "My job is to serve His Majesty's government, and if that entails telling them they're blooming fools to their faces, I'd do it!"

MacKenzie clucked his tongue. "More treason! You ken the government's stance on women's suffrage."

"And I know our stance on the government!" she said, keeping up the masquerade of offense.

"Dinna worry, Audrey. I can keep a secret," MacKenzie said. "I am, after all, in intelligence."

"Thank you, sir." She smiled, causing MacKenzie's heart to flutter.

"You ken, Audrey, I'm about to go to dinner and..." He stopped.

"And?" she said.

He hesitated, then drew himself up. "And I'll expect your full attention to your duty tomorrow."

"Never one to shirk a task, sir!" she said defensively.

MacKenzie's face flushed. "I ken that," he said.

He broke away, stifling a sigh. That had been a near-run thing, and his retreat left something to be desired. This was the closest he had come to asking Audrey to go with him anywhere (though he had thought of many places). He knew he could never do that. What if she said no? Knowing her, she would be at the pamphlets for the rest of the day. Then, every time he saw her, he would be reminded of how he had made a fool of himself. That day had cost him his courage around women just as much as in combat. He wished, though, he could have backed out without insulting her.

MacKenzie left the office and climbed the steps up to ground level. His stomach sickened more with each step.

Mausers! Those confounded Mausers! With the Kaiser dead set on outshining Britain, it was only a matter of time before those Mausers he had read about were pointed at Tommies like him.

He locked the building's door behind him as he stepped into St. James's Square. The friendly May sun still bathed London in light, but it reminded MacKenzie of its harsher mood toward him and his comrades on that day.

He considered his stomach. It felt somewhere between indigestion and seasickness. He did not want to eat feeling like that, but he considered it a duty. He needed strength. Perhaps a visit to Stromboli's was the very thing. It was the best food he could afford.

He made his way north along Regent Street, pausing every now and then to glance about him. He took care that no one made eye contact with him; the eyes were the easiest thing to remember about someone.

On both sides of the street, buildings rose to four or five stories. Jammed together, they resembled cliffs presiding over a river of pavement. Space came at a premium in this crowded city, so the only way to go was up.

He had never really gotten used to the structures crammed as close as herrings in a barrel after the solitary dwellings and small villages he had grown up with in his father's parish in Easter Ross in the Scottish Highlands.

He and his brother had run many a race in the wide-open landscape, but now they would race together no more this side of the New Jerusalem.

And he would certainly never get used to the lavish buildings lining Piccadilly Circus. In the center of the circular road stood the Shaftesbury Memorial Fountain, splashing under the supervision of the winged statue of the Greek god Anteros, his bow in hand. Every inch of these buildings spoke of grandeur and dominion, paid for by the blood of soldiers like MacKenzie.

MacKenzie leaped at the blare of an auto's horn, the sound bouncing off the buildings. A man on a bicycle swerved for cover. A more congenial horse-drawn omnibus clopped, rumbled, and whined in the opposite direction around the circle. MacKenzie veered northeast onto Shaftesbury Avenue.

Four blocks, and the quality of buildings slackened off. The designs appeared less grandiose, the houses not kept at the same pristine level of repair. Farther east, the buildings became positively dilapidated, even dangerous. MacKenzie turned north well before he entered those neighborhoods.

He caught sight of the orange candlelight in Stromboli's window. An awning with bars of green, white, and red that resembled the Italian flag stretched over the doorway. White calligraphy advertised the name of the proprietor on the glass windows, behind which sat a display of cannoli arranged so that they reminded MacKenzie of stands of Lee-Enfield rifles. By now, his boots had become as muddy as an elephant. He would have to polish them when he reached his flat.

He turned into the restaurant, evaluating if he still felt like eating.

A young boy, just old enough to have long trousers and a faint attempt at a beard, stood at the entrance. He was a few inches shorter than MacKenzie, but he carried himself with a posture like a muzzle-loader's ramrod. He wore a brown corduroy blazer with a polka-dot bowtie.

Inside, diners occupied about half the tables, which were clothed in red and white checkers. They chatted quietly. They were frugal middle-classers, not poor like the inhabitants of this part of London. The lad smiled broadly at him.

"Capitano MacKenzie! Not in the mood for haggis tonight?"

MacKenzie forced a smile. "No, Enrico. Just show me to my usual table. It doesn't look occupied."

"Right this way, capitano," he said with a bow. "And what Stromboli masterpiece can we provide tonight?"

"Spaghetti, please."

"Much better than haggis, signore! I tried haggis once—just once. It was the most revolting thing I ever tasted."

"Aye, weel, you have to be born to it, I suppose. Where did you go that you had it?"

"Last summer, I took a trip to the Highlands with the money I had saved. The place was beautiful; the food was rotten. Nothing like home in either case. What wine would you like?"

"I've already had something to drink."

Enrico jumped to a salute that approximated MacKenzie's to Connally. His hand brushed the black hair he had parted to the right. His green eyes darted to MacKenzie's medal for a second's admiration, as always. Enrico dreamed of martial glory. So had MacKenzie—before that day.

MacKenzie's Directorate of Military Operations now had the task of making sure Enrico and the other young lads like him were never called up for a European war. Failing that, it had to make sure the empire stood as prepared as possible. It could not afford a hash like the South African War when fighting against a Great Power like Germany. The British had barely gotten away with their comedy of errors against 40,000 South African Boers; they would stand little chance with a repeat performance against Germany's millions.

A vision flashed across MacKenzie's mind of Enrico in a khaki uniform, then of gray-clad Germans with shouldered Mausers parading down the street right outside. He had to glance out the window to make sure it was not real.

MacKenzie scarcely felt in a state to eat when his plate of pasta arrived.

"Especially good tonight, signore!" Enrico said. He raised his hand to his mouth and kissed his fingertips.

"Thank you, Enrico."

Enrico jumped to another salute and went off to tend to other customers. MacKenzie did not want to disappoint him by leaving the plate half-finished. He choked the food down. When he got up, MacKenzie left Enrico his usual, large tip. A little contribution to his next holiday in Scotland.

MacKenzie used an omnibus to get to his flat in Finsbury. Entering the red-brick building, he ascended the back stairway to the third floor. He checked the slip of paper he had placed in the doorjamb. It remained in place; no one had opened the door while he'd been gone.

He fairly well collapsed into his armchair, his body exhausted from his mind's wrangling. In his prayers that night, he petitioned God for a good report from Gibson. Somehow, though, his mind returned to Colonel Connally's words: "I'm sure the Kaiser will find a way to put all Europe on tenterhooks before long."

CHAPTER 2: THE SECRET AT ST. JAMES'S SQUARE

MacKenzie jolted awake. He looked around like a rabbit caught in a trap before realizing with relief that he still lay in bed in his flat. But all the same, he could not restrain the pounding of his heart. That cursed report had brought on the dreams again. His right side ached afresh.

His hand trembling slightly, he fumbled for a match to light the lamp. The orange glow that soon illuminated the room was a mixed blessing. The scarlet pimpernels on the wallpaper both settled and unsettled him. At least it proved he was not there, but on the other hand, he could not bear the sight of red at the moment.

No sooner had he calmed his heart down than it started racing again in shame. How long did he have to put up with this before he would be due in at the headquarters? He glanced at the clock. 3:00 a.m. Far too early.

He had to do something until 5:00 at least. He was not due in the office until 11:00, but he preferred to stay awake if he was going to have dreams like *that*.

He slid into his slippers and groggily pulled on his crimson robe. Now the red enveloped him. He opened a drawer in his nightstand and withdrew a deck of cards. A red and white floral pattern decorated the back, while the worn edges indicated how many sleepless nights the cards had kept him going.

Wear and tear surrounded him—in the cards, in the wallpaper, and in the sheets. Worst of all was the wear in his uniform. One more thing to be ashamed of.

Sitting down at his table, he dealt the cards out in seven rows for solitaire. Since his heart refused to settle down, he grabbed his bottle of Dewar's that sat on the corner of the table. He poured a shot and gulped it. Barely stopping for breath, he drained another shot before shame filled him again. What would the people back home in Easter Ross have said to his drinking?

He flipped card after card as he lined up the suits for half an hour. His arithmetic skills ensured him victory after victory. As long as he could keep the number-crunching part of his brain occupied, he could draw his focus away from the memories.

The window drapes, closely fastened, kept the dim light of the gas lamps outside at bay. The light outside also had to contend with a shroud of a dense fog, ensuring that MacKenzie's room remained shadowy. He did not particularly care for the dark, but he craved privacy more. Few things unnerved him as much as the feeling of being watched. What if someone was reading reports on what he was doing like he read reports of what others were doing?

He glanced up at the clock again. 4:00 a.m. Maybe there was no reason he couldn't show up early after all. He splashed cold water over his face, shaved, and donned his faded uniform.

It was still dark when he arrived at Vittoria House in St. James's Square. Across the square sat Winchester House with its whitened bricks. MacKenzie spared a passing glance at the balcony atop the building in case any silhouetted figures were watching.

Anyone would have expected MO3, the special duties section of the Directorate of Military Operations, to be in the same building as MO1 and MO2. The secret, however, remained locked away in Vittoria House, built in red brick and white stone dressings to celebrate the British victory at Vittoria over Napoleon's legions in 1813.

MacKenzie made his way up the steps to the porch of Vittoria House. His key opened the lock, but he immediately relocked the door once inside.

What a fortune a burglar could make here, he thought wryly.

He followed the circle of light from his torch as he stepped around display cases and over richly-woven carpets. The house's cover story as an eccentric nobleman's townhome meant that the place had knickknacks lining the shelves like an undisturbed pharaoh's tomb. It was an eclectic collection.

Before long, he reached the rearmost room of the house, where artifacts from the Highlands lined the front wall. He stopped and gazed for a few minutes at the weaponry. In a glass box atop black velvet lay a claymore from the battlefield of Culloden. It had a dark blue, broad blade. It was an elegant weapon, but one capable of the most horrific wounds. The only thing worse were the Dumdum bullets shot from Mausers. MacKenzie shuddered.

The room was vacant aside from any Highland ghosts lingering over their possessions. He reached under the table on which the artifacts lay and pressed a button. He swiftly disappeared behind the red curtain at the back of the case, where he pushed on a panel in the wall. The panel swung to reveal a wooden staircase. Gloomy shadows shrouded the steps, but at the bottom stood a doorway, gleaming with electrical light from behind.

MacKenzie hesitated. Who could possibly be here this time of night?

Feeling his Webley revolver, MacKenzie made his way silently down the steps. His already jumpy mind flitted from awful scenario to awful scenario. Had the secrets of British intelligence fallen into enemy hands?

As he reached the middle step, MacKenzie's stomach churned. MO3's secret agents might be compromised. Would he have to kill?

He flung open the door.

"Blimey!" a woman gasped.

MacKenzie almost seized his Webley, but he recognized the woman in time to stay his hand. She sat at her desk as usual, albeit at a very unusual hour.

"Audrey, what on earth are you doing here this time of night?"

"'Pon my soul, Captain MacKenzie, what are *you* doing here this time of night?" she asked.

"I asked you first. Besides, I outrank you."

Audrey saw the smile on MacKenzie's face and laughed nervously. "In faith, Captain, I stayed up all night working on these blooming pamphlets. It's an idea I've been mulling over for weeks."

"And the colonel won't suspect something when there's another stationery requisition two days after the last one?"

"What he don't know won't hurt him," she said with a wink. "Which one of us fills out those requisitions anyway? And, now, I expect you are here because you had a dream about that day."

MacKenzie's eyes darted away from her gaze. There was no point in denying it. "How did you ken?"

"You show up early and all clammed up, I've noticed, the morning after. This is earlier than I've ever seen you, though."

"My subconscious didn't let me sleep in as late as usual before starting in on me."

"Do you even have anything to do here this time of morning?"

"No."

"Then you can help me. Bundle these copies I've made, and tie them up, if you please." She turned back to the typewriter and was soon feverishly typing away.

MacKenzie marveled that she looked so immaculate after staying up all night working. Her white linen blouse still looked pressed, and the garnet brooch at her throat still remained perfectly centered. He glanced down at her red-and-black plaid skirt below the desk. It was the same one that had reassured him during his panic the previous day.

Her rosy face showed no signs of stress. He wondered if Audrey ever actually did feel stress. Passion, most assuredly, but it always seemed to result in confident eagerness rather than strain.

She had dazzled the directorate ever since the committee had opened the intelligence division to women typists the prior year. She was the only one not secluded behind bars on the top floor of the headquarters across the square under a matronly supervisor.

Confound it! He was staring again!

Many times, he had felt the urge to flirt with Audrey or to ask her to join him at Stromboli's, but he always knew better than that. Last night was the closest he had ever come to it. With Audrey, it was all work or the Cause. Happily for her, she went about it in legal ways as a member of the National Union of Women's Suffrage Societies, or else she never would have gotten the job. But would anyone so dedicated want him when she knew how cowardly he was?

"So, every day I'm quiet, you conclude I've had a nightmare?" he said hesitantly.

She did not turn back to him until the bell rang, signaling the end of her line. "There ain't no other reason, is there? Normally, as is, you're a friendly chap, always ready with a kind word. Then some days you come in here, plop down at the desk, and don't say nothing until you leave."

"It's nothing personal."

"I know," she said softly. "If I'd been through something like that, like as not, I couldn't talk at all. Are you going to get those pamphlets bundled before the colonel sees them?"

How much did she know? He had deliberately concealed everything he could from her. From almost everyone. Maybe she had heard him discussing it with the colonel.

He leaped to his task. Unconsciously, he wanted to atone for any hurt feelings he had caused. Or maybe it was because he had caught himself staring at her.

"I'll tell you, Audrey, even if we never let women vote, they should make an exception for you. You should get points for effort, at least."

Again she finished her line before turning back to him. "Thank you, Captain MacKenzie, but I don't believe in making exceptions in place of rights."

MacKenzie stacked the pamphlets and tied them. He did not know where to stand on the question of women's suffrage. Certainly, he would not mind if Audrey and her constitutional comrades in the National Union of Women's Suffrage Societies could vote, but the idea of some of those fire-breathing radicals in the Women's Social and Political Union determining Members of Parliament...

That was not his job, fortunately. His job was to make sure that women's suffrage and Irish home rule remained the most urgent issues facing the politicians. It seemed that some MPs thought a German invasion would be preferable to women voting and Ireland governing itself, but MacKenzie knew better. If they had been there on that day...

Audrey had just ripped a pamphlet from the typewriter and handed it to MacKenzie when the colonel stepped in. They jumped to salutes.

"Good morning, MacKenzie, Audrey. Hard at work already?"

"Just saving the government, sir," Audrey said.

Connally strode into his office. He closed the door behind him.

"From itself," she muttered to MacKenzie.

MacKenzie laughed softly, lest the colonel should hear him.

He decided to use the time to look over some recent clippings from foreign publications in the library. Once his quota of six foreign newspapers would arrive that morning, he could peruse them for matters of military significance.

He opened the rear door and pulled the string to turn on the light. Long rows of bookshelves with cutting books filled the cramped space. He drew the latest Russian cutting book out and returned to his desk.

The first clipping was propaganda for the war with Japan. It even had the audacity to defend the Baltic Fleet for firing on the British fishing boats at the Dogger Bank!

He unconsciously gnashed his teeth at the Russians. Anything to keep up the Great Game against Britain—that was how his brother had died. Serve the buggers right if the Japanese sank the whole fleet. They'd ken soon enough the outcome of the clash; the Baltic Fleet had almost reached the Sea of Japan.

MacKenzie read for a few more hours until the corporal dressed in a servant's suit dropped off his six newspapers. On top of the newspapers sat an envelope with a Berlin postmark. Knowing it was Captain Gibson's report, MacKenzie opened it first. At the top ran a header: Urgent and Top Secret. MacKenzie produced his codebook and set to work methodically.

> *I met with my anarchist contact this morning who provided me a telegram from the Kaiser to the Tsar on October 27, 1904, together with the code it was written in. It talks of war against Britain if we object to Germany coaling the Baltic Fleet and desires Germany to act in concert with Russia and France, the Dual Alliance.*

MacKenzie dropped his pen. That could not be! He scrutinized each word against the codebook again. It read exactly as he had decoded it the first time. It took only a heartbeat for him to realize the direness of the situation.

With Russia and Japan waging bloody war in the Far East, and Russia's ally France and Japan's ally Britain trying to stay out of it all, Germany might spy an opportunity. It already had alliances with Italy and Austria-Hungary, but what about the other two great powers in Europe?

Rivalling Britain had become the Kaiser of Germany's obsession, and his aggressive actions were always raising the temperature of the diplomatic water closer toward full boil. The directorate had as its chief concern the preparation for another European war.

If such a thing did happen, nothing could be worse than what the telegram implied—Russia pouring troops through Afghanistan into India, the Italians threatening the Suez Canal, and Germany and France hovering to invade the

Isles. Britain's small professional army would never stand a chance against so many conscripts. With Britannia gone, the world would have to pick between German militarism and Russian autocracy.

Urgent and top secret, indeed! This could not wait.

He leaped from his black leather chair, seized the blue stationery with the decoded message, and strode to Colonel Connally's door. He pounded on it with a franticness he regretted as he heard it. He thought he saw Audrey jolt out of the corner of his eye. Connally, however, remained his imperturbable self.

"Enter."

MacKenzie forced himself to stride in coolly. Connally sat at his desk, the lamplight gleaming on the varnish. He still had a telegram on yellow paper in his left hand. MacKenzie jumped to a salute.

Connally glanced up from under his mop of black hair. His lips turned up under his bushy mustache, and his eyes brightened when he saw MacKenzie. As he rose, he put the telegram down and returned the salute. "MacKenzie, my boy! What is it?"

"Very troubling, sir, this report from Captain Gibson."

Connally gestured to the chair across from him. "Sit yourself down."

MacKenzie sat down but remained straight as a ramrod at the edge of the chair.

Connally settled back in his red leather seat. He dropped his head to his chin and stared straight into MacKenzie's eyes.

"Yes?"

MacKenzie hated it when Connally did that. The man scarcely blinked. It made him feel like Connally were giving him his full attention, but it was also unsettling, like Connally could see through every facade.

"As you ken, Gibson's been tasked with monitoring the Kaiser's correspondence through our anarchist contact at the Kaiser's home—the Neues Palais. There's a telegram from the Kaiser to the Tsar suggesting war against us if we object to Germany's coaling the Baltic Fleet on its way to the Pacific to fight the Japanese. He wants to bring France in under the terms of the Dual Alliance. It's dated October 27 of last year, so who kens where they've gone with that?"

Fear flashed across Connally's face. In an instant, his eyes returned to their accustomed, narrow gaze. Connally only ever displayed fear for an instant, even in battle.

"Balderdash!" he scoffed with a sweep of his large hand. "Have you been reading the latest invasion novel too seriously? Back to reality, MacKenzie. Why would Russia cozy up to Germany against us? Which is more valuable to her, the godforsaken steppes, which we could invade from India, or the wheatfields and oil wells of the Ukraine and Caucasus that Germany threatens?"

Connally leaned back slightly in his chair. "She signed an alliance with France fifteen years ago against Germany precisely for that reason. I still remember how shocked we were that the most repressive autocracy in the world would ally with the most liberal republic. *That* should tell you how much she fears Germany."

MacKenzie put his finger on the desk. "But that's just it, sir! Suppose Russia did join Germany out of fear. If she didn't think she could beat Germany, she might join her. Then France would be the one fearing. It'd be Germany, Austria-Hungary, Italy, and Russia allied. Would France really stand against that, or would she cave in and join that bloc against us?"

Connally folded his hands. "Really, MacKenzie, do you think France would ally with Germany while she still wants Alsace-Lorraine back? I don't think you understand how rankled the French soul can get, my boy. They lost that territory because they went to war over an insulting suggestion in a telegram, for pity's sake! It's simply against everyone's interest for Germany to ally with Russia and France."

"I submit, sir, that what you say is completely true if we were dealing with logical, rational statesmen," said MacKenzie. "Instead, we have to consider the Kaiser's pathological envy of our greatness, the Tsar's vacillating indecision, and the Frogs' spinelessness. I dinna think Captain Gibson would have misconstrued the telegram he intercepted."

Connally paused and drummed his fingers on the desk. "What about you? I know the way you feel about the Russians."

MacKenzie's face flushed. "It has nothing to do with that, sir. I wouldn't set my country on the road to war just because of what the Russians did to my family."

During the South African War, a Russian volunteer with the Boers had killed his brother with a Mauser's Dumdum. That war had been a quarrel that MacKenzie regarded as no concern of Russia's. The Russians had snuck support to the Boers simply out of malice toward their imperial rival.

"MacKenzie, this telegram, if we can believe the source, was sent more than six months ago. I think we would know by now if anything had come of it."

Connally leaned back in his chair and put his fingertips together. His eyes darted aimlessly about the small office as he considered MacKenzie's words. For a moment, it seemed as if the colonel would chalk the warning up to MacKenzie's jumpiness.

MacKenzie second-guessed his instincts. Did his concerns arise solely because he had read about Mausers in yesterday's report? He could still see the wounds the Boers inflicted with those German rifles every time he closed his eyes.

Connally was taking too long, so MacKenzie decided to speak. "Sir, I feel compelled to point out that the possibility of all Europe arrayed against us is so horrendous that we ought to take the faintest whiff of it with all deadly seriousness. His Majesty's efforts and our foreign policy have been focused since the South African War on keeping us from war with all of Europe at once. Ask the DMO, sir. General Grierson would definitely want us to investigate anything that might cut us off from France. We must be sure."

Connally nodded slowly, his chin pressing deeper into his chest. "That's true, my boy, that's true. Very well. I want you to coordinate our efforts in Berlin. Insist upon regular reports from Captain Gibson. Agent Field has recently returned from Berlin; we should get his thoughts. Maybe we should send him out again." He paused. "I'm putting you in charge of this. Keep me informed."

MacKenzie jumped to a salute and strode out of the office. He hoped he had not just made a colossal threat out of a simple red herring.

He returned to his desk and withdrew his codebook to compose instructions for Captain Gibson. He checked them over three times before placing the letter in the envelope to give to Audrey.

"Audrey, I'm afraid I'm going to spoil your fun. I need the dossiers on our agents in Germany and Russia. I'm going to see if I can call any of them in on my little matter. I'm going to pull our clippings on Germany and Russia."

Audrey smiled with a curtsy. MacKenzie felt a flutter in his chest.

He opened the rear door again and turned the light on in the library. He withdrew the Dewey decimal catalog and began flipping through it, looking for all the relevant cutouts he could find on Germany and Russia in the past seven months.

With catalog in hand, he strode down the shelves and snatched the desired books, stacking them at the entrance. Soon he had a stack like a ziggurat. It took him several trips to get them all to his desk.

When he got the last of the stack to his desk, Audrey had a whole other stack of files waiting with a cup of coffee. The woman was as efficient as she was passionate. Too bad there could never be anything between them...

As he read the foreign newspaper clippings, he had a hard time focusing. His eyes glided over the lines like they were slippery to his sight. He wanted to read more slowly, for he rarely forgot things he read deliberately, but his anxiety whipped him on like a merciless cabby.

He feared his nerves were robbing him of comprehension. Nothing seemed to indicate that Germany and Russia were reconciling. The Kaiser had recommended that the Baltic Fleet sail to reinforce the remnants of Russia's Pacific Fleet, and the Russians had taken that suggestion. But they'd had no other option once Japan had decimated the ships they needed to defend Port Arthur. That did not evidence any intent to form an alliance.

Germany had forced Russia to remove its retaliatory tariff on German manufactured goods to keep Germany from threatening its western borders. Germany, meanwhile, cranked up its duty on her corn to 78%. Surely that was no sign of trust.

Whatever was going on, the Kaiser and the Tsar had not involved the German and Russian cabinets. Could anything succeed without the approval of the chancellor of Germany and the ministers of Russia?

But surely the Kaiser had this in mind: Britain alone against the Continent again. If Russia signed an alliance with Germany, surely the Frogs would cave in and join them rather than fight every European power east of the Rhine.

Britain would have Japan as its only ally, clear across the world. The small Royal Army could not defend every corner of the empire at once. His Majesty King Edward had tried to prevent this contingency for four years. He had succeeded in reconciling France and Britain, but would the Kaiser's threats prove more persuasive to the Frogs? German militarism or Russian autocracy—the choice was as simple as that.

Time to look at the network. MacKenzie slowly perused the files. No obvious transfers presented themselves. He had set up a network perfectly positioned to detect any military activity in Germany or Russia, and that seemed at least as important as any treaty. A piece of paper was worthless unless the sovereigns decided to act on it. If they did, he would have plenty of warning. He could spare no one from that network to join Gibson at the Neues Palais.

At a quarter to eleven, the door opened, and in stepped a spindly, fair-haired man. He had the first wrinkles of middle age, and he wore dark-rimmed spectacles that resembled owl eyes. His disheveled hair continued the owl analogy as it stuck up like two ear tufts.

The man stopped at MacKenzie's desk, forcing him to look up, then smiled a toothy grin and held out his hand. "Ronnie, how are you?"

"I'm fine, Archie," MacKenzie said as he took the man's hand. "You're late this morning—even for you." He instantly repented the handshake, since Archimedes' hand was stained with dark grease that transferred to his own.

Archimedes laughed sheepishly. "Forgive me! I did some repair work this morning on a personal gadget of mine, not the directorate's. Come with me. I want you to see something. I was about to call it a night when I realized my latest device worked. I stayed late putting on the finishing touches."

He took MacKenzie by the elbow and led him to the door of his work lab. He opened the door to reveal a prime example of creation out of chaos.

Blueprints lay scattered everywhere, hanging from desks or draped over the backs of chairs. Scraps of metal and wood were strewn amid piles of sawdust. Contraptions only half-finished sat abandoned in corners. Archimedes had had his share of lectures from Connally on his disorderliness, but this office never remained tidy for long.

Archimedes made his way around a desk and purposely snatched something up from his worktable. "My proudest invention yet. Every time, I make them smaller."

In his palm, he held a small device that looked like a thin brass disc with the crisscrossing of a microphone on top of another thicker, wider brass disc. In all, it measured only a few centimeters in diameter and a centimeter and a half in height.

"This is a wireless listening device. We'll call it a 'bug' since it's literally a fly on the wall. Remove this backing here, and there's adhesive for you to place this somewhere, or you can nail it into a wall or desk too. It has a range of twenty-five hundred yards. No one would think to look for this, but you could listen in with your ring. I trust yours is still in good condition."

"I guard it with my life."

Archimedes laughed. "Yes, well, make sure you do if you ever go out into the field. You should see the kinds of broken devices some agents bring back and expect me to fix! 'All the King's horses and all the King's men,' and all that. Dear me!" He sighed. "Well, that's well and good. Gibson broke his, and I haven't had a chance to fix it yet. He's still sending paper reports, isn't he?"

MacKenzie nodded.

"Anyway, I have something else I wanted to work on today," Archimedes said. "It's a special chemical compound."

Placing the bug back in his pocket, Archimedes rubbed his greasy hands and disappeared into his lab. MacKenzie closed the door behind him and returned to his desk in the center of the small office just as Audrey placed another stack of papers on it. His heart had strained when Archimedes mentioned MacKenzie's going into the field, though whether it was from anticipation or anxiety, he could not tell.

"I expect this is the lot, Captain," Audrey said. "If you don't mind me asking, why are you looking up our networks in Germany and Russia? They're allied to each other's rivals, as is, and there ain't no chance of them joining against us, is there?"

"Maybe. It's just a hint right now, but I want to make sure it goes no further than that."

"Ow, I can't decide whom I detest more—Huns who wipe out populations of Africans or Ruskies who wipe out villages of Jews."

"You ken, Audrey, you certainly do have concern for the downtrodden. I've always admired that about you."

She smiled. There was a pause. "Will that be all, Captain?"

MacKenzie realized he had been staring for longer than she had liked. He darted his glance away and felt his cheeks flush. "Er, make sure you ken where the files on the French agents are. This might involve them too."

The Honorable Spy

The more he looked at the files, though, the fewer options he seemed to have. MO3 had no better agents than Field and Gibson, and there were none closer to the Kaiser than they. Doubtless, the Kaiser would play his cards as close to his chest as possible. Any agent MacKenzie moved from watching the German or Russian militaries would mean less vigilance toward any threat of mobilization. Perhaps they did have to rely on the anarchist contact at the Neues Palais.

An explosion suddenly shook the headquarters. MacKenzie's leaped to his feet with his ears ringing. His heart jumped into his throat. He glanced back at Audrey to see if she was all right; she had taken cover under her desk. The whole building reverberated—where had the noise come from?

An acrid stench filled the office. It smelled like a chemical and stung at every part of his body that came into contact with air.

Archie!

MacKenzie looked across the office toward the door to his friend's lab. Yellow smoke billowed out through the jamb. MacKenzie dashed across the room and flung the door open. The full force of the gas struck him like a tempest. He coughed and gagged. It took all his strength to remain on his feet.

He drew his handkerchief to his nose and mouth and dropped to the floor. His eyes watered, blurring his vision. He closed them. He would have to crawl and feel for Archie as best he could.

He tried to call out, but he could not open his mouth without hacking. He felt for the desk, hoping Archimedes had been working at it when the explosion occurred. He bumped into it and grasped for a corner. A few seconds later, he found another corner and reached behind the desk. He could feel the chair give way at his touch. He reached out and felt Archimedes' shoulder. The man lay unconscious on the floor.

MacKenzie grabbed Archimedes's arm and draped it over his shoulders. He worked his way back around the desk. He retched so forcefully that it brought him to a standstill. When it was over, he forced himself to keep going. He hoped he was pointed toward the door and kept crawling.

He emerged into the main office and rose to his feet. He barely had the strength to hold Archimedes up, but Connally appeared and took Archimedes' other arm. Audrey was snatching up the files on MacKenzie's desk.

"Come on!" Connally said. "Leave the files."

They dragged Archimedes to the entrance and rushed up the steps. The air grew less poisonous as they ascended. When they reached St. James's Square, MacKenzie collapsed.

The next thing he knew, he was waking up with his head in Audrey's lap. Someone had loosened the collar on his uniform. He coughed until he almost vomited.

"If that weren't the bravest thing to see, Captain," Audrey said when he had finished. "It's one thing to brave bullets, as is, but what about when you can't even breathe?"

Praise from Audrey felt reward enough for the chance he had taken.

"Pray God our soldiers never have to fight in something like that," she said.

"How's Archie?" MacKenzie asked.

"He's coming around," Connally said.

Archimedes coughed and opened his eyes.

"What the deuce were you thinking?" Connally demanded.

"The compound wasn't as stable as I thought. Even Diesel blew up his own lab, you know."

"What in the world were you working on?"

"It's an acid to burn through locks. Some of them can't be picked, you know."

"How long do you suppose we have to stay out of the headquarters?"

"A week to be safe, if we can ventilate the place. We'll have to go to our contingency plan."

"Next time, be more careful, man!" Connally said. "I took this desk job so I wouldn't have to risk life and limb!"

All four of them managed a laugh.

London
May 22, 1905

The contingency plan meant that while the headquarters below Vittoria House was ventilated and evacuated, their division handled affairs at the main directorate headquarters across the square in Winchester House.

MacKenzie felt like he was wearing sackcloth amongst the others. Connally, Archimedes, and Audrey, the only permanently assigned members of MO3, knew him as a conscientious officer despite his uniform's condition; these strangers had only the uniform to judge him by.

"Captain MacKenzie?" a fellow captain saluted as he entered.

"Aye. Phillips, is it?"

"Yes, sir. I was just wondering, if it's true that you saved the little scientist from the fumes in the lab?"

"Aye."

Phillips grinned from ear to ear. "Then my next question is why you haven't been in the field since you were an intelligence officer for the Number Five Flying Column in South Africa. Surely an officer of your undisputed bravery... Or is it because Colonel Connally knows of your reputation for panicking?"

"Captain, are you trying to be impertinent?"

"How can I, sir, when I simply state facts everyone in this directorate already knows?"

By now, his grin had become a leer. MacKenzie gripped his VC and held it out.

"Do you see this, Phillips?"

"I do, sir. Did you spend all your funds on that such that you couldn't afford a proper uniform?"

MacKenzie almost slugged him. He forced himself to express only the emotion contained in a disappointed sigh. "So that's what this is really all about. I have a scar that speaks louder than this medal and this uniform. If you could see it, you would note that it is in my chest and not my back."

"I shall confirm that, sir, when that uniform finally falls off of you."

"That will be all, Phillips. I am on the most important assignment in the empire right now."

"Yes, *of course*, sir," he said with a mocking lilt. Phillips saluted and strutted away.

When he had passed out of earshot, Audrey showed up. "I heard Captain Phillips just now. What an insubordinate—"

"You ken better than anyone about my tendency to panic."

"He didn't have no right to talk to you like that! Maybe if he'd been there on that day, he'd be jittery too. He wouldn't have lasted two minutes there; you had to stand it all day."

MacKenzie looked into her eyes. They shone with kindness. He did not deserve it. Phillips had been right.

"Anyway, Connally knows what you did in that lab. I'm sure he'll send you out into the field for it."

MacKenzie did not know what to think of that. He felt a reaction to the idea in his gut, but he could not determine what it meant.

Toward the close of the day, as MacKenzie packed up, he saw Phillips sauntering up to Audrey's desk. Phillips leaned over it and looked her in the eyes.

"Say, love, you're with the special duties section, aren't you? What's your name?"

"Audrey," she said coldly.

"Well, Audrey, I must say I'm sorry you're only with us for such a short time. *You* look like someone who's worth getting to know better. Do you have dinner plans?"

"Before you go any further, Captain, I think you ought to know that I'm a close associate of Captain MacKenzie's."

"What? The deskbound coward? How close are we talking here? I'll bet he's real timid in bed."

"I don't know nothing about that. I do know he's a gentleman, as is, which, I'm sorry to say, not everyone in this office is."

"A gentleman? Have you seen his jacket, love?"

"Let me make this simple for you: I'm married to my work, and even if I wasn't, I sure as eggs is eggs wouldn't be married to you."

Phillips leaped back. "You're a saucy one! I wouldn't say such things if I talked like you! How'd a girl with your accent ever get a job this important?"

"I don't know. Why would they admit someone like you into a job with this much trust?"

Phillips snarled. "You must be a suffragette."

"As a matter of fact, I am!"

"One more confirmation for me that you're all harridans. Well, take care when you go back into that basement office of yours. I know how much you lasses are prone to fainting."

As he turned to leave, MacKenzie caught sight of Audrey's face. He had never seen such anger in her features before. As soon as Phillips had departed the office, MacKenzie walked over to Audrey's desk.

"He has his own way about making friends, for certain."

"I hope he gets sent on a mission so the Huns can see to their duty."

"It's only for a few days," MacKenzie said reassuringly. "I'll see you tomorrow."

"Goodnight, Captain."

Before MacKenzie could reach the door, a khaki-clad courier burst in with a brown envelope. He saluted as he caught his breath.

MacKenzie returned the salute. "Is there something I can do for you, Corporal?"

"I'm looking for Captain MacKenzie, MO3."

"You've found him."

"I was told to deliver this at once. It's from Captain Gibson, sir. Urgent, he says."

MacKenzie took the envelope and ripped it open. He withdrew the report and took it to his desk for decoding. Furiously he jotted down the decrypted version.

MacKenzie gasped.

CHAPTER 3: THE TSAR'S TELEGRAM

The news only got worse as MacKenzie continued decoding the telegram. Europe had just come several steps closer to world war. He re-read it again to make sure he understood it correctly. It looked like the Kaiser would get his way after all. The Royal Army was on the verge of another day like that day.

Audrey came up and laid a hand on his shoulder. "Is it as bad as all that, Ranald?"

MacKenzie looked up. She had never called him Ranald before. She had a tender expression in her eyes. He could not tell if it was concern for her country or for him.

"Is Connally still in his office?"

"Yes."

"This can't wait."

He leaped to his feet and raced to Connally's temporary office. Once again, he pounded with more franticness than he would have liked.

"Enter. Ah, MacKenzie! Bad news?" Connally rose to return MacKenzie's salute.

"Horrible news, sir. I asked Gibson to copy down the exact wording of any further telegrams so there would be no confusion. This has been recovered from a telegram from the Tsar to the Kaiser on October 28th: 'I agree fully with your complaints about England's behavior concerning the coaling of our ships by German steamers, whereas she understands the rules of keeping neutrality in her own fashion. It is certainly high time to put a stop to this. The only way, as you say, would be that Germany, Russia, and France should at once unite upon an arrangement to abolish Anglo-Japanese arrogance and insolence. Would you like to lay down and frame the outlines of such a treaty and let me know it? As soon as it is accepted by us, France is bound to join her ally.'"

Connally collapsed back into his chair. It let out a creak like a scream. For once, fear seeped into his flinty features and stayed there. "It's unthinkable!"

"Nevertheless, sir, the Kaiser and the Tsar have drafted a treaty. Gibson goes on to say that he would stake his life that nothing's been signed—yet. He's trying to recruit new contacts to confirm all this. He's certain from what he's heard that the Tsar and Kaiser haven't canned it either. It's hanging over our heads."

"So it seems. Very well, how would you feel about returning to the field?"

MacKenzie hesitated.

"Me, sir? Why?"

"Aren't you fluent in German, French, and Russian?"

"Aye, sir. I wasn't sure whom we'd be fighting in the next war, so I learned all three."

"It's up to you, my boy, to make sure we *don't* end up fighting all three! Besides, you're the best handwriting analyst I've ever known. I want you to compare Gibson's copies of these telegrams with something genuine from the Kaiser's personal telegrapher. I'm not fully convinced this isn't some anarchist scheme. Maybe they want us to think war is imminent so that we'll nurture the anarchist movement so we'll have a fifth column to strike against Russia and Germany. Those countries are crawling with the vermin! After all, to sit on a treaty that earth-shattering for seven months..."

MacKenzie shared Connally's concern that the anarchist contact might be playing his own game. He was the only one disloyal enough in the Kaiser's household to work with Captain Gibson, but if he could be disloyal to one master, he might prove disloyal to his new friends as well. That was the problem with working with the scum of the earth.

"With respect, sir, if this is so important, why are you sending me? Or is it that you still dinna take the threat seriously enough to assign Agent Reilly? He's the best we have."

Connally leaned back in his chair. "This job requires the highest order of trust, and there's no one I trust more than you. Reilly would sell us out for the right price, especially when he has so many irons in the arms-industry fire. I only trust him when he thinks peace is in his best interest. He never proved his loyalty to his country like you did on that day. He isn't even British!"

"With respect, sir, what of my propensity to panic? Does your trust in me take that into account?"

Connally shifted forward. "There's no shame in Soldier's Heart. I'm sure you'll come through when your nation is depending on you."

MacKenzie wondered if he deserved Connally's trust. Certainly, he was as loyal to His Majesty as anyone. He wanted to serve him in the field but doubted he could. Would he bolt and run at the sight or sound of another Mauser? The cursed things still haunted his dreams, and he knew the reaction the mere mention of them had produced in him the other day.

"Please, sir, send someone else!"

Connally frowned. "Now, look here, MacKenzie. I've explained that there's no one else better suited for this. I want a copy of this treaty that the PM can present to France before the Tsar signs it. Hopefully, the Frogs will call for a conference of nations before she gets sucked into the mess. I know France doesn't want that, and Austria-Hungary could never stomach being allies with Russia again, so there's three votes against it if we get the word out in time. We may even get President Roosevelt involved!"

He leaned back with a deep breath. "Or we might just scotch it without the need to make anything public. You know how they say that the last man to speak with Tsar Nicholas is the most powerful man in Russia? We want one of our friends to be that last man. His Majesty has done so much for our Entente Cordiale with France. I don't want to see it all go up in smoke. Seems to me, there's a world war brewing, and you've got to stop it!"

No getting out of it now. MacKenzie had an order, and he had no intention of disobeying.

"I'll try, sir."

"Now, you go home and get some rest. Audrey and I will stay up tonight and set the details. Dismissed."

MacKenzie saluted and departed. He went over to Audrey's desk. "Your turn, Audrey. You and the colonel will work out the details for my assignment."

Her eyes brightened. "*Your* assignment? You're going back into the field?"

"Against my better judgment, aye. I just hope I'll return to see you again."

"Ow, you will, Ranald! But just in case you don't, I do want to tell you I think you're the finest bloke I know."

MacKenzie's heart fluttered. He almost blurted out how he felt. He was going to die, so why not? Instead, he clammed up. He feared the awkwardness on the remote off chance that he returned more than he dreamed of the romance if he did not. Just the same, he reckoned the odds much greater that he would not return.

A haunting question popped into his mind: if British intelligence was just becoming aware of the secret negotiations, what did German intelligence know?

CHAPTER 4: THE REICH'S BEST INTERROGATOR

Outside Berlin
May 23, 1905

Leopold Tirpitz could not keep from running his fingers along his black handlebar mustache. He knew that if he stopped, his long fingers would simply drum out Prussian marches on the upholstered seat of his jostling carriage. And if he stopped himself from doing that, he would begin humming the bass parts of those marches quietly to himself.

He felt trepidation like this every time he received a summons from the Master. What if today the Master called him to account for that day, when he had forfeited his peace of mind for all eternity?

He knew he had proven the best spy in the Order. He was a master of disguise and interrogation. No target of his had ever not talked in the end. He had just successfully uncovered a dangerous French agent, whom he had rendered... *harmless* to anyone.

He left behind the streets of Berlin, shaded by bushy chestnut trees dotted with pink or white plumes of flowers. Normally, at this time of day and at this time of year, he would have been strolling with his neck craned at the explosion of delicate colors, or he would have been eavesdropping on conversations from over hedges in café gardens, where Berliners lingered over their coffee or beer. He might even have visited the hotels with their splendid gardens, where everything was ordered just so. Just the way he liked it. Nature under control of the German race.

His carriage, however, stopped at an entirely different location. If Berlin was the pleasant heart of Germany, Hlidskjalf Castle was its brain. Here, the Order of Siegfried had its headquarters. Here sat the head of the octopus where the information from tentacles dug into all corners of the globe found its way to the Master's vast desk.

The varnished oaken piece of furniture was so wide that the Master would have to slide his chair on its wheels from one end to another to retrieve a telegram placed in one of his inboxes. He had one for each Great Power he had decided upon war with—Britain, France, and Russia—with others for less strategically significant groups of nations, like the Balkans.

Leopold Tirpitz enjoyed the chestnuts and lilacs of Berlin, but the grim beauties of Hlidskjalf enthralled him. Like Neuschwanstein to the southwest, this castle had been constructed recently, so the designers had felt free to furnish it with features fitting their fantasy, rather than serving any practical purpose for defense.

The Master, though, had left Hlidskjalf with its dark gray, foreboding limestone, like a medieval castle. This set it starkly apart from Neuschwanstein's inviting, fairytale-esque exterior. Grotesque gargoyles fashioned from nightmares presided over every corner. Hlidskjalf had a military-enough purpose, just not a defensive one—here, the Order planned the war, or wars, that would make the German Reich a worldwide power, the only sovereign nation under the sun.

Tirpitz took a deep breath as he stepped out of the carriage. The flutter of a raven overhead got his attention. *A sign*, he thought excitedly. It could mean death, for ravens often passed before heroes doomed to die, but it might also indicate that Odin was watching over him through Huginn or Muninn. Tirpitz's life seemed governed by caprice, either Odin's or the Master's. He swallowed hard.

He proceeded up the tall, gray stone staircase to the gatehouse, which stretched between two rows of statues of Germanic warriors. Unlike the gargoyles, these outsized stone sentinels represented the heroes of pagan Germania. These men had humbled Rome and ravaged monasteries from the mists of the North Sea.

Many had just tunics and trousers for protection, with no helmet to obscure their long, flowing hair. Some, though, wore full armor, with mail coats and conical Viking helmets. These lacked the horns gracing the singers in a Wagnerian opera. The Master loved Wagner, but he remained a stickler for his own version of Germanic history.

At last, reaching the precipice that marked the edge of the moat at the top, Tirpitz handed his pass to the gray-clad sentry, who had snapped to attention with his Mauser, his rifle butt smacking on the stone slab. The sentry called to the gatekeeper, who lowered the drawbridge, its chains clanking all the way down. With a boom, it struck the stone at Tirpitz's feet. Behind it, several portcullises rose to allow him into the castle's main hall.

Tirpitz crossed the drawbridge and heard it clank its way back up behind him. The pointed portcullises dropped down again. If this was his day of reckoning, he could not avoid it now. He prayed to Forseti, the god of justice, that he would not meet the fate of the countless souls he had led through this hall to the torture chambers and oubliettes below those towers. They never reappeared above ground alive. If the Master was calling him to account for that day, no one could save him.

Pounding fear pulsated through him. The hall echoed faintly with the chatter of Order agents and staff congregated in groups, either leaning on the cold walls or around desks. If not for the copious electric lights, the hall would have been as dark as a medieval castle's.

He quickened his echoing steps past the offices lining the hallways and found himself by a massive door of rough oak panels. He banged on it with the iron knocker.

The sentry drew back the small panel at eye height. "Who approaches?"

"Hauptmann Leopold Tirpitz," Tirpitz replied smoothly with his oily voice.

"Your summons, Herr Hauptmann?"

No one ever saw the Master without a summons. Tirpitz passed his paper through the watchman's hole, his tongue flickering out of his mouth like a serpent's as he licked his parched lips. The sentry opened the heavy door slowly.

"He's expecting you, Herr Hauptmann."

Tirpitz swallowed as he crossed the sparse waiting area to another, smaller door. He rapped on it tentatively.

"Who's there?" a gravelly voice demanded.

"Hauptmann Tirpitz, Herr Oberst."

"Ah! Enter."

Tirpitz fumbled with the door handle and stepped inside. His eyes needed to adjust to the dark. As usual, the Master had drawn his curtains, and the only light came from a lamp shaded such that its narrow beam fell exactly on the current paperwork on the desk and no more. Even the Master appeared as little more than a shadow, albeit a bulky and foreboding one, in a capacious, thickly cushioned chair.

Tirpitz saluted with his arm outstretched and palm down, like a Roman officer.

"You summoned me, Herr Oberst?"

"*Ja.* We have two problems that need your flair for counterintelligence," the Master said. "For one thing, I have heard talk of friendly exchanges between the Kaiser and the Tsar. Not just familial chit-chat between cousins, but actual offers of alliance. We're not supposed to know about it, as they have not even told the cabinets."

Tirpitz was surprised the Master knew of it then, but then, the Master knew everything.

"For His Imperial Majesty and the Reich's sake, we cannot allow this," the Master said. "It is self-evident that Germany and Russia cannot remain friends forever. What fellowship have Teutons with Slavs? What does civilization have to do with savagery?"

Tirpitz knew the Master despised Russians more than almost any other race.

"I fear, though, that by the time the war inevitably comes, Russia will have industrialized," the Master continued. "Her numbers are a might we cannot match. We want war sooner rather than later, as soon as the Kaiser has seen to it that we can match England at sea."

Tirpitz remained at attention, staring at the top of the Master's chair. "With respect, Herr Oberst, do you truly fear that we will have to fight England and Russia at the same time?"

"Fifteen years ago, we said the same about France and Russia. A republic and an autocracy? Impossible! And yet, that ingenious fellow Rachkovsky managed to persuade them that they could be friends, and now we have enemies on two fronts. If Rachkovsky digs his tentacles much further into England—and I've heard of English agents working for him—who knows if he'll do the same there?"

Normally, Tirpitz would have relished the chance to match wits with Peter Ivanovich Rachkovsky, the Russian secret police's foremost spymaster, but he did not like where this was going.

"The French seem eager to get England into their bed," the Master said. "You must ascertain the Kaiser's intentions."

Tirpitz looked around fearfully.

"With respect, Herr Oberst—spy on the Kaiser? Isn't that treasonous?"

The Master thumped his fist on the desk. "If you don't have the stomach for the job, we can reveal the truth of that day to the police! You forget that I have your life in my hands and that you owe your highest loyalty to the Order."

Tirpitz's heart was racing. Become a criminal again by spying on the Kaiser or be prosecuted for his former crime?

The Master seemed to perceive his fear, for he settled back in his chair.

"Hauptmann," he said somewhat soothingly. "When the Kaiser formed the Order after his accession seventeen years ago, his charter tasked us with making Germany as ready as possible for the next European war. He trusts my counsel. When I explain to him that he is putting his 'place in the sun' at risk by this policy, he will understand. There'll be no questions about how we knew. He never asks any questions about our methods—he'd rather not know."

"*Jawohl!*" Tirpitz snapped back to attention. "I'll do it—for the Order."

"*Gut*. Now, second, we have discovered a leak of the Kaiser's personal telegrams to the Tsar. Copies of several in the Kaiser's own handwriting have gone missing. We don't know where they've gone, but we can't allow England or France to find out about this. It might provoke war before our navy is ready."

The Master thumped his desk again.

"By the gods' favor, I am the only one with enough wisdom to decide when it should begin. When I judge that the omens are auspicious, the planets and nations have aligned rightly, and the gods have decreed it, I will arrange a diplomatic incident that will bring the swords of the *Aesir* and *Einherjar* slashing down on the *Untermenschen*. We can't have anyone else interfering with my divinely ordained wisdom! If you find an English or French agent at the end of this trail, I want him silenced. Understood?"

"Jawohl."

"Your first task will be to interrogate a Herr Johann Schilling. He needs your special technique. Completely effective, it's proven. What a pity we can't patent it."

Tirpitz saluted. "My pleasure, Herr Oberst."

Having confirmed that he was free of the system of torment he had perfected, Tirpitz turned to go mete it out to someone else. He stepped lively out of the office and strode back down toward the main hall.

He soon found Heinrich von Papen, his favorite associate in the Order, standing around with his nose in a file. In one of his rare departures from Germanic mythology, Tirpitz liked to call him, "the Patroclus to my Achilles."

Heinrich sported a long, bushy mustache that extended well beyond his jawline. It seemed calculated to make up for his high, balding forehead. The redness of the mustache also seemed calculated to make up for the almost complete lack of color in his complexion.

Heinrich snapped to attention and gave the Order's salute as he approached.

"Heinrich, my good fellow. I understand we have someone in custody for interrogation."

"Jawohl. I take it you are eager to start?"

"Who else can do it half so well?"

Heinrich grinned. "No one, Herr Hauptmann."

"Lead the way."

Heinrich smartly about-faced and almost pranced down the hallway. Tirpitz followed with a less giddy gait.

The Master still needed him! Nothing bad would befall him while he was needed.

They followed the narrow hall to the Heime Tower. Suddenly, Tirpitz stopped.

"One moment, Heinrich," he whispered.

Tirpitz crept up to a woman behind a desk. From behind, he could only see her neatly dressed blonde hair and crisp white blouse, but that was enough. Suddenly, he wrapped his arms around her waist and kissed her neck. The woman jolted, but her blue eyes lit up when they met his.

"Poldy, you're back!" she said. "Successful mission, I trust?"

"Could it be otherwise when I was assigned to it, Hilda?"

"You must give me a chance to welcome you back to Berlin. Your flat, tonight?"

"I would love to, Hilda, but I have a rather pressing engagement right now, and I don't know how long he will last—I mean, how long *it* will last. Perhaps two nights from now. He'll surely be dead by then."

"All right, love. See you then," she said with a wink.

Tirpitz stroked her cheek, then fell back in beside Heinrich.

The smile faded from his lips. This was a far cry from what he had originally learned his skills for. It would be one more memory to haunt him every time his eyes closed. He knew he wouldn't sleep well for several nights.

The gods will it. More than that, the Master wills it.

How foolish he had been on that day. Would he ever sleep peacefully again? At the Heime Tower, a guard in field gray and a pickelhaube helmet saluted.

"I understand I have a patient expecting me?" Tirpitz said.

The guard laughed. "He's in such need of your *tender* care, Herr Hauptmann."

Everyone seemed to be enjoying this but Tirpitz. The guard unlocked the door and opened what seemed like the abyss of the underworld. The winding stairway descended within a few steps into utter darkness. Heinrich switched on a torch and led the way down.

The musty air assaulted Tirpitz's nose. An even worse stench wafted up from the cells below. The stench inevitably resulted from shutting away prisoners to starve without cleaning between incarcerations. It was like descending to the bottom of a latrine.

If only there was a way that did not offend his senses so! Tirpitz knew, however, that the stench of unwashed humanity played into the effect as much as the impenetrable darkness. He reckoned the assault on his smell a small price to pay for security from the Master's caprice.

At the foot of the stairs, Heinrich led Tirpitz to a cell. His keys jangled in the lock. Tirpitz stepped in and yanked out the prisoner.

The prisoner stank of sweat. Tirpitz had seen worse, though. Some of the prisoners' clothes draped from them like voluminous robes after they had been properly starved. This one still filled out his soiled clothes nicely. Evidently, he was a recent addition to the oubliette. If his limbs did not reveal enough, he still had defiance in his eyes—a sure sign of a recent addition.

Tirpitz had to be strong.

"This is the man we suspect of leaking information?" he asked Heinrich.

"Jawohl, Herr Hauptmann. He is part of the Kaiser's household staff, but we found anarchist writings from Kropotkin and Kravchinsky in his personal effects."

"Herr Schilling, do you realize what you are?" Tirpitz asked gently. "You may be an anarchist, ja, but from this point on, you are a dead man. It's not a question of *if* you will die, but rather *how*. I'll give you a bargain by my oath to Thor: Tell us what we want to know, and you can have the death of your own choosing—poison, a bullet, you name it. If you don't, I swear another oath that it will be the most painful, lingering death possible. I feel I should advise you upfront that no one has ever not talked after undergoing my special treatment."

Schilling clenched his jaw sullenly.

"I admire your confidence, if not your wisdom," Tirpitz said. "I hope you'll admire my skill in turn."

***

Fourteen hours later, Schilling managed through his shrieks to cry, "Enough, *bitte*! I'll tell you anything, I swear!"

Tirpitz concealed a sigh of relief. "That's better. Now, did you steal the Kaiser's telegrams?"

"Jawohl, Herr Hauptmann!"

"Whom did you give them to?"

"Captain Arthur Gibson. He's a British agent."

"And where might I find him?"

"Charlottenburg."

"I say, the British are investing a lot in this spy for him to afford such quarters," Tirpitz muttered. "Or, more likely, he's a man of means since they don't reimburse their agents' expenses worth a fig. Did Gibson tell you anything of what he would do with them?"

"Nein, Herr Hauptmann."

"And who else belongs to your anarchist circle?"

Schilling pressed his trembling lips together.

"I said..." Tirpitz began threateningly.

Tears pouring from his eyes, Schilling recited every name he could think of.

"Are any of these others working with the English?"

"Nein, Herr Hauptmann."

"And what did the English offer that corrupted you so thoroughly?"

"A guarantee against extradition if I killed the Kaiser if it looked like he was going to make war inevitable."

Tirpitz snapped back. "King Edward agreed to that, did he?"

"I don't think so, Herr Hauptmann! Just the ones who know the truth in the Foreign Office."

"I thank you, Herr Schilling. You've been most helpful, if not entirely cooperative."

"Now, please, a bullet to the brain!"

Tirpitz nodded. "See to it, Heinrich."

Heinrich put down the pliers and dragged Schilling to his feet. "Come, traitor."

Tirpitz locked the nausea in his gut until Heinrich and Schilling were gone. He burst into Schilling's cell and vomited. He vomited again. He wiped his mouth with his handkerchief and wound his way back up the stairs.

From the castle courtyard came a shot. Tirpitz returned to his office and wiped the sweat and mingled blood from his brow with a scarlet handkerchief. Next, he proceeded to scour the gore from his fingers. He began to curse that day that had landed him here.

Soon, Heinrich reappeared.

"That was splendid!" Heinrich said. "Wrung it all out of him, by Thor!"

"The Old Scoundrel didn't teach me much, but he did teach me there's no motivator like pain," Tirpitz mumbled.

Heinrich glanced down in sympathy. When Tirpitz referred to the Old Scoundrel, he meant his father.

Tirpitz tucked the handkerchief back into his pocket. "He also taught me that there's no nepenthe like beer. I'm going to have a few rounds. Would you care to join me?"

"Shouldn't we issue orders based on the information we received?" Heinrich said.

He held out his transcript of information from Herr Schilling. Tirpitz realized he had focused so much on the torture that he had forgotten the whole point of it.

"Ach, ja! Where is my head? Pass his list of anarchist compatriots along to the police. That's hardly a matter we need to concern ourselves with. More immediately, put Captain Gibson under surveillance at once. I wish to know him better. I want to know what brand of cigarette he smokes; no detail is too insignificant."

CHAPTER 5: AGENT FIELD

London
May 24, 1905

MacKenzie slept poorly that night. He hit the pillow and spent much of the night staring up at the gray ceiling. Sometimes, he turned on his side and gazed at the wall. Every time he closed his eyes, an alarming thought would cause them to shoot open again. He had not taken to the field in three years, and now he had been given the most sensitive of missions. Surely, he would not come back alive.

His mind kept flitting back to Audrey. The thought of his dying and her marrying someone else bedeviled him. He knew it was irrational. He had no intention of courting her, so why should that notion horrify him? Aye, no intention, to be sure, but that did not equate with no desire.

He awoke so early that he had no difficulty in reporting on time to Winchester House. Audrey looked her impeccable self. Entering Connally's office, he found a different story.

Colonel Connally sat amid a pile of papers drawn from the open filing cabinets. His face showed lines of wear and concern, which MacKenzie had not believed possible of his even-tempered commander.

Now MacKenzie became even more anxious. His heart jumped into his throat.

"I want you on the first boat out of here on the 26th, as soon as your passport is viséd in case you need to travel through Russia," Connally said. "In honor of your fine work in South Africa, your codename will be Cheetah while you're on the spy. The DMO is personally concerned, since possible war with Germany is involved. This will get Parliament and the army to take us seriously! Pull this off, and maybe we'll get the funds we need."

MacKenzie cleared his throat. A world war was brewing, and Connally was still considering the bureaucratic rewards to be gained. It was true, though, that MO3 was badly underfunded.

"What are your instructions, sir?"

"You will go with Lieutenant Field. He's been back from Berlin for two days and will be attending an anarchist meeting in Whitechapel tonight. You will meet with him afterward to discuss his findings. He may have news after the meeting. Then I want you two to meet with Captain Gibson. He's been told to expect you at the Royal Opera House in Berlin in three days' time at the performance of *'Die Walküre.'*"

A small perquisite—MacKenzie loved Wagner and Norse mythology.

"You will greet him with the code phrase, 'I wish I was shooting in the Highlands,' and he will reply, 'The sport is better in the Vienna Woods.' You will both be in civilian garb, of course. Gibson's also been instructed to procure a handwriting sample from the Kaiser's telegrapher; you are to compare it to what he already has. I won't feel satisfied we aren't being set up until you confirm these telegrams are genuine."

MacKenzie had no doubts of his abilities on that score, at least.

"When you pack, include the German guard uniform that will be delivered by courier in case you have to sneak into the Neues Palais. Archimedes has forged German military identification for you. If need be, you will be Hauptmann Wilhelm Kleber. You, Gibson, and Field will have no connection with the Embassy or our military attaché. You are working in no capacity for the British government or the War Office. We want no diplomatic incidents. In fact, if things do go sour, and something's found out, you will be punished upon your return—for the sake of appearance. This is officially an unofficial mission."

Connally paused. "Unofficially, though, I must tell you there's no one's loyalty to his king and country that I trust more than yours, and I know your German and Russian are the best in the department. Now, Archimedes has something important for you."

He took MacKenzie by the elbow and ushered him to Archimedes's temporary lab. It had not taken the inventor long to messy it up like his old one. Papers draped every inch of desk and worktable space. Some had even spilled out of the wastebasket.

Archimedes hammered away at something with a jeweler's loop in his eye. A half-eaten sandwich lay on a plate, wrapped in blue paper on the desk. Connally cleared his throat. Archimedes leaped up to greet them.

"Ronnie!" he said as he shook MacKenzie's hand vigorously. "I owe you my life, so I am going to recompense you the best I can. Here's the bug I've designed and now entrust to you. This version is, I hope, indestructible—well, as much as anything can be. It's waterproof and fireproof. As I said, listen to it using your ring. It still transmits correctly, does it not?"

"Aye." The ring MacKenzie wore on his right hand featured a ruby that could be tapped in its setting as a wireless radio transmitter, or the ring could be tuned as a receiver. Though miniscule, it produced and read crystal-clear signals, something no wireless could boast except Archimedes's.

Archimedes produced a pair of boots. "And here are these. They're your size. In the heels, you'll find a vial of acid. It's the substance that blew up in the lab the other day."

MacKenzie stepped back from the gift. "Archie! You ken I'm allergic to that stuff. I had a very bad reaction."

Archimedes laughed. "No, I wouldn't give you anything dangerous after you saved my life. That just exploded after being left on the burner too long. It's perfectly safe, as long as it's in the vial, but if you need to destroy a lock, it'll prove more than capable of that."

"Archie, you think of everything."

Archimedes smiled. "I have to, to stay ahead of the Huns. As the Red Queen said, 'Here, you see, it takes all the running you can do, to keep in the same place.'"

MacKenzie grinned at the reference to *Through the Looking-Glass*. Both he and Archimedes had loved that book as schoolboys.

"Thank you, Archie. Sir!" He saluted to Connally, about-faced, and marched to the door.

"Ranald?"

Again, the use of his first name from her surprised him. "Aye, Audrey?"

MacKenzie turned to look at her. His heart sank to find her blue eyes glistening. They reminded him of the lochs in the Highlands reflecting the morning light.

She laid her hand on his. "I... I just wanted to say"—she choked—"that is, I want you to take every precaution. Who else will help me distribute my pamphlets with you gone?"

Tell her how you feel! MacKenzie opened his mouth but shut it just as quickly. He only allowed himself to take her hand in his and raise it to his lips.

"I want to be there when you vote for your first MP."

Audrey blushed.

***

MacKenzie checked his watch. It had not moved more than three minutes since he had last looked at it. Still, that was three more minutes that Agent Field was late by. He began quietly whistling the Boer song, "Sarie Marais."

He tried to think on his time as an intelligence officer for the Number Five Flying Column. He had never let anyone down when he had filled that position; that was why he had received his assignment to MO3. Surely, he still knew how to conduct himself on the spy.

He groaned at Agent Field's tardiness but reassured himself that he remained a good man. A little prone to impertinence, perhaps, but thorough in his work. MacKenzie intended to let him take the lead. He had more experience and a leveler head. MacKenzie would simply analyze the handwriting and leave the heavy lifting to Field.

This place appeared even more dilapidated than his flat. Definitely a blue mark on Charles Booth's poverty map of the city. Paint peeling, shutters drooping from their hinges, cracks in the brick and mortar, dirt in piles—it looked like no one had bothered to rebuild since the Great Fire of 1666. Earlier, he had followed the smell of a wood fire to find a woman burning her furniture. What a hopeless place to be born and to die in.

MacKenzie fought to keep all of Britain from becoming like this under German or Russian heels, and he prayed for God's hand to bring peace with justice to this part of the city. Hopefully, these would prove just growing pains. Already the government and charities like the Salvation Army were striving to relieve this gaping wound in Britain's side.

He looked out from the alley where he waited. No sign of Agent Field or, for that matter, anyone. What he would give to be on holiday shooting in the Highlands! His west highland white terriers would exult to be let off the leash after a badger or rabbit. They were obsessed with hunting, ruthless even. He would shoot his prey, and then all three would enjoy a hearty bit of meat that night. He found it much more fun when the prey could not shoot back. If they could...

He heard footfalls on the pavement. He checked his watch again. Agent Field was late by twenty-five minutes.

A figure in a black overcoat with his collar turned up and his hat brim pulled down sidled into the alley. MacKenzie could just barely make out his stiff, auburn mustache from the shadows on his face. The figure pulled his hat back and undid his collar. It looked like Agent Field.

"Scotland always moves them," MacKenzie said.

"But none can stay like England."

Field held out his hand. MacKenzie took it but held up his watch in his other.

"Lieutenant, do you ken what time it is?"

"Sorry, old boy. Our lecturer went on about the evils of Russia's war with Japan past schedule. With the Baltic Fleet nearing its destination, he's afraid Russia will impose its autocratic will on China and Japan after all."

"Speaking of anarchists, how reliable would you say our man in the Neues Palais is?"

Field shrugged. "As trustworthy as any anarchist, I suppose."

"He wouldn't, say, want to set Britain and Germany at war with each other?" MacKenzie said.

Field shook his head. "Anarchists shy at imperialist warfare, sir."

"But not at blowing up imperialists themselves?"

"They know the common people they claim to look out for would be the ones fighting another European war." Field paused to grin broadly. "Can't be *complete* hypocrites, can they?"

"It's just that Captain Gibson has reported something incredibly dangerous," MacKenzie said, "and I want to make sure his contact is reliable."

Field's eyes flitted around. "What did he say? My instructions didn't spell out why I was being sent back to Berlin—only to ask you."

MacKenzie nodded. "Gibson reports that our contact in the Kaiser's palace has just given him a telegram from October 27 of last year. With Germany wishing to coal the Baltic Fleet on its trip around the world, the

Kaiser proposed to the Tsar that they and France join forces against us and Japan."

Field jerked back. "All three against Britain?"

"Aye. You've met the Kaiser; you monitor him. Do you think he's capable of that?"

Field rolled his eyes. "*Everyone* knows he wants war with Britain, sir."

"Dinna be impertinent, Lieutenant! I mean, would he bring Russia and France in on the deal? Which does he crave more, our territories in Africa, or Russia's in the Ukraine and France's industrial towns?"

Field shrugged again. "All of them. I don't see those as mutually exclusive. If he defeats us, who will there be to stop him from trampling on France and Russia?"

"Is he smart enough to con Russia and France into bleeding for Germany before he turns Germany against them?"

"I wouldn't put it past him."

"But you dinna think anything's happened yet?"

"I know for a fact the Kaiser has not met the Tsar in person since then. They certainly haven't signed anything—at least, not together."

MacKenzie stroked his chin. "Why do you suppose we are just now learning of this?"

"Our contact at the palace does his best, but he's not in a trusted position. He has to take what information he can get when he can get it."

MacKenzie sighed. "I hope we're in time."

"I don't think much has happened between those two *eminent* sovereigns since October of last year," said Field. "That's my impression."

"We must be sure," said MacKenzie. "After the war in South Africa... why, it'd be, 'Out of the briar into the thorns,' as we say in the Highlands. Is there anywhere other than the Neues Palais we could gather this intelligence?"

Field nodded. "Gibson's been monitoring a castle outside of Berlin. Hlidskjalf, its name is. They say it's privately owned, but it's run like a military installation. Gibson can't get into it or get anyone to talk about it. They all clam up when it's mentioned."

"I read about that in his report. He said it's been stocked with Mausers"—he shuddered—"Obviously, a military installation. Do you suppose they're the Kaiser's secret police?"

"Who knows? I suggest we look into that while we're there."

"Och, aye. Our cover story is that we are looking to invest in German plastics. Are you all ready to gang?"

"All Sir Garnet, sir," Field replied.

"Good. I'll see you at 7:30 a.m. tomorrow at King's Cross Station. We'll catch the train to Lowestoft and sail on the *Islay* to Hamburg. Sharp next time, Lieutenant."

"Yes, sir."

Field saluted and rearranged his wardrobe. He pulled his hat down and his collar up like any self-respecting anarchist and stepped out into the street.

From somewhere in the darkness, a shot rang out. As the bang echoed off the buildings, Field crumpled to the ground.

CHAPTER 6: RUTHLESS BEAUTY

MacKenzie froze. Was that a Mauser? Of course not! Whatever it was, Agent Field was dead as a mackerel. A flow of blood oozed from his breast. MacKenzie's racing heart poured horror through his arteries.

He heard a rapid succession of footfalls on the cobbled street. He glanced up and spied a silhouette with a pistol dashing away like a gazelle. MacKenzie drew his Webley revolver and took off after him.

"You there! Stand still!"

The figure darted a glance back and fired a shot. *Two*, MacKenzie thought. The bullet sang past his ear.

The fellow kept running. He had a good start on MacKenzie, but MacKenzie did not have the codename Cheetah for nothing, and he rapidly closed.

His man cut down a side street between two glass-front brick stores. MacKenzie matched his agility in the turn, his reflection dashing across the window and disappearing like a vengeful ghost. Another abrupt redirection into a claustrophobic alley. They had left the gas lights illuminating Whitechapel Road. If MacKenzie had not closed the distance, the man would have disappeared into the shadows.

MacKenzie spun on the balls of his feet. The man had halted at a red brick wall several feet taller than he. He jerked around and fired twice.

Three! Four!

The man's exertions told on his marksmanship; MacKenzie barely heard the bullets whip past. They must have missed him cleanly.

Clambering onto a pair of crates, the figure climbed the wall. As he pulled himself up, he kicked the top crate to the pavement with a crash, then disappeared behind the brick.

The Honorable Spy

MacKenzie dashed to the wall. He holstered his pistol, jumped up, and grabbed hold of the brick. He pulled his elbows up and then used them to pull the rest of himself over.

He glanced around. He could not see the man anywhere in the alley, but neither did he see any cover for him to have hidden behind. MacKenzie leaped to the ground and ran down the alley, back onto Whitechapel Road. The man could not have hidden anywhere here either, as all the shops on the street appeared closed and locked. He scanned the storefronts for broken windows or doors that the man might have busted open.

There he was! The figure stood about sixty yards away, MacKenzie judged. The man looked back to see if he had lost MacKenzie. Spotting him, the villain fired again.

Five!

MacKenzie had had enough. He drew his Webley from its holster, thumb-cocking as he did. Gripping it with both hands, he stiffened his arms. The sight aligned, and MacKenzie pulled the trigger. The enemy's pistol went flying from his hand.

One!

Now he had two sums to keep tally of in his racing mind. The figure stopped and glanced around frantically at the road. MacKenzie ran to catch him before he could retrieve the weapon. He cocked the pistol for another round.

Instead, a shot rang out from a storefront just across the street from his opponent. MacKenzie startled, but it was Field's assailant who collapsed with a shriek. As he clutched his leg and writhed like a worm in a bird's beak, MacKenzie heard a door creak open.

He glanced toward a fish shop with its displays behind glass emptied for the night. It was vacant of anything except for a silhouette that emerged from the door like a spirit.

Before MacKenzie could reach the fallen body, the shadowy figure had raced to the suspect and crunched its shoe on the man's arm, which had been reaching for his pistol. MacKenzie could tell now, as he drew nearer, that the figure was a woman wearing a working dress.

MacKenzie stopped. The wounded man called out to her, but before he could do anything else, she leveled her pistol at the suspect's head and fired off another shot.

The woman looked up from her kill and rearranged her hair. Panting, MacKenzie sprinted the remainder of the way. The toe of his boot slipped on the man's brains on the pavement.

As he looked up at the executioner, he realized she deserved the codename Cheetah more than he. She was the most beautiful killer he had ever seen.

Golden locks glimmered in the moonlight, framing a healthy complexion (one that did not blush at being discovered with a smoking pistol at the head of a corpse). Her lips, as full and red as a rose, betrayed no emotion at the sight of him. Most of all, he noticed her large eyes, blue as St. Andrew's flag. They had a predatory hardness when he first met them, but in an instant, they softened into friendliness.

MacKenzie could do no more than gasp to catch his breath. Words had fled from his mind. He did not know which surprised him more—the fact that this gunman was a gunwoman, or that that gunwoman was breathtaking.

No London workingwoman could shoot like that. From her neck dangled a fourteen-carat gold chain holding up, not some locket from a sweetheart, but an exquisitely crafted, albeit threatening, golden dog's head. It had closed eyes and jaws set in a permanent howl under pinned back ears. As MacKenzie hesitated, the woman took the initiative.

"I'm Catriona Cameron," she said with a Highland brogue. "Captain Ranald MacKenzie, Black Watch, I presume?"

"Aye."

"A pleasure to meet you, Captain MacKenzie," she said in Gaelic.

MacKenzie had never met Catriona Cameron, but he knew the name. She was one of the civilian agents the Foreign Office paid for, not directly under the command of MO3.

Catriona held out the hand that had just killed a man, and MacKenzie drew it to his lips.

"The honor is all mine," he said in the same tongue.

"You ken, Bannockburn could have been an English victory," she said in English.

MacKenzie's jaw dropped slightly. Now she was giving him the code phrase Connally used among his Scottish agents!

"But the MacDonalds were on the right flank," he returned. "Now could you please tell me what is going on here?"

"This man was a Fenian working for the Germans. I shot him because he was reaching for his pistol."

MacKenzie scrutinized the corpse. Why would an Irish revolutionary want to kill a man just come from an anarchist meeting? On the other hand, there was no love lost between the Catholic Fenians and the atheist anarchists, and who knew what vendettas went on in the revolutionary underworld? Could Field have provoked him earlier while posing as an anarchist? Or, if this man had worked for the Germans, perhaps he knew the truth about Agent Field. But then, why had he not shot MacKenzie too?

English authorities had no quicker way of depriving a man of his due process than saying he was an Irish rebel—years of history backed that up. Was Catriona using that as a cover for skipping formalities? He felt fairly certain that she had stood in a perfect position to deny him the pistol without blowing his brains out.

"You've been assigned to study the Tsar's negotiations with the Kaiser, have you not?" she said.

"Aye."

"I'm to accompany you as your support," she said. "Connally assigned me a little after you left. I was coming to meet you when I heard the shots. I'm sorry I was too late to save Field, but I think he's been avenged properly."

If you hadn't shot him, we could be interrogating him and getting to the bottom of all this, MacKenzie thought bitterly.

"Why did Connally not tell me?" he asked. "I already had Field with me at the time. If he wanted three agents, surely he would have said something to either of us."

She sniffed. "He told the Foreign Office, who insisted on having one of their own agents assigned. A womanly touch, too. Perhaps I can go unnoticed where you can't."

"Connally wouldn't have neglected to inform me."

"This is rather last minute, you'll agree. We've got to leave tomorrow to meet with Gibson on time."

That was true. MacKenzie himself had only been given one day to prepare. He still did not quite believe someone as efficient as Connally would make an omission this glaring, though.

But she did have a point. Disguised as a serving maid, she could go about as she wished, as unnoticed as a phantom. And she had used the correct code phrase.

"I'll be leaving aboard the *Islay* from Lowestoft with you," she said. "I take it you'll be on the morning train there from King's Cross Station."

"Aye."

"Splendid. I'll purchase a ticket. I think it would be least conspicuous if we travelled as husband and wife sightseeing in Berlin. The chestnuts are lovely this time of year, I hear."

"Very weel."

Shrill police whistles stabbed into their ears. Down the street, a collection of faint lights from police lanterns glowed like a constellation.

Catriona tugged on his sleeve. "Come on. Let's get out of here," she said.

"I think we can explain ourselves to the peelers."

"Maybe you can, but I'd rather not," she said rapidly. She turned and dashed down the alley MacKenzie had just come from.

"Halt! Stay where you are, man!" the lead inspector shouted.

MacKenzie threw his arms up and let the police approach.

"What's going on here?" the inspector said.

The man was on the short side for a London bobby. He had blond hair and a rather aquiline nose over an unkempt goatee. His teeth showed yellow tobacco stains as he spoke.

MacKenzie slowly drew his identification papers out of his pocket. "Secret business, inspector. Captain Ranald MacKenzie, MO3, Directorate of Military Operations. This was an Irish revolutionary trying to evade custody. He killed a lieutenant named Field in an alley off Whitechapel Road back several blocks that way. The body's still there."

The officer held up his lantern to MacKenzie's papers. He squinted as he studied them.

"Right," he said. "But we'll still have to call the coroner. I'm sure you won't mind waiting around for his report if what you say is true?"

"I'm on state business, and I must be about it as soon as possible. If you take me in, you'll disrupt His Majesty's intelligence work of a most important nature."

The inspector locked his eyes on MacKenzie's face. MacKenzie froze, his countenance like ice.

The inspector shrugged. "All right. Go on."

MacKenzie about-faced and marched off. Now the police would not waste their time chasing rabbit trails, looking for another elusive Jack the Ripper. Also, he had ensured that his name remained clear.

What on earth is going on?

He knew only one thing for certain; he could not rely on Agent Field anymore. He would have to do the heavy lifting himself. He certainly did not intend for a lady to bear the brunt of this task.

The same question flashed across his mind that had haunted him for months after that day: had he failed a comrade? Perhaps, but he would see to it that Field had not died in vain. MacKenzie was going to get that treaty.

MacKenzie fumbled with the lock on the door to his flat. The paper in the jamb remained undisturbed. He entered with that reciprocating engine in his chest again. He was panicking about panicking.

He fingered his Victoria Cross for comfort but didn't find any. He reached involuntarily for his flask, but then realized that for the rest of the mission he could not imbibe alcohol.

He drew the flask from his pocket and poured it out in the wash basin. Not even one final sip. He might need the camera Archie had rigged in it, but he had to carry it around empty. What consolation could he take?

His mind flitted to an auld Highland saying his father, the minister, had taught him. The man had never proven short on Bible verses or auld Highland sayings. This one did not come straight from the Bible, but it accorded pretty well, he thought: "Do your best, and God will help."

He thought of the two storms that had struck the Apostles on the Sea of Galilee. Twice, they had found themselves in peril as their little boat had tossed on the water. It would have either capsized or foundered, leaving the disciples to the less than tender mercies of the waves. But both times, Christ had intervened and stilled the storm to perfect calm. He did not often intervene so miraculously these days, but He remained no less in charge.

Indeed, now He sat enthroned over the entire universe. Certainly, history since the New Testament had shown what great works He could still do with humble, obedient servants. Another Highland saying flashed through his mind: "Everything must be as God will have it."

MacKenzie flung himself to his knees and clasped his hands together. His mind raced, and he found it hard to settle down on a prayer. What should he ask for? Protection, obviously. Global peace, assuredly. The Kaiser's repentance—difficult, but definitely. Wisdom and quick wits, of course. God's glory and the fulfilment of His plan in this, most of all.

When he finally climbed into bed, MacKenzie drifted off to slumber in nearly perfect peace.

The next morning, he decided to verify what he had heard the previous night from Catriona. Connally not informing him of his intended backup? Catriona gunning down a suspect needlessly? It would be best to double-check her story.

He leaped to the task of shaving and dressing in his white linen suit for spring. Alas, it looked in little better condition than his uniform. Confound it. Had a moth eaten a hole in this jacket's elbow too? At least the crease in the front looked crisp and the waistcoat untouched.

He tied his ankle boots with the cloth tops and set to picking out his tie. Happily, he ran less risk of censure for a faded tie since fashion dictated that it be inconspicuous. His pale-blue, striped tie should prove the very thing. He topped it off with his Panama hat.

He had packed everything else the prior day while he had waited to meet with Agent Field. He had stashed his Lee-Enfield, emptied of all rounds and its ammunition, as unobtrusively as possible.

It occurred to him that he could radio the headquarters for confirmation of Catriona's story. He had too little time to visit in person. Of course, he had to transmit in code. He withdrew his codebook and jotted down what he wanted to say.

If MO3 could use radio signals that their agents could hear around the world, Connally took no chance that transmissions would be understood if intercepted. Only a handful of people in the world could read the codebook, for Archimedes had written it in an alphabet fashioned from his limitless imagination. To keep frequency from betraying the letters, the alphabet contained more than one symbol for the most common English letters.

MacKenzie tapped on his ring with Connally's call sign.

"Connally, here. Read you, Cheetah," came the reply in code.

"Have met with backup Catriona Cameron from Foreign Office," he tapped out in encrypted Morse code. "She is coming with me to Germany."

No reply came from the ring. MacKenzie waited, uncertain if Connally had received him. Finally, the ring started up again.

"Stand by," it said.

MacKenzie could not wait. His train would depart very soon. He would have to get the reply on the way. He rotated the ruby to diminish the volume to what would be an inconspicuous level when the response came. Leaving his flat, MacKenzie hailed a cab to convey his trunk with him to King's Cross Station. No message came while he was in the cab.

What is taking the colonel so long?

Upon arriving, he checked his watch out of habit before he remembered the large clocktower overlooking the station from between the two massive arched windows. The train was scheduled to leave in half an hour.

He unconsciously whistled "Sarie Marais" again as he made his way to the departure platform on the western side. He hurriedly glanced in the waiting rooms but could see no sign of Catriona. He mumbled an apology about his wife to the porter and pulled out his pocket watch again. She was cutting it close. He could always hope she had misunderstood what he'd told her.

That would solve a lot.

He went to the waiting room nearest the western entrance and sat down.

He felt his ring vibrate and heard his call sign faintly. Leaning his head on his hand so that his quiet ring was right by his ear, MacKenzie copied down the message and decoded it: "Have verified with Foreign Office. Catriona Cameron missing for two months. Disappeared on assignment in Germany."

CHAPTER 7: FAREWEEL TO ENGLAND

MacKenzie had no idea what to do now and no time to think about it. He could not miss the train to Lowestoft. And more, Catriona Cameron, or whoever she truly was, would be on it as well. There still remained a possibility that she was a British agent; she certainly knew the department's secrets. But she had lied to him about Connally knowing about her assignment.

Maybe Connally had not checked with the right person at the Foreign Office. That seemed unlikely. Even if she were German, he could not leave her on her own now; he wanted his eye on her. She knew about the meeting with Gibson, and if he left her alone, she could prepare a very nasty surprise for them.

"Och, Ranald!" a voice cried behind him. "Forgive my tardiness. Couldn't decide on that last gown to include."

MacKenzie spun about and saw her. Her clothing now could not have contrasted with her working dress from the night before any more. She wore a wool Redford suit with a jacket and skirt in vibrant pink and a white shirtwaist. She sported earrings like roses with gold stems and leaves, and ruby petals. She had arranged and piled her hair far higher under her small, matching hat than he had seen the night before.

The only thing that matched yesterday's attire was that golden dog's head necklace. Glimpsing her in daylight and clad in fine apparel took MacKenzie's breath away. In this light, he noticed a miniscule mark on her jawline that looked like a burn scar.

He could not think of anything to say, and she seemed to enjoy his dumbfounded expression. Unlike Audrey, she clearly welcomed his admiration.

She leaned in as if to kiss him on the cheek. "I have my passport. It says I am Mrs. Catriona MacKenzie," she whispered at last.

That abruptly brought MacKenzie's mind back to more important matters. "Less conspicuous as husband and wife?" he asked. "Do you believe anyone will buy that when they see your suit compared with mine?"

Catriona scrutinized his worn suit and frowned. "In my defense, it was dark when I saw you. I can't change my attire now—or passport. I take it you dinna ken much about luxury."

"No."

"While you're with me, you shall learn. My father keeps me in funds. He's gey and wealthy, but it hasn't always been that way. As the Apostle Paul said, 'I ken how to be in poverty, and I ken how to abound.'"

"Aye, weel than, I see."

"So shall you, Ranald MacKenzie. I have a first-class ticket for us. I would imagine the Secret Service funds allocated to you couldn't cover that."

She kens at least that much about British intelligence.

They boarded the train in the second car behind a sleek engine. As the train whined and rumbled along, MacKenzie and Catriona spoke very little. They faced each other on the opposing bench seats, but neither wanted to speak first.

He did not want to say anything further about the mission, and she seemed reticent as well. They were like two armies drawn up in battle array, weighing the other's strength before deciding to initiate battle.

The staring contest made MacKenzie nervous, so he grabbed a newspaper and kept watch on her from behind it. She took the hint and shifted her gaze out the window to the green countryside. MacKenzie redirected his gaze occasionally in that direction as well.

Little cottages and villages dotted the landscape, like remote islands in a sea of green. Sheep and cattle fed on the lush verdure.

MacKenzie darted his glance away. The prospect of sea traveling had made him think of the ocean, and he grew nauseous at the thought of sailing. MacKenzie might have relished the salty aroma of the air as they neared the coast had his mind not associated it with misery. Seasickness—yet another reason Connally should never have sent him. In all the turmoil of the morning, he had forgotten to take Archimedes's seasickness cure.

To MacKenzie's approval, the train reached Lowestoft on the North Sea coast precisely on time. The *Islay* was a beautiful ship. Its hull was painted black, with white on the uppermost decks and its funnels a stately red-and-black. She had a rakish look to her as befitted a Scottish ship. The ship's horn bellowed just as MacKenzie and Catriona stepped off the train and arranged for their luggage under a cawing flock of seagulls.

Procuring a steward, they got their luggage on his cart and approached the gangplank. Catriona slipped MacKenzie their upgraded tickets so he would appear the one who had bought them. Beneath the gangplank, the waves lazily slopped at the hull where the black paint met the red at the waterline. The ship's horn blew overhead again.

MacKenzie boarded the ship with trepidation, as if he stepped into Charon's ferry. He could not back out now, for he could only get off in Germany.

The steward led them down the carpeted hall and opened the door to their cabin. Catriona entered nonchalantly, but as MacKenzie took a step inside, he froze. He had never seen anything so luxurious.

The room had an emerald-green carpet, and its upholstered chairs pled to be sat in, promising comfort in return. The curtains featured a lovely floral design, its pastel colors glowing with the sunlight behind it like a summer garden. Atop the rosewood table sat a dark ice pail. Inside was a bottle of champagne with a name MacKenzie knew he had never heard of. Catriona stopped and turned around.

"What's the matter, dear? Did you forget something?"

"Er, no, I..."

"You're not leaving much room for the steward, darling."

"Och, sorry, sir." MacKenzie stumbled in to let the steward drop their luggage off.

As soon as the steward had left, Catriona could not restrain a laugh. "What's the matter, Ranald? Not accustomed to such fine accommodations?"

"Haven't seen the like since I shipped out to South Africa," he said sarcastically.

Catriona laughed. As the tugs towed the ship out to sea, she handed MacKenzie the bottle of champagne. "Here, darling. Uncork it, please. I should like a toast."

MacKenzie popped the cork and poured them each a glass. He was sparing with his and liberal with hers. If he wanted anyone to have too much alcohol on this voyage, it was she. She glanced at the glasses and smiled. She clinked hers to his.

"Fareweel to England, and may Germany keep no secrets from us!"

MacKenzie raised the glass to his lips and felt the bouquet waft into his nostrils. As he sipped it, an even more enjoyable taste teased his senses. He froze again. Catriona laughed.

"Never had a champagne this fine, I suppose!"

"Weel, it's not Dewar's whiskey."

"You can afford that?"

"That's a necessity."

"I propose that this be the last drop of alcohol we touch until we're safely back at Vittoria House, presenting our report," Catriona said.

"I quite agree, Miss Cameron."

"Catriona, please!"

The pleasantries did not last long before MacKenzie felt himself growing queasy. Soon, his body felt every sway of the ship pulse through his being. He staggered to his trunk and nearly ripped all his packings apart looking for Archimedes's seasickness cure. He needed the bottle with its thick, purple liquid.

Catriona glanced up from the newspaper she was reading. "Everything all right, Ranald?"

"Seasick... Forgot to take Archie's cure before... Now, I, I... can't find it in my trunk."

He could barely get the words out through the lump in his throat. He knew if he spent another second on his feet, he would throw up. He made his way to the bed and plopped down on the cream comforter and pillow.

She rose and went over to the trunk, which was now surrounded by articles of MacKenzie's clothing. She laughed. "A guard's uniform! Anticipating a masquerade ball in Berlin?"

"Just at the Neues Palais. I'll repack it once I—"

"Shhh! Dinna talk. It'll just make you feel worse. I'll take care of it."

She knelt down and carefully repacked everything MacKenzie had cast aside. If she was looking for any secrets of his, the trunk would disappoint;

he had everything on him but his Lee-Enfield. She rose and walked to the door to the cabin.

"You just lie still. I'll get you some Triscuits."

She returned and sat down on the bed as she handed him a plate with the crackers the manufacturer billed as the "Traveler's Delight." MacKenzie began to nibble on them.

"Strange, isn't it?" she said.

"What?"

"The MacKenzies were a naval clan, and the Camerons weren't. Your ancestors had galleys to travel and go a-raiding, but mine did their cattle theft on dry land. Yet here, you're the one seasick, and I'm fine."

Probably because you're not a Cameron.

"You just rest easy," she said with an encouraging smile. "I'll keep watch until you're weel."

She turned the chair to face the off-white cabin door and sat down.

"Thank you," MacKenzie moaned and closed his eyes. He had no choice but to accept her proposal.

As he lay as still as he could, his mind plumbed the depths of his danger. If Catriona was German and had associates aboard the vessel, he was all but powerless against them. He fingered his Webley as he imagined a gang of German agents bursting into the room. He reasoned, though, that she probably would not spring a trap until they met with Gibson, and she could get two agents for the price of one. Like a piece of flotsam amid a gale, his mind grasped the tiny hope that she really was Catriona Cameron.

***

She surprised herself with how nurturing she felt. That feeling had never been part of her nature. Perhaps, once upon a time, she'd had the ability to be, but that was before that day. Perhaps this Scot's handsomeness and helplessness had stirred something in her heart. His golden hair, gray eyes, and firm jaw were a pleasing combination. After all, protecting the helpless was the basis of her job.

Just the same, the world she lived in meant that helping the helpless involved hardening herself into a pillar of granite. Still, she could smile at her kindness to an enemy. Was that not a noble thing to do?

The complacent Brits and their Splendid Isolation!

She knew what that meant, being a friend to none and a thorn in the side of all. What great power had they not almost gone to war with since she had been born, including her own? They couldn't even resist picking a quarrel with their Yankee cousins, all while they otherwise patted the American eagle's head to get a friend against Germany. Over South America, of all places! What was *that* to them?

Of course, MacKenzie's country and her own found plenty of obscure corners of the world to squabble over, like vultures over the last remains of a squirrel. She found herself praying that she would not wind up having to kill this agent.

She went to dinner while MacKenzie lay in agony. The first-class saloon had stately furniture with the finest tablecloths possible. The pillars looked simple but elegant and blindingly white. A string quartet played a collection of lively compositions, especially Strauss. She forced herself to drink only water when she knew finer beverages were available. The lamb tasted so savory with the mint sauce!

When she returned, she went into the water closet. She soon emerged in a nightgown and approached the bed on the side opposite MacKenzie. He weakly held up his hand.

"One moment, please. I'll get up."

She smiled. "That's very gallant of you to consider my honor, Captain MacKenzie, but if a German agent bursts in on us, we're going to have a hard time convincing him we're a husband and his wife on a sightseeing trip if you're sleeping on the deck instead of in bed with me."

"What about *my* honor?"

She smirked. "I won't try to take advantage of you."

MacKenzie sighed and laid his arm over his eyes. He seemed to acquiesce. She climbed into the bed beside him.

How naïve he is!

Berlin
May 26, 1905

Tirpitz was still filled with excitement that night. He could not wait to get Hilda into bed! He might not even pause to remove his boots.

As he reached his flat's door in the twilight, he paused. Should he feel guilty? On the mission, he had already slept with two other women since his last assignation with Hilda.

Bah! Odin would feel no guilt, so neither should his most important servant.

Christ made Himself so unreasonable, he felt, for punishing mortals for doing what only came naturally. A minister had once remonstrated with him about his philandering. The man had given those stock, clichéd Christian reasons for chastity succeeded by monogamy.

Love between a husband and a wife took Christ and the Church as its model, and Christ had no Church but one, and His bride had no God but one. But the old Lutheran had really turned him off to chastity when he had said that God had designed physical relations such that they reached their deepest consummation and highest satisfaction in a level of intimacy and trust that was only possible between two people oath-bound to one another.

Trust? Trust no one—not even the gods.

That motto had stood him in good stead all his years. Leopold Tirpitz was on Leopold Tirpitz's side, and his duty was to procure for Leopold Tirpitz whatever Leopold Tirpitz desired. He served and glorified the gods so that they would find it in their best interest to serve and glorify him.

Why would anyone make up a God like Christ, one who needed nothing from His people? He had only love to motivate Him to do them good, and experience had long since taught Leopold Tirpitz not to put much stock in that. Love always proved a broken reed upon which, if a man leaned, it would pierce him and go into his hand. The Old Scoundrel and the Old Woman had beaten that into his brain.

Satisfied that he had no need to weaken himself with that unnecessary and debilitating emotion, guilt, Tirpitz opened the door to his flat.

All dark. Had Hilda forgotten? His heart leaped in alarm until he heard her humming, *"Deutschland über Alles."*

Tirpitz turned the shadowy corner to find his table lit faintly by maroon candles in golden holders. The white tablecloth glowed orange, but the rest of the room remained dark as a cave. The savory smell of veal wafted into his nostrils.

As his eyes adjusted, he could finally make Hilda out. She had dressed in a wine-colored evening gown, and she wore her blonde hair loose. Discerning his silhouette in the doorway, she stopped humming and beamed brighter than the candlelight.

"Poldy! I thought, since we haven't been together in a while, a nice, romantic dinner was the very thing—a chance to catch up!"

So much for making love with his boots on. That was the problem with Hilda—she always wanted to talk.

Smiling, he took his seat beside her. "Splendid idea, *Liebchen!*"

"Veal cutlet—your favorite!"

"You remembered."

They began to eat. Their silver clinked on the plates as they cut the meat.

"The Master was in a foul mood today," Hilda said.

Tirpitz smirked. "You said you wanted to catch up. What's actually *new?*"

"I meant worse than usual. Do you think it's because of the leak in the Kaiser's telegrams?"

"You know of that?"

"Everyone in Hlidskjalf knows of that after the way he shouted when he learned of it."

"I can assure you that the leak has been plugged." Tirpitz sighed at the memory.

"Then perhaps it's because England is drawing closer to France? What will the Reich do if she ever has to fight England, Russia, and France?"

Another crazy idea from Hilda. No wonder he didn't want to talk all night. "That is something that will never happen, Hilda. The Entente Cordiale is just a marriage of convenience between two cowardly governments who don't want to get dragged into a war in East Asia. Just you wait—when the Baltic Fleet meets its doom, England and France will go back to loathing each other like they have for the past eight hundred years."

"But, if they don't, and instead grow closer, won't France try to reconcile England and Russia?"

Tirpitz suppressed the urge to roll his eyes. He kept his tone civil. "Liebchen, no countries hate each other more than England and Russia. Their empires compete over wide swathes of the same territory. England ended five decades of so-called 'Splendid Isolation' by entering into an alliance with a far-off empire that can do her no good—I mean, of course, Japan—just to contain Russia in forsaken places all the way across the globe. Do try—that is, don't be so fearful, Liebchen." He had almost said, "Do try to think."

Something like pride flashed in Hilda's eyes. Her eyebrows arched for an instant. "We're going to have one less thing to be fearful of quite soon," she said. "The chief of police is investigating some terrible crime that happened on December 13, 1895. He wouldn't tell me what it was exactly, but he showed me an order from the Kaiser himself to pull any files the Order may have on it. I found one buried away in the basement archives, and tomorrow, I shall deliver it to him."

Tirpitz felt the blood drain from his face. He hoped the darkness concealed his paleness. Hilda seemed not to notice.

"Did you—did you read anything in it?"

"Not really. Just enough to know it was what the chief was looking for. He said it was top secret, so I didn't read beyond the first page."

"Hilda, Liebchen, I don't think you should hand that file over to the police," he said, straining every muscle to keep his face and tone even.

"Oh? Why not?"

"I believe the Order may have been involved, if I remember correctly. It could be extremely embarrassing to—" He caught himself. "I mean, the Master may take it very badly."

Hilda jolted slightly but recovered herself. "It's a command from the Kaiser!" she said. "And I promised the chief I would do my best to help him."

She has so much more integrity than I!

"Then I'll take care of it for you!" Tirpitz said. "Just give me the file, I'll dispose of it, and then you can say truthfully you don't have anything on that event, whatever it was."

Don't do this to me!

Hilda sighed. "I'm sorry, Poldy, but I would still have to tell the chief that we at one point had a file. What do Germans hold more sacred than orders from a superior or our own oaths? I must do something now that I know! If I don't, why, I might as well be a loathsome anarchist!"

Tirpitz jammed his chair back and leaped to his feet. He held out his hand. "Liebchen, you're absolutely right! You astonish me with your devotion to duty. Come, let's adjourn to the boudoir right now while my blood is hot with your fire!"

Hilda grinned. She rose gracefully to her feet. Tirpitz drew her into an embrace and began frantically planting kisses on her neck. He grasped her shoulders tenderly. Anything to get her into bed at once!

***

Hilda's devotion to duty deprived Tirpitz of all the delight he had intended to derive from her. His mind was elsewhere the whole time. As soon as he could hear her breathing heavily in sleep, he raced back to Hlidskjalf. Far from hot with love, his blood was boiling in rage. Why would the gods (and the Master) not cleanse him of his deed on that day? His fists clenched. He wished he could burn that file. The Master kept the evidence about that day to hang over his head. The Kaiser, if he knew, would never forgive Tirpitz for what he had done. He must never know. Thus was Tirpitz ever forced to do the Master's dirty work.

He unclenched his fists long enough only to seize the file and stash it back in its place in the basement. He couldn't destroy it; if the Master discovered it was missing, it would be obvious who had done it. In the darkness he thought he heard the groaning of the prisoners in the oubliettes nearby. Back in his office, he feverishly typed up a new report purporting to cover that terrible crime in detail.

His fingers practically glided over the keyboard as he imagined how things could have turned out differently—how he wished things had turned out now. It had to be as misleading as possible without losing credibility. His guilt followed him like a ghoul stalking at every turn, whipping him on.

As the bell rang at the end of the line, Tirpitz paused for one moment. No wonder Christians were willing to humble and attenuate themselves with those unnecessary hindrances of love and peace if they could be convinced they were free of their guilt. Could their God forgive even Tirpitz? If he asked forgiveness like that murderous King David of theirs...

Nein! He demands too much in return.

Odin might not purify him from guilt, but he decreed no change in behavior. Tirpitz's loins would be his to do with as he pleased—and every other part of him too. Besides, if he were Christian, he'd always be finding new sins to repent of. To be forgiven one minute and then feel guilty again the next... How futile! How foolish! If he was to make it to Valhalla, he had to save his ponderings for how to deceive the police, not how to make a weakling of himself.

May 27, 1905

MacKenzie and Catriona had disembarked the *Islay* in Hamburg. From Hamburg, they had traveled by first-class train to Berlin, where they presented their identification to the authorities and explained that they were sightseeing. MacKenzie had never seen the inside of the Savoy Hotel in London, yet here, in Berlin, he now stayed in one.

He experienced his first ride in an elevator. In the room, he found a carpet softer than he had thought possible under his shoes. Everything white glowed in the bright lighting. The bright flowers on the wallpaper seemed to dance in one vast choreographed pattern.

The rooms made his flat look like the slums in Whitechapel by comparison. For the first time, he did not have to heat his own water for bathing, since a device somewhere out of sight took care of it for him.

For dinner, they had courses so rich that MacKenzie made himself sick on the unaccustomed sauces. The cooks had stuffed one thing into another for so many layers that MacKenzie could scarcely bear the overload on his tongue from so many delicious tastes. Definitely a step up from the brose and butter he had grown up on in Easter Ross. He could not hope to offer to pay for the dinner, however much that might have counted against his gallantry.

Catriona insisted on strolling in the hotel's gardens, pink and white with blooming chestnuts. MacKenzie noticed a tall, imposing hauptmann standing straight as a ramrod in his gray uniform. He instinctively averted his eyes and ducked into the shadows as they crossed paths, strolling past a particularly vibrant, shady tree.

Lower down rolled a flood of red, gold, and white roses. Catriona leaned down to better fill her senses with the aroma. Her graceful movement, the red rose matching her lips...

Confound it! He was staring.

Catriona rose and held out her arm. MacKenzie gulped and took it in his.

That night, they ate in the hotel restaurant with water from a spa, the most refreshing MacKenzie had ever drunk.

Next morning came the day they were to meet Gibson. MacKenzie heard a newspaper delivered outside the door by one of the bellhops. He retrieved it, glanced at the headline, and froze.

CHAPTER 8:
A NIGHT AT THE OPERA

Berlin
May 28, 1905

The newspaper crinkled in his hand.

"Bad news, Ranald?" Catriona asked.

"No, not bad... just surprising, I'd say. The Baltic Fleet's voyage is at an end. It wound up at the bottom of the deep."

"What?" she gasped.

"It's been annihilated in the Straits of Tsushima."

"What? How could that be?"

"The Japanese based their navy on ours."

Catriona sat stunned and silent. He noticed her face redden. MacKenzie's own revealed a subdued, philosophical satisfaction.

"There's a bit of good news," he said. "The Russians have been humbled. Maybe now the war will end, and they'll stop causing trouble."

"What? Och, aye, aye. But that the Japanese could defeat a world power..."

"I'd say they're a world power themselves now."

"You dinna come back from isolation and stagnation like that so quickly," Catriona said defensively.

"Except they did."

"What time do we meet with Gibson tonight?" she said hurriedly.

"Seven o'clock in the Royal Opera House. Hopefully, we'll finish our meeting in time to catch the fine music."

"Revolutionary racket," Catriona said. "Haven't you ever considered how Odin is the capitalist and Götterdämmerung the revolution that topples his empire?"

"I find it best not to drill too deeply into artists' personal lives, for the vast majority are disreputable wretches at heart. Wagner, for instance, was a vicious anti-Semite."

Catriona glanced away as though unimpressed.

"Handel—now there's a man you can admire as an artist and a musician."

"If it weren't for him, there wouldn't be any great songs in English," Catriona said with a wink. "But we all ken the best songs are Scottish."

MacKenzie sensed an opportunity. "And what's your favorite?"

"'Up and Waur Them A', Willie,'" she said without hesitation.

MacKenzie's lips parted. "That's mine too!"

It's also one not too many people ken about.

She grinned. "Come on, Ranald, start us off!"

MacKenzie began to sing, and Catriona immediately joined in:

> *When we went to the field of war and to the weaponshaw, Willie,*
> *With true design to serve our king and banish Whigs awa', Willie.*
> *Up and waur them a', Willie, waur, waur a'.*
> *The lords and lairds came there bedeen,*
> *And wow but they were braw, Willie.*

They sang all eight verses flawlessly. Her voice was mellifluous, the performance eminently enjoyable. Every test MacKenzie gave this woman, she passed with perfection. Maybe she was Catriona Cameron after all. But then, how could Connally have confirmed with the Foreign Office that she had not been heard from when she had in fact returned? That seemed possible but not plausible.

And she appeared disappointed and angered by the news she had just heard. No patriotic Brit would mind the Russian bear receiving a good drubbing at sea, especially not at the hands of Britain's ally. But a Frog, a Hun, or a Ruskie could.

The Kaiser had proposed sending the Baltic Fleet in the first place, and the French were Russia's allies. He could not let his guard down fully, but then, it might come to the point where he had to trust her fully. What then?

For now, he had no intention of letting her meet with Gibson. If she was planning a trap, that would be the place to spring it. He quickly thought of how best to distract her.

"This article contains information that might be useful to our mission, however distasteful you find it," he said as he brought her the newspaper. "Please read it and see what you think."

She took the newspaper as MacKenzie returned to his seat and drew out a notepad. As she read, he jotted down a message.

"I just heard from Gibson on my wireless ring," he said. "A contact of his has slipped a new telegram from the Kaiser to the Tsar into a doctoral dissertation by a Georg Stuckart on the Battle of the Teutoberger Wald and its connection to the Siegfried myth. He can't go there himself since he believes they're both under suspicion. I'll meet with Gibson if you retrieve the telegram. It's just across the street. You can be back in time for the opera. Here's the approximate shelf it's on."

He handed her the note with a random set of directions he hoped would be confusing enough. She nodded and stashed the instructions in her handbag.

***

MacKenzie had to remind his heart to beat when he glimpsed Catriona in her evening gown later that night. The gown was the color of claret, with ruffles at the waist and flared sleeves that draped down from her elbows. The chiffon fabric and taffeta underneath made an enchanting whisper as she walked.

Much to his surprise, she seemed to requite his astonishment. For once, he wore the highest quality in fabrics—a dark suit with tails, a white waistcoat, and a silk top hat. For a moment, neither could say a word.

Catriona recovered her voice first. She clasped her hands.

"That's the style, Ranald!" she said. "Would that you could dress like that all the time!"

"It's in good condition because it doesn't get worn that much."

"I'll certainly not be ashamed to go out with you in public like that."

"And you were before?"

She laughed. "You said it yourself, Ranald. The two of us as husband and wife wasn't very believable by sartorial comparison. Pity you couldn't wear your dress uniform. I'd wager you'd look like a knight in shining armor."

MacKenzie's heart leaped at the compliment, but then he remembered his instructions. "We have no connection to War Office Intelligence on this mission."

"I ken that, Ranald! Just take the compliment."

They got a cab over to the Royal Opera House. MacKenzie hummed to himself something he remembered by Wagner.

Catriona laid her hand on his. "That's 'Tannhauser,' darling. We're going to see 'Die Walküre.'"

MacKenzie sighed. She played the part of his wife splendidly.

The cab pulled up in front of the Royal Opera House. The structure had a pale pink exterior, which reminded MacKenzie of azaleas. The zinc tympanum featured a selection of the relevant muses and a frolicking satyr. The entrance stood between two iron stairways on the right and left, and as they walked toward the door, stone statues kept watch over them. MacKenzie glanced across the plaza and caught sight of the Royal Library, which someone had said looked like a giant chest of drawers made for holding books.

"See you in time for the 'Ride of the Valkyries,'" MacKenzie said cheerily.

She walked over toward the library. MacKenzie stepped inside amidst the chattering of the waiting spectators. Ivory columns supported the balcony with capitals and trim of gold. MacKenzie peered around the crystal chandelier at the balcony for any eavesdroppers. He glanced at the column where they were to meet. Where was Gibson?

He checked his watch. He was a little early. Gibson still had time to show up without demonstrating impertinence.

MacKenzie instinctively looked back to see if Catriona had returned. If only Gibson would hurry up! He had to get their conversation done before she returned. He glanced at his watch again. Minutes were slipping away.

Finally, a man in a well-tailored suit over a white waistcoat approached him. MacKenzie recognized him as Captain Gibson.

"I wish I was shooting in the Highlands," MacKenzie said.

"The sport is better in the Vienna Woods," he replied.

Gibson held out his hand. MacKenzie grasped it and felt the piece of paper hidden in his palm.

"So how are our favorite cousins?" MacKenzie said. "Still on speaking terms, no doubt?"

"They have not confided anything in me," Gibson said. "And I couldn't read any of their latest telegrams, even if I tried."

"How are you getting on at the New Place?" MacKenzie said, avoiding the name Neues Palais. "Making any friends?"

"None that can unburden their soul to me. This ominous 'Order' keeps cropping up in their talk, though. Every time someone disappears, they're convinced the Order has something to do with it. I haven't heard from my friend from the New Place. I had intended to meet with him this morning for breakfast."

MacKenzie's heart sank. "What Order?" he asked.

"Not sure. I think they have something to do with that new castle that's been built a few miles down the road from the New Place. I think they might also be connected with the Place itself. I've learned that there's a two-story red brick house just north of the grounds of the New Place that's being used as an armory in case of an emergency at the palace."

"How many guards?" MacKenzie asked.

Gibson clammed up and looked over MacKenzie's shoulder. MacKenzie turned to see Catriona right behind him. If there was a trap brewing, now would be the moment. MacKenzie felt the blood rushing to his cheeks.

"That didn't take long, darling," MacKenzie said.

"You must have been mistaken, dear. The Dewey decimal catalog was quite clear that there was no dissertation in that part of the library."

Confound it!

MO3 had adopted that system soon after its invention, but he had not expected someone outside the department to be so familiar with it. Catriona held out her hand. Gibson forced a smile and kissed it.

"You have a very beautiful wife, Captain Cheetah," he said. He leaned in and whispered in MacKenzie's ear, "You brought your wife along?"

"You weren't expecting Catriona Cameron?" MacKenzie whispered back.

"Who?"

MacKenzie felt hollow in his chest. What could he do now? He had to get the information from Gibson while the conversation around them blocked out the sound to any listeners. But now he had even more reason to suspect that Catriona Cameron was not who she claimed to be.

An acrid odor suddenly stung MacKenzie's nostrils. Catriona and Gibson wrinkled their noses. In another breath, MacKenzie recognized what it was. Chloroform! He had not smelled it since that day. Flashes of memory slammed into his head. His right side ached. His eyes watered.

Wait a moment! Why on earth am I smelling chloroform in an opera house?

CHAPTER 9: THE TRAP

MacKenzie saw two men approaching Catriona and Gibson. Rags dangled from their hands, dipped, no doubt, in chloroform. They had been set up! MacKenzie quickly looked behind him.

He was not disappointed. A third figure with a rag crept right behind him. He dropped the telegram and jabbed his elbow into the fellow's diaphragm. The man crumpled over. MacKenzie turned back. The other two had already seized Catriona and Gibson and had pressed the rags to their faces. Both struggled futilely, trying to pry the rags away.

MacKenzie's sense of honor sent him instinctively toward the man assaulting Catriona. He swung a left-handed "hay-maker" at the attacker's right ear. The man dropped to the floor, releasing Catriona.

The third assailant was already dragging a thrashing Gibson away. The stunned crowd receded from them like a tide. MacKenzie lunged after him. He had almost reached them when he heard shots ring out. Several of the operagoers screamed. MacKenzie froze. He glanced around as his mind darted back to that day.

Catriona had withdrawn a pistol from her handbag and shot both of the fallen men. A succession of four shots rang out in reply. Mausers! This time they really were Mausers!

MacKenzie's heart raced as quickly as his thoughts. The echo in the opera house made it seem like the gunfire surrounded them. He panicked.

Several German soldiers emerged from behind columns with their rifles. The situation was getting far too hot for one wide-awake agent backed up by a half-drugged one. At least one thing was clear—Catriona was on his side. He grabbed her wrist.

"Come on!"

As they made a run for it, Catriona proved rather sluggish. As the Germans pursued, however, she fired another shot that cut the lead one down. The others hesitated.

The spies emerged from the opera house into the night, and MacKenzie experienced an epiphany. He observed three black automobiles of the Benz & Cie. Wolfhart design. The gas lights lining the street gleamed off the glossy black frames.

The small, sleek racecars were top secret assets of the German military, but MacKenzie thanked heaven that he'd had experience with them. An agent had infiltrated the company the prior year and smuggled one for MO3 that MacKenzie had tested.

The auto had four seats, as the generals intended for them to carry messengers and officers about the battlefield in the quickest manner possible. He and Catriona could both get away in one.

MacKenzie dashed to the leading auto as quickly as Catriona's legs could manage. Shots rebounded off the steel exterior, which was armored for protection in battle. He spied the crank and thanked heaven for the enemy's oversight.

"Get in!" he said as he released her and snatched the crank.

"You can drive this thing?"

"Aye."

MacKenzie inserted the crank and pulled for his life. A bullet rushed under his arm; a second's difference and it would have hit him as he brought his arm down. He did not have the presence of mind to hold the crank correctly, but this vehicle had safety mechanisms to keep the crank from breaking his hand as the engine roared to life.

The Germans rushed out of the opera house. Catriona fired a shot that brought another Hun down. MacKenzie leaped into the vehicle and floored the gas. He could see soldiers in the mirror leaping into the other two cars before he reached second gear.

Catriona had fallen asleep in the passenger side from the chloroform. Not even the ringing of shots from the car behind could rouse her. Since the Germans were after her as well, he would protect her while she was so vulnerable.

***

Back in the opera house, Tirpitz stepped out from his place in the corridor and surveyed the damage. That had not worked out as he had hoped. Drugging Gibson and reading his instructions for this meeting had seemed like a good idea at the time, but he had just lost two agents and gained only one enemy agent in return. Besides, what good was Gibson? He had served Tirpitz's purposes perfectly, simply by being surveilled. Tirpitz had really wanted the two spies who had gotten away.

Heinrich saluted and handed him the telegrams. "We have recovered the Kaiser's correspondence," he said.

"Yes, at quite a cost." Tirpitz sighed as he regarded the two dead agents and the fallen soldier. "You didn't read these, did you?"

"Nein, Herr Hauptmann, not I."

"Good. I'll see they're sent to Potsdam in the morning. Did they take the right car?"

"Yes, sir. They took the car with the device fixed to it. We can follow their trail of phosphorescent paint at our leisure."

"I want a squad assembled on the double, Heinrich. You and I will handle the pursuit personally."

At least his backup plan had worked. Truly cat-and-mouse, for the enemy had thought they would get away, but Tirpitz would disabuse them of their illusion soon enough—assuming, of course, that the pursuers in the Wolfhart vehicles did not catch them first.

***

MacKenzie could not go beyond third gear in the Wolfhart, controlling his speed as he swerved around cabs and omnibuses. At least the Germans in the following cars would have a hard time shooting straight. The bumpy roads were making control difficult, but it would also affect their aim. How many soldiers were trained to shoot out of autos?

An omnibus was straight ahead. In a split-second, MacKenzie brought the auto around just to the right of it. His vehicle skidded. MacKenzie turned the wheel into the skid and regained control just in time to pass a horse-drawn cab turning into an intersection. The horse took fright and bolted with the cab, a chorus of shouts arising from down the street.

MacKenzie and Catriona jostled back and forth as he pulled right and left, dodging every obstacle. He was practically leaning on the four-key hornet horn—just like His Majesty. He kept looking in the mirrors. The other Wolfharts clung close behind.

A bicycle careened off the road as the cyclist made way for the speeding vehicles. MacKenzie had no time to feel guilty. He only thought of escape.

Shots rang out. A ping meant that one had hit the exterior, hopefully not penetrating anything vital. MacKenzie slammed on the brakes to make a sharp right down another street. The car screeched, but he kept it from skidding. The Germans matched his maneuver. MacKenzie accelerated to the speed he had had before the turn.

An ox cart came lumbering up from an alley on the right. The driver, seeing the mad pack of cars racing down on him, leaped to safety, leaving the cart in the middle of the road. MacKenzie made the tightest left turn imaginable. He hit the brakes and, at the last minute, turned the car down the alley. He had barely straightened out the wheel when he heard an almighty crash. He glanced behind in the mirror.

One of the Germans had slammed into the cart. Splinters fell everywhere like wooden rain. The oxen shrieked hideously.

The other Wolfhart kept on him like a foxhound. MacKenzie could not spare a glance at the speedometer. He focused his attention straight ahead. Shots rang out again and pinged off the armor.

He passed onto a bridge. The structure rumbled beneath his tires. He spied one vehicle moving slowly ahead of him and another several yards away heading in his direction on the other side of the bridge. He had seconds to turn the gear into fourth, giving a burst of acceleration and passing around the auto in front of him. The other car honked and slammed on its brakes to avoid a head-on collision. MacKenzie cleared it by mere inches.

MacKenzie glanced in his mirror. The blasted Huns were still on them!

Another Mauser shot. MacKenzie's left mirror shattered. Glass went everywhere. MacKenzie wished he could fly on a kelpie since there seemed no escape in this thing.

A bullet hissed between him and Catriona and went through the dashboard with a clink. He finally reached the end of the bridge and swerved right. The Germans followed.

A new odor wafted into MacKenzie's nostrils. Burning paint! The engine was overheating. Something had to give, or the car would shut down, and he would find himself at the mercy of the Germans. He had to think of something.

"Catriona, wake up!" He took his hand off the steering wheel long enough to give her a quick jolt.

"Och!"

"Catriona, can you shoot the tires out from their car?"

"If I dinna drop the gun out the window..."

"Mind the bumps."

She turned and leaned through the open window. With the cars swerving, MacKenzie wondered if she could get a clean shot. She had to do it quickly, for their opponents had begun shooting at her. He scanned the road ahead.

"There's nothing ahead. Shoot now!"

For an instant, the two cars went straight. Either the Germans or Catriona had a clear shot. Catriona fired, and the report of the gun was followed by the boom of a blowout. The enemy's car swerved with an ear-piercing screech as its momentum carried it along with only three sound tires.

Catriona fired again, and a second boom proclaimed her success on the other tire. Their foes' vehicle lurched forward and shrieked to a stop on two flat front tires. MacKenzie laughed with relief. He worked the car back down to first gear.

"It's not over yet," Catriona said. "They've rigged something to this car that's trailing phosphorescent paint. They'll track us, so we can't go straight back to the hotel. Take us to another, and we'll walk back to ours. Och, if only I weren't half-dead from this chloroform!"

She broke her pistol open to reload with ammunition from her handbag. MacKenzie glanced over long enough to get a glimpse of the other contents.

Behind the ammunition pouch lay a little booklet with a chilling title in Cyrillic: "The Manufacture and Use of Gelignite Grenades."

CHAPTER 10: THE AGENT'S SECRET

The whistle of a skylark awakened MacKenzie. He was embarrassed at how late he'd slept. Catriona's soft breathing indicated that she was still sleeping. Of course, that was probably the chloroform. Hopefully, the effect wouldn't last much longer. They needed to be moving on.

He had driven them three kilometers from their hotel before leaving the car with a valet at the Grand Hotel Alexanderplatz. He had felt like a barbarian making Catriona trudge across Berlin in her state, but he had helped her to the point of his own exhaustion. He turned his head on the pillow to confirm that she was still asleep.

Everything about this woman took his breath away—the dignified stillness of her features, the elegant cast of her face. She resembled the sleeping Valkyrie from the opera they had intended to watch the previous night. Certainly, she was as fierce as one. Shame stabbed into his heart. He was no hero worthy to wake her like Siegfried, not haunted as he was by the shades of that day.

He was a captain of the mess of the Black Watch, to be sure, the finest regiment in the finest army on the planet. The regiment that had lost two-thirds of its men rather than admit that the French breastworks at Ticonderoga could not be taken. The regiment that had stopped the entire French I Corps at Waterloo (with a little help from their fellow Scots in the Gordons and Greys, he conceded generously). He even had a VC to pin on his chest. But did that make him a hero?

And what of Gibson? His chest suddenly felt hollow as he gave the poor fellow his first thought since he had heard those first shots. He had lost his nerve, and now a comrade had fallen into the hands of the enemy.

Surely, he could have rescued Gibson with a few more strides and a swift blow like the one that had saved Catriona. As he had on that day, he had let a countryman down in the worst of all ways. He did not even have the Kaiser's telegram or the telegrapher's correspondence! He realized now that he had dropped them in his effort to escape.

He prayed for forgiveness. He had not acted with the boldness of one trusting in Providence's perfect ordering of events. Had he let God down too? Of course he had; he always did. He had to pray that next time he would have courage.

After all, what did it matter if he died? The Apostle Paul, who had faced dangers at least as great as that day, had written confidently, "Who shall separate us from the love of Christ? Shall tribulation or distress or persecution or famine or nakedness or peril or sword? (As it is written, 'For Thy sake we are killed all the day long. We are accounted as sheep for the slaughter.) Nay, in all these things we are more than conquerors, through Him that loved us."

Someone who believed in that would not flinch if the entire world arrayed against him. His mind flitted to the auld Highland saying, "He who intends no evil, dreads no evil."

Suddenly it occurred to him how providential his escape last night had been. Panicked by the Mausers, somehow, he had had clarity of mind enough to drive through the bustling streets of Berlin without an accident. Catriona, though drugged, had still shot better than the Germans. No bullet had touched either of them. There was much to be grateful to God for.

He sighed. If only God had been so merciful to Gibson. Surely Gibson deserved it more, not cowardly Ranald MacKenzie.

He glanced back over at Catriona. Diplomacy weighed on his mind just as heavily. He had put the pieces together; he knew now what she truly was. His country and hers had become as close to sworn enemies as one could get without declaring war. The politicians had narrowly averted that cataclysm in the past, but how many more times could the two great powers back down from their standoffs?

If not for the seriousness of the crisis, he would have dissevered himself from her. Yet, she remained his only ally now on the Continent, and he had to ensure that that Continent did not unite against Britain. If he could not engineer a conference... It would be that day a million times over around the world. Europe would wallow in the bloody throes of death.

Certainly, Catriona had proven her worth in a crisis. While he had panicked and let a comrade be taken, she had practically held off an entire German squad. She had aimed perfectly with her pistol at the tires despite all the motion.

But what he knew she was repelled him to his core. It was bad enough she was a Russian subject, but to be an Okhrana provocateur... She belonged to the Tsar's secret police, and her task entailed tempting anarchists into committing heinous crimes so they could be arrested and so that a horrified world would turn against anarchism.

And all this for a regime that would send men and women to a life of hard labor in freezing Siberia just for reading the wrong book. It was a regime that allowed mobs to riot against unhappy Jewish communities to distract from the problems it had created itself but would open fire on peaceful protesters who came to petition the Tsar at his palace.

He had to wake her. The Germans had no doubt followed their trail all night. They had had to sleep in the hotel out of necessity from fatigue. Now they needed to be on the first train they could get. They would have to try again in Russia.

He tapped on her shoulder. "Catriona!"

Her eyes remained closed. "Mm. Ranald, what is it?" she mumbled.

"We need to be going. We've slept too long. They've no doubt been looking for us all night. We'll take a train out of here, all right?"

"All right. Where?"

"With the Germans on our tail, I suppose the safest thing to do would be to carry out the mission in Russia," MacKenzie said. "I trust it will be pleasant for you to return home."

Now her eyes shot open. "Home? What on earth are you talking about?"

"I ken what you are, lassie. You're an Okhrana agent provocateur."

"Wherever did you get such an outlandish idea?"

"That revolutionary you shot in the East End called to you like he kent you. Then I got a glimpse of bomb-making instructions in Cyrillic in your handbag. You are clearly involved in the Russian underworld. The fact that you betrayed anger about the Battle of Tsushima indicates you are on the Tsar's side, not the pacifist anarchists. I want answers, or I'm going to arrest you with that treasonable material on your person."

She sighed. "All right, what do you wish to ken?" she said as she revealed her Ukrainian accent.

"For a start, your real name." He took her hand in his as if to kiss it. "Whom do I have the honor of addressing?"

"I am Svetlana Petrovna Rachkovskaya. You can call me Sveta or Lana. Peter Ivanovich Rachkovsky is my adoptive father. I'm part of his network in Britain."

The way he held her hand, he could tell that neither her pulse quickened nor her hand grew cold, evidencing that she was telling the truth at last. Now he knew where she got her skill (and heartlessness) from if the Okhrana's greatest spymaster had adopted her.

"Why did you kill that man in Whitechapel?"

She looked away with a cold air. "He had it coming. I would have sent him to Siberia eventually anyway. It became more pressing at that moment to keep him from blowing my cover with you, though. He thought I was a fellow anarchist, not Catriona Cameron, of course."

Her ruthlessness chilled MacKenzie's blood.

"Why are you pretending to be Catriona Cameron?"

"Do you ken Vladimir Burtsev? He's a revolutionary, and he decided to keep a dossier on every suspected police agent just like we keep a dossier on every suspected anarchist. He was finally arrested in the British Museum, but your Parliament insisted that his files not be handed over to the Okhrana. My father wanted that list, so I worked my way into British intelligence to get it. Since then, it's just easier to access other information I want from your British liberals by pretending to be one of them."

"I'll give you some advice. Catriona Cameron went missing in Germany two months ago."

Svetlana muttered something in Ukrainian.

"Why are you working with me?" MacKenzie said. "Why not one of your Okhrana chums? How did you even ken about my mission?"

She laughed. "I'm a frequent visitor to your Winchester House. I just happened to learn of your mission when the special duties section was stationed there temporarily. But under present circumstances, I would actually rather work with a British agent, distasteful as that might be, than an Okhrana one. Too many have turned traitor and worked for the revolutionaries. You can't tell who to trust anymore. And even if they are on the Tsar's side, they might not be on my father's. The Tsar restored him to power, yes, but he and the Tsaritsa dinna like him. The Tsar only took him back into the Okhrana because of the emergency with the Grand Duke Sergei's murder, and the last thing my father needs is for some opponent of his to learn that he assigned me to spy on the Tsar, especially if he's a Russian who already doesn't trust me as a Ukrainian. They feel threatened now that we're starting to develop an identity of our own. They'll lose their great power status if ever we break away."

"And why would the Okhrana be interested in a treaty between the Kaiser and the Tsar? What does that have to do with anarchists?"

"My father's afraid Wilhelm is going to lure our Little Father away from France. If that happens, our job will become much more difficult in keeping track of the revolutionaries there. Not to mention all the work my father has invested in the Franco-Russian alliance. I can state with pride that no one did more to encircle Germany than he. Anyway, the Little Father is keeping the treaty secret even from us, so I was tasked to look into it. My father believes there are several members of our cabinet he can confide in who will dissuade the Little Father before any treaty goes into effect. He trusts me with his most important missions. Now, do you have any other questions?"

MacKenzie had held her hand the entire time and detected no signs of stress or lying. He was satisfied. He let her go. "No."

"Then I have one. Can I still rely on your collaboration?"

"I suppose."

"No supposing, Ranald! Our countries are mortal enemies, and we both ken how far we can trust one another. I give you my oath that I will back you up until we get the treaty in return for your own promise. I won't go another step with you otherwise. Will you take it?"

MacKenzie bit his lip. He would rather have a Boer in front of him than a Russian subject behind him. As she said, he knew how far he could trust a servant of the Tsar. Even if she was Ukrainian by birth, she had joined his secret police and served the empire that dominated her homeland. The Russians had as their ultimate objective the Russification of their subject peoples. How far had they gone in turning this one?

A Russian volunteer with the Boers had shot and killed MacKenzie's brother after his commando had pretended to surrender. The fact that the Russians had been willing to fight the British in a war that was not their own seemed downright spiteful. He had a hard time forgiving that. If they had not hated Britain so, and he could think of no cause why they should have, his brother would have still been alive to this day. And how many oaths had Svetlana doubtless given the anarchists she intended to betray to the police?

But then, did he have any choice? Could he proceed on his own when she knew about his mission? They apparently wanted the same thing. Did he really think he could get as close to the Tsar without her? Shouldn't he leap at the chance to torpedo this thing within the Russian cabinet without making a public show of it all?

He took her hand again. "I accept it. As the auld Highland saying goes, 'I will not be one day for you, and another against you.' Now, if we go down the street to the Friedrichstrasse Station, we can catch a train to Breslau and then change to one going to Warsaw. Hopefully, the change will make us harder to track. I think it would also be less conspicuous if we took third class this time. I hope you dinna mind."

"I'll manage. I ken how to be in poverty, remember?"

From what he had seen, MacKenzie doubted she knew what poverty truly was.

A swift walk around the block brought them to the Friedrichstrasse Station. Above and between the masonry walls with their arches rose a steel train shed that covered the platforms.

As they made their way in from the north, MacKenzie looked up at a magnificent cupola. In fact, the whole area was dotted with cupolas. He scanned them as he entered the station for any watching eyes. Hopefully, this was not the obvious next place for a spy to go to from the Grand Hotel Alexanderplatz.

Train whistles and the chugging of engines reverberated in the train shed. A pair of dark-blue uniforms off to the side of the platform caught MacKenzie's eye. He saw two burly men with thick mustaches. They stood motionless, their eyes surveying the station like a cheetah from atop an anthill. Their eyes shifted, but the rest of them did not stir. They waited for prey.

"Police," he whispered in Svetlana's ear.

MacKenzie pretended a mild coughing fit so he could raise his handkerchief to his face. Svetlana raised her fan to cover hers. For good measure, MacKenzie purchased a newspaper in case he needed to hide behind it. Svetlana kept an eye over her fan on the police as MacKenzie purchased the tickets to Breslau.

MacKenzie thought Svetlana would be horrified by third class, but she disappointed him. She sat down on the plain bench-like seat next to MacKenzie with a contented sigh and fanned herself. The train whistled again and began steaming through Berlin. Majestic buildings streamed past the windows.

German words buzzed all around them like a hive of bees. The packed train meant they could not speak in any commonly known language. Fortunately, MacKenzie knew that they possessed a rare language between them.

"Let's see what your marksmanship is thought of in the press," MacKenzie muttered in Gaelic. He turned to see the front page of the paper. The paper crinkled.

"What?" he exclaimed. "British anarchist slays three German soldiers!' 'German ambassador to the Court of St. James's to issue formal protest!' I didn't kill anyone!"

"If they can't accept the notion of a lethal markswoman, that's, as the Poles say, 'Not my circus, not my monkeys,'" Svetlana said in Gaelic.

She was never at a loss. MacKenzie thought that if he had addressed her in Kaffir, she could have responded. He grudgingly admired her quick wits but tugged at his collar to release the heat under his shirt like steam.

"And how many of those Poles have you sent to freeze in Siberia?" he said.

She looked him coldly in the eyes. "Probably a few more than the Irishmen your government sent to bake in Australia."

"You've painted a target on my back better than Rembrandt could have! There's even a description of us. You and your pistol. That's a fine thank you after I saved your life."

Svetlana's eyes flared like an explosion of fireworks. "Excuse me, but if you saved my life, I saved *yours* with that pistol. Remind me, which of us shot the tires out of our pursuers' car?"

MacKenzie shifted to the edge of his chair, looking about to explode in response, but his mind left his body hanging. For a moment, he sat still. His eyes flitted as he tried to think of some snappy comeback, but they searched in vain. Finally, he sat back. "All right, you have me. I just wish you hadn't shot the two men when they were down."

She laid a hand on his shoulder. "It was a snap-judgment—maybe a wrong one, but maybe also a right one," she said gently. "Who's to say now?"

MacKenzie sighed.

Svetlana's lips parted. "So you suspected I was a Russian subject when you saved me instead of Captain Gibson?"

"I suppose so."

"So why would you rescue a rival nation's spy rather than a countryman?"

"Instinct. Something to do with the damsel being in distress." He did not want to mention that he had panicked before he could get to Gibson.

Svetlana frowned. "Distress—I dinna suppose I could argue that. Damsel—I dinna ken about that. But I do sense a frostiness toward Russians in your eyes. I suspect that would extend to Ukrainians like me as weel."

"You serve the Tsar of All the Russias, don't you?"

"Aye, he has my oath. Much as I'd prefer for him to let Ukrainians be Ukrainians, he is the force I support to keep the anarchists in check. My countrymen strive honorably to preserve our language and our culture, but I draw the line at revolution against him. I'll guard him against his foes like a brother Cossack warrior unless there's a way for us to depart in peace. Then I would serve my homeland with the same sense of honor as to him."

"Weel then..."

"So you *do* look down on me?"

"Can you blame me? Our countries have hated each other for nearly a century. Your government represents everything we fought civil wars and revolutions to escape from."

She laid a hand on his. "Oh, come now, Ranald, can't you appreciate anything from my country?"

"Weel, your music can hold its own with any nation's. I'd put Tchaikovsky right up there with Strauss and Wagner."

Svetlana's eyes brightened. "I love Tchaikovsky too! The elegance of our aristocratic culture is one of the things I fight for. I love a good ball and dancing into the wee hours of the morning. Fun is not something I'm allowed to have much of, so I relish every moment of it I can snag. Your country has some excellent pastimes, I must say: tennis, cycling, foxhunting. And who could possibly be funnier than Gilbert and Sullivan or Harry Lauder and his 'ower thrifty wee mannie'?"

MacKenzie glanced down. "I love concerts and the theater too, but I probably spend more on them than I should."

She stroked his arm. "Dinna feel bad, Ranald. Weel-done art is one of the glories of mankind—an aspect of God's image in us. But however you feel about Russia as a country, I'd wager the aristocrats of our two countries live very similar lives. Music, dancing, dressing up, shooting…"

"Aye, shooting," MacKenzie said, "I often go badger-shooting with my five terriers in the Highlands."

Her brows wrinkled. "You dinna seem like you can afford that."

"Connally underwrites it with government funds. Best target practice in the world, he says. I usually bring a bag full of books when I do. I'm a soldier because I bought into Scott's depiction of soldiering as glorious."

"And you no longer think it is?" she said.

He sighed. "I saw the reality in South Africa."

She patted his hand. "Give yourself a little credit, Ranald. If soldiering isn't glorious, what can possibly be so? You Highlanders in your regiments ken what awaits you in battle—agony, mutilation, and possibly death—and yet you rush into it to protect your homes and family! You fight for each other like a band of Cossack brethren. Soldiers live every day by the rule that, 'Greater love hath no man than this, that a man lay down his life for his friends.'"

MacKenzie's eyes watered as she spoke. She had reawakened the feelings he had not felt since that day. She had made his heart glow again to wear the khaki.

"Why do you think I serve my country in the Okhrana and face the same risks, if not for the same reason?" she continued. "I ken full-well what a revolution would mean for my homeland. You can't let just any yobbo rule Russia. Why, you get a loathsome scoundrel in charge, and how long do you think he'll keep his mitts off our wheatfields, oilfields, and industry? Or put the workers in charge instead of the landowners, and how long do you think it will take for them to make a pig's breakfast of the best farmland in the world? We've been feeding civilization for millennia, and I'll see to it we do for millennia more!"

MacKenzie frowned. "If only you didn't go about it in such a dishonorable way!"

She laughed. "Oh, and you are so honorable as a spy?"

"Aye, fairly! I avoid all the vices soldiers and spies fall prey to. I dinna gamble. I drink, but not to excess. I dinna visit houses of ill-repute. I try to live by Christ's precepts as best I can in my feeble way."

She laughed, and her lips formed a foxy smile. "I notice, though, even your code of honor lets you lie to accomplish the mission. You sent me on a wild-goose chase last night on purpose."

He glanced away. "It took some soul-searching when I first became a spy. I subscribe to hierarchicalism. I believe certain moral commands take precedence over others. Take David's oath to Saul not to cut off his posterity. Years later, David had to break that oath to avenge the Gibeonites to whom the Israelites were bound by an earlier oath. And everyone kens that we shouldn't honor the authorities by obeying them when their commands conflict with God's."

He turned back to face her. "I believe that the ten commandments are ranked in order of importance: our duties to God first and to man second. It begins by forbidding idolatry, the sin that underlies every sin, and ends by forbidding coveting, which is just a thought. A rebellious, wicked thought, to be sure, but surely not as bad as outright idolatry."

Svetlana nodded charitably.

"The commandment to preserve life comes before the commandment against lying. You see, several saints lie to protect themselves or others, and in the case of the Hebrew midwives lying to save the baby Israelite boys, the text says they lied, then it says God *therefore* blessed them. It would seem the reason He blessed them includes the lie if it precedes the 'therefore,' wouldn't you say?"

"I take it you mean more saints than Rahab and the midwives, then," she said.

"Aye, it's not just them, often as they are presented as the only examples. Elisha lies to the Syrians, I would say. Some say he didn't lie to them because he had left the town he had told them he was not in. But anyone can see he's saying something very different from the obvious truth: 'I'm right here in front of ye loons!' He tells the Syrians, 'This is not the way.' Aye, it surely was, since they've come right upon him."

He backed up his point by counting on his hands.

"Jael lies to Sisera, David lies frequently to save his hide, Jonathan lies to Saul, Hushai lies to Absalom, and the woman in II Samuel 17 lies to protect David's spies. It seems to me, when life is on the line and we are at a disadvantage, we can try to deceive our way out of it, or we can tell the truth and hope God intervenes miraculously. I can think of plenty of saints who did the former, but not one saint who did the latter. Now, of course, we should never lie about our faith in Christ like Peter did because we have no higher duty than to honor God, so no hierarchy could possibly rank anything before it."

Svetlana pursed her lips. "Sometimes, we have to go further than that to protect the Tsar. I take it there's no double-dealing in your system."

"No!"

Svetlana smiled. "Hm. I wonder how long you can last as a spy thinking like that. Your Sidney Reilly plays all sides, you ken. He works with us just the same as he works with you. Even I have to disclose a little secret or two from my nation to stay credible as Catriona Cameron—or whoever I will have to be now."

"I am loyal to God and to His Majesty! I serve them and them only."

Svetlana smirked like a mother whose child had just said something sweet and sincere but hopelessly unrealistic. "Do you even have much experience in espionage?"

"I was the intelligence officer for the Number Five Flying Column in South Africa. I captured the infamous commandoes Miguel van der Veer and Jacob Tromp."

"How?"

"I gathered a group of Uitlanders who kent enough Afrikaans and customs to pass for Boers. They infiltrated the commando and kept me apprised of when they were near the telegraph wire I wanted to use. I sent an uncoded message about a train of rations and medical supplies to the nearest British camp, then sent a coded message ordering them to fill the train with soldiers. I kent our scorched-earth tactics meant they couldn't resist that bait.

His eyes brightened. "When they struck, they found the train full of Lee-Enfields and more carbineers scattered throughout the countryside. My Uitlanders had warned me where they were going to strike. We shot their horses and then rode them down. I kent van der Veer and Tromp by sight, so I captured them personally."

She fanned herself. "Bravo, Ranald! Maybe you have what it takes to make a spy after all."

"I just hope the telegraph isn't our undoing as weel. Anywhere we go in Germany, they can send a telegraph long before we can get there. If they amass troops along our route, I fear it will be like the auld saying: 'A stone in place of an egg, and a knife in place of a sword.'"

They said nothing for a moment. Both realized that if the Germans anticipated their route and telegraphed ahead, they would find themselves in an unspeakable position. They were passing through a forest between two thick canopies of leaves.

Svetlana yawned. Before long, she fell asleep with her head on MacKenzie's shoulder. MacKenzie sighed. She was an engaging companion and crack shot, but as soon as the mission concluded, he would have to sever all connection with her. Definitely report the presence of an Okhrana agent in British intelligence.

Their countries hated each other bitterly, and she possessed a vicious personality under that gorgeous exterior. She would shoot anyone she considered an opponent—if she could not get them sent first to a frozen prison. Under that beautiful skin flowed ice-cold blood.

Would he miss her? Of course not! Not a Russian subject!

At Breslau, they switched to the railway toward Warsaw and Russian territory. MacKenzie would have to trust that Svetlana would not betray him to her countrymen, not yet at least. Surely, she seemed capable of betraying those who put their trust in her (that was her job as an agent provocateur). But what would be the point of that? He had nothing that she could benefit from.

Maybe Providence had directed that he had dropped the papers Gibson had given him. Until they had the telegrams they wanted, they needed each other. Once they had achieved their goals, MacKenzie would have to watch himself as he returned to Britain. In Russia, it was said, everyone was either a spy or one who was spied on.

***

The train had stopped. MacKenzie checked his watch. They could not have reached Warsaw yet. They had not nearly steamed on the track long enough, and besides, the view out of the window remained forest. The pines, several yards off, seemed to stretch their needles out to the train.

He looked out the window. He could see no fence that demarcated the border between Germany and Russia. If they had stopped to take Russian border guards on board, he would have expected to see some mark of the border. Something felt odd.

He nudged Svetlana awake.

"Ranald, what is it?" she asked in Gaelic.

"Something's up."

The door to their car slid open. His heart sank. The electricity of the telegraph had in fact preceded them. In came not Russian police in khaki uniforms and peaked caps, but Imperial German soldiers in field gray and pickelhaube helmets.

CHAPTER 11: STOPPED AT THE BORDER

The German soldiers, a sergeant and a *soldat*, began making their way down the aisle, demanding passports from each passenger. Entering Germany, they probably would not have needed any, but entering Russia required it. The soldat had a Mauser slung over his shoulder. MacKenzie's heart jumped at the sight of it.

Svetlana laid a hand on his. He swallowed his heart back down his throat. He needed to protect Svetlana as best he could, never mind the treaty or the conference.

Yet he saw no way to sneak past the soldiers. It was too late to leave the car and jump—even if that would not make crossing into Russian territory awkward.

MacKenzie and Svetlana exchanged glances.

"Play it calm," Svetlana whispered. "Maybe they dinna ken our names on our passports."

But what if Gibson told them?

MacKenzie reminded himself of the Webley in his shoulder holster. He prayed it would not come to that. His heart pounded against it. He couldn't panic. Not now. He tried to control his breathing. He checked his watch to give him somewhere to put his eyes. He could not bear the sight of that Mauser with its straight bolt.

Remember me, O God, for my good!

The soldiers drew nearer.

He pushed his hat brim down on his forehead. Little good that would do. The newspaper and fan would be too obvious. The man in the seat in front of them handed the soldiers his passport. They looked it over, returned it to him with a nod, and stepped to MacKenzie and Svetlana.

"Mein Herr, Meine Frau, you will come with us, bitte," the sergeant said in German.

MacKenzie nodded and rose. The soldat reached to unsling his Mauser. MacKenzie raised his hand to his mouth as though to cough. With the fist he had made, he swung a backhanded blow at the soldat, who had not yet readied the Mauser.

Simultaneously, Svetlana punched the sergeant, who did not expect such resistance from a woman, in the throat. The two soldiers went crashing to the railroad car floor, and MacKenzie and Svetlana dashed for the nearest door in the rear of the compartment. Their footfalls thumped down the aisle.

"Halt!" the sergeant coughed. "Stop them!"

A passenger almost stepped out of his row to confront them, but Svetlana had drawn a pistol, and he wisely stepped aside. MacKenzie threw his weight into the door handle, and they burst out of the car and leaped into the night. Shouts came from within the car, and MacKenzie looked back to see German soldiers pouring out of the other cars like hornets from a hive.

"Into the woods!" MacKenzie said in Gaelic.

"I have this pistol, and I'm sure you have one too!" Svetlana called back. "That's twelve shots, and there can't be as many of them as that. We can shoot it out."

"By all means, if you want to provoke another diplomatic incident."

"Wait!" Svetlana said.

They paused long enough for her to wrench her high heels off. A flash cut through the night in the corner of their eyes, and the blast of a shot rent the air. A bullet sang past them. Svetlana ducked.

"It's no good to duck," MacKenzie said. "By the time you hear it, it's past."

MacKenzie pulled her back to her feet, and they dashed through the grass together for the woods. The startled crickets leaped in all directions from the grass, like sparks dancing from a fire.

Several shots rang out behind them. MacKenzie instinctively counted the bullets, but he realized that there was no point in that. Each soldier had a clip with five bullets, and he did not know how many of them there were in total, so that meant that there were any number of total bullets left for all he knew.

Their only hope was to make it to the woods. It offered the best chance of sanctuary. The grass hissed as they ran through it.

A volley rang out. MacKenzie heard the bullets thud and rustle through the grass. He could hear Germans shouting orders, but he could not make out exactly what they were saying at this distance.

Bullets smacked into the trunks of the trees; bits of bark splintered in all directions. Then they made it among the foliage. Now they could slow their pace. Quick wits now became more important than quick legs. Most of all, they had to keep from running into tree trunks in the darkness.

The leaves formed a dark blanket blotting out most light from the stars or the moon, save isolated patches of silvery light. MacKenzie took Svetlana's hand as they navigated the maze of trunks. Twigs snapped on their legs. MacKenzie remembered the dark advance the night before that day when they had used ropes to stay together... No, he would not think on that. He had to think of getting Svetlana safely through this.

"Split up! Use your torches!" he heard voices say to their left.

They had sent soldiers in from the north! Surely the west, where they had entered the woods, was no safer.

Just to be sure, MacKenzie glanced back. Glowing lights, like the shining of predator's eyes in the night, sprang into life back at the tree line. The pincer would catch them if they kept going this way.

"Southeast!" he hissed.

He pressed Svetlana's hand even harder as he veered to the right to make sure they did not get separated. He wished he could use Archie's compass, but it glowed in the dark, and the last thing he wanted right now was light.

His eyes were growing accustomed to the darkness. He could make out the trunks' silhouettes against the moonlight, their branches impeding them like shades from the underworld, trying to snag them with ghostly appendages.

MacKenzie stopped and looked back to count how many lights were closing in on them. He counted nine lights forming a rough semicircle running from west to north. At least nine soldiers.

"Broken twigs!" they heard in German.

"Wait!" Svetlana whispered.

She halted, let go of MacKenzie's hand, and began fishing in her handbag. With a muffled cry of delight, she withdrew a cluster of small, silvery spheres strung together and tied to what looked like a fuse to MacKenzie.

"Quick! Strike me a match!" she whispered.

MacKenzie shrugged. "I dinna smoke."

"Confound it, Ranald! Do you do *anything* like a normal soldier?" she hissed. "Hold this."

As MacKenzie held the bombs, Svetlana dug through her handbag. She produced a matchbook and immediately lit the fuse. Just as quickly, she blew out the match.

"Throw them that way!"

MacKenzie hurled the bombs as far to the northwest as he could, and they resumed running through the woods. Svetlana tripped on a root, but MacKenzie caught her. Then he slipped on something, and she broke his fall.

"We better slow down, or we're going to get a crippling injury," MacKenzie whispered in her ear.

They felt their way forward, testing each step and reaching out with their hands for any encumbrances. The torches were closing. The Germans could light their way through the trees, but MacKenzie and Svetlana had to cautiously work their way through them. The contest couldn't go on much longer.

The lights behind them swept back and forth like scent hounds zigzagging to pick up the trail. *What about dogs?* If the Germans had them, there'd be no escape through the trees. MacKenzie spared just enough of his attention to listen for the baying of hounds.

They were catching their breath as they felt their way through the tangle. They were practically groping. The only way to go was deeper. Whatever surprise Svetlana had in store for the Germans, when would it go off? Or *would* it go off? It could have been a dud.

"The trail leads this way!" they heard a German shout behind them.

"They're almost upon us!" MacKenzie said. "Quick, find a tree that can hide both of us."

No sooner had he spoken than the dim shape of a large, gnarly oak with a wide reach presented itself just in front of them. *Thank You, Lord!* MacKenzie bent over and lowered his hands together to give Svetlana a leg up, but she jumped for the lowest branch and pulled herself up without any help. MacKenzie followed.

Svetlana found one branch and clung to it while MacKenzie took the one beside it. The rough bark dug into his chest and arms, but he grasped it as tightly as he would a buoy in a turbulent ocean. Now they had only to wait. They tried to control their breathing.

Maybe the bombs would catch some of the Germans as they pursued them.

The lights drew nearer. They would reach them in a matter of seconds. MacKenzie thought the Germans had passed where the bombs had landed. So much for that hope. They had nearly reached the tree…

A series of bangs popped off from the bombs. They sounded like pistol shots. A cacophony of bird cries erupted through the forest. The Germans went to ground.

"Behind us!" the sergeant shouted once he had recovered from his surprise. "You two, stay here in case they come back this way. We'll fan out back to the northwest."

The Germans made their way cautiously toward the source of the blasts, rifles pointed at the thick darkness, leaving two soldiers behind. In no time at all, the tree trunks swallowed up the lights. The two soldiers slung their Mausers and sauntered over to MacKenzie and Svetlana's tree.

MacKenzie realized he was holding his breath as one of them stepped under the limb he clung to. He exhaled as slowly and as faintly as he could. They had only to turn the torches upward, and MacKenzie and Svetlana would be sitting ducks. The soldiers held their Mausers at the ready. MacKenzie's heart pounded at the sight of it. He could barely swallow. Was it loaded with Dumdums?

"What do you suppose they're up to?" one asked the other. "English spies trying to make it into Russia from Germany?"

"They'll find no friends there, to be sure," the second said. "Come to think of it, do the English have *any* friends on the Continent?"

The first one pursed his lips. "The French, maybe, but with friends like that, who needs enemies?"

They laughed.

"They're welcome to each other," the second said. "Just as the French are welcome to the Russians."

The first swatted at a mosquito.

"Hey!" he said.

"What?"

"You don't suppose they want to assassinate the Tsar?"

"Why would they do that?"

"Seems to me it would bring an end to the war with their Japanese ally."

"If they don't, there's plenty of anarchists who'd do it for them," the second said.

"They assassinated one Tsar already. Best of luck to them on this one."

"Ach, Hans, shame on you!" the second said as he gave him a shove.

"What?"

"Don't be stupid! You know it's best for Germany that the Tsar of Russia be an idiot like Nicholas."

They laughed. MacKenzie looked back at Svetlana to make sure she wasn't about to shoot them. She had daggers in her eyes but stayed as still as he.

"Know what I would do if *I* became Tsar of Russia?" the second asked.

"What?"

"Abdicate."

The second slapped his face and muttered a curse at the mosquito. A twig snapped. The Germans spun around and flashed their torches into the trees. A doe darted out of sight.

"Must be a Russian deer," the first said.

"How can you tell that?"

"It's running away from the Germans, isn't it?"

"What a day it will be when we face them in battle!"

MacKenzie had another battle on his mind. This agony of waiting brought memories of that day rushing back. As before, he could only stay as rigid as a dead man and pray for deliverance. He could almost see the muddy field laid out around him again. He expected a Mauser's crack any second.

He shook his head. He mustn't panic. Surely God was with him even now. He had seen MacKenzie through that day for a reason.

Mosquitoes whined about his head and bit him, but he dared not swat them. A thousand mosquito bites were preferable to a Mauser wound. When would the Germans leave? When would one of them look up? He clenched the branch all the tighter. Little bits of moss and bark trickled down to the forest floor. Some brushed the second German soldier on the shoulder. MacKenzie had to stifle a curse in his mind.

The soldier swatted at his ear. "These confounded mosquitoes," he said. "Let's head back inside. They've either caught them and not come back to us, or they've lost them and won't be missing us."

"Ja."

They marched back toward the distant tree line. Before long, their voices, now indistinct, had resumed joking and laughing. MacKenzie waited until he was positive they had left earshot, then he decided to wait a little longer.

"Ranald, I dinna ken about you, but I dinna intend to sleep in this tree," Svetlana whispered after a while. "Surely the way to the border is clear."

MacKenzie worked his way down and held his arms up to help Svetlana. She let him lower her to the ground.

"Thank you," she said perfunctorily.

MacKenzie reached into his pocket and drew his compass out. Archimedes had rigged it with phosphorescent paint.

"I guess we just head east now."

She smiled impishly. "What does your gallantry call for? 'Ladies first,' or, 'Be the point man?'"

MacKenzie glared at her. "Just because you never exhibit any civility..."

She waved charitably. "Go ahead, Ranald. You've got the compass."

"We have a proverb in the Highlands: 'Civility never got anyone a broken head.'"

Svetlana scoffed. "Aye, so I've heard. There's only one proverb I need to ken, though: 'To Hell or to Siberia.'"

"What were those bombs anyway?" he asked.

"A gift from a revolutionary admirer of mine. They're supposed to distract Russian police. I was wondering what I was going to do with the little crook's present."

They cautiously made their way through the woods, Svetlana grasping MacKenzie's hand. Twigs snapped under his boots and leaves crunched. MacKenzie tuned his ears like a radio receiver for any sound of Germans. He couldn't hear anything. Thank God for the mosquitos! He would itch tomorrow, but he owed his life to the Germans' annoyance at the insects. God could work good from anything.

"Wait!" Svetlana said.

Kneeling down, she tore strips from her dress and wrapped them around her feet.

"Is there anything I can do for you?" MacKenzie said.

"Thoughtful of you, Ranald, but what can you do? It hurts, but I'm accustomed to hardship such as you wouldn't believe. I spent four months in a Siberian prison."

"What happened?"

"It was quite deliberate, I assure you. It happened right after my greatest success. You remember the plot back in '01 to explode a bomb on London Bridge?"

"That was you?"

"Aye. Dinna look at me like that, Ranald! I assure you, I never had any intention of letting them go through with it. I simply needed a plot such as would stir your British liberals to action against the revolutionaries. Anyway, out of a circle of thirty-five, twenty-five were rounded up by your Special Branch. I escaped with the other ten back to Russia."

She looked upwards haughtily. "Obviously, I had to inform the Okhrana. I couldn't let them walk scot-free in Russia with those explosives on them. But then I had a tremendous idea! I would let myself be taken with them to Siberia and then 'escape.' What's the one thing that's bound to expose a police spy? He never gets caught. This way, if anyone ever doubted my credentials, I could point to my Siberian exile. Even Burtsev would never guess my true identity.

"I talked it over with my father. He was against it, but I won him over. He kent I'd been toughened by that day such that..."

She stopped midsentence. MacKenzie arched an eyebrow.

"Anyway, he didn't doubt my toughness or my devotion to the oath I'd sworn against the revolutionaries," she resumed. "These feet you seem so concerned for carried me across thousands of barren miles—in chains, mind you. We walked over trails where you wouldn't see a human tenement for miles. We had to use sledges when the weather turned to its winter viciousness. It was a cold no fire could bring relief from."

She sighed. "My father had insisted on supplying me with a cloak of otter fur, and I believe I wouldn't be here without it. It's a cold you couldn't imagine, three billion versts from the sun. You can't move a muscle away from your chest, because you want to keep everything as close to your torso as possible. You shiver until you nearly faint. Then there's the hunger gnawing at your stomach like a rat. Sometimes, all you have to give it is a crust of bread begged from the local peasantry. So dinna you worry about me, Ranald MacKenzie!"

MacKenzie turned to look into her eyes. "I'm so sorry, Sveta. I had no idea..."

"You thought I was just a pampered rich girl who has never kent hardship. Weel, I have!"

"And you send others to suffer that same fate?"

She halted. For a moment she hesitated, then sighed. "Aye, Ranald, I do. I must to maintain order. How else will our Ukrainian grain feed millions of hungry mouths unless the Tsar remains in power?"

"I think he uses rather a heavy hand. Some of the anarchists' ideas seem downright virtuous to me. Giving workers Saturday off to enjoy culture and personal enrichment? If we could purge out the bomb-throwers while leaving the basic desire to improve the human condition—"

"Ranald, can you think of a revolution, however well-intentioned, that didn't lead to something worse?" she cut in. "Yes, monarchical France treated its peasants terribly, but it didn't guillotine its opponents by the thousands or load its rebels on barges and sink them. They wound up with a dictator-emperor, as these revolutions always do, who wasn't satisfied until he had drenched every corner of Europe in blood. No French peasant was as miserable under King Louis as the Portuguese peasants your ancestors passed as they chased Napoleon's troops out."

MacKenzie had to grant her that. He kent what his regiment had seen in 1811 as they pursued the French army from their Portuguese ally. The French had tortured, murdered, and burnt their way from the outskirts of Lisbon back to Spain, where mutilation and massacre awaited any stragglers at the hands of the guerrillas. And all this after the British had already devastated the countryside themselves to keep the French from "living off the land." No one would have dreamed of such things in peacetime, but when a man started a war, he birthed a monster that would grow and assume an uncontrollable life of its own. A pox on anyone who would dare start one for his own selfish gain!

She shrugged. "Who can say who was right in all the Roman civil wars, but they wound up with a system that put absolute power in the hands of men like Nero and Domitian. And dinna get me started on the savagery of the Zealots. Revolutions always lead to something worse. The only change a nation can better itself by is an organic evolution linked with its finest traditions—the Anglo-American way and Tsar Alexander II's!"

"Aye, that's what Edmund Burke thought of the French Revolution," MacKenzie said. "But I see no need to send people to a frozen wasteland just for reading a book. And how violent do you think most of them would be if they didn't have provocateurs like you stirring them up?"

"If we can so easily lead them to such crimes, it would only be a matter of time before they came up with them themselves. We didn't start this war, but we'll end it, to be sure!"

MacKenzie couldn't question her sincerity to her cause. That she would go to Siberia to protect others… Was that laying down her life for her friends too? He couldn't imagine what a "that day" would be for one who was so wealthy. She wasn't a soldier, so she would have seen nothing like what he had seen on his own "that day."

They emerged from the woods into a field with long grass. They paused to survey the landscape, but a stiff breeze whooshed into them, carrying with it the rumbling of thunder. Lightning flashed across the sky.

"So much for staying amid the trees until first light," Svetlana muttered. "How certain are you we're not in Germany anymore?"

"I've guided hundreds of men across the veldt on nights with new moons under Boer noses," MacKenzie said. "And always on time. Granted, they dinna have many trees there."

"But you'd stake your life on it?"

"I dinna think we have any other choice with this storm coming on. There! That farmhouse. How about we pass the night in the barn and depart before anyone kens about it?"

"Very weel."

MacKenzie set his face toward the yellow glow in the house's window. The silhouette of the barn just stood out against the blanket of the night sky. Keeping the compass in his right hand, he took Svetlana's hand in his left. The thunder around them spurred his steps toward shelter like an artillery barrage. He heard a snap and felt Svetlana drop. He broke her fall. Svetlana swore in Ukrainian.

"What a stupid place to leave a branch!" she said.

"Do you ken any Polish?" MacKenzie said. "I dinna, but we're in what would be Poland if you three empires had minded your own business."

Svetlana scoffed. "Dinna need any. They teach all the children Russian in school these days. Russians can't stand to share the empire with other languages. They can't even stomach one as similar as Ukrainian."

The barn scarcely looked any better than a Whitechapel lodging. Cracks and chips ran through the wood planking like fault lines in the earth, and the roof had nothing more than thatch. MacKenzie glanced around for any observers as they reached it. Seeing none, he opened the door for Svetlana. The earthy scent of grazers and their fodder assaulted their noses. Svetlana crinkled her nose but rushed in nevertheless.

The rusty-colored cattle raised their heads from their stalls but soon ignored the newcomers. All her talk about enduring hardship aside, Svetlana plopped herself down on a pile of straw and laid her head back with a groan.

With the anxiety passing from his veins, MacKenzie felt exhaustion seep into his muscles. Svetlana folded her hands and laid her head on them. MacKenzie lay down next to her. The drip-drops of light rain pelted the roof.

"Not a minute too soon!" MacKenzie said.

Svetlana opened her eyes and looked up. "I hope the roof doesn't leak." She closed her eyes and lay back down.

The door opened, and a girl in her teens stepped in, leading a white-faced calf. She wore a gray dress with a scarf over her head. Seeing the two spies, she gasped and froze. MacKenzie leaped up and held out his hand reassuringly.

"Please, miss, we mean you no harm!" he said in Russian. "Can you understand me?"

"*Da.*"

"Jolly good," MacKenzie muttered in English under his breath.

Returning to Russian, he said, "We are just unfortunate travelers whose coach has been upset and need shelter for the night. We'll leave tomorrow morning. Please don't tell anyone we're here."

The girl regarded Svetlana with pity in her eyes. She looked exhausted and totally disheveled.

"Very well," the girl said.

"What is your name?"

"Tirzah."

The name was Jewish. MacKenzie darted a glance back at Svetlana. A Russian peasant would feel nervous enough if she knew an Okhrana agent sheltered in her barn, but a Jewish one would become downright petrified. The Okhrana's anti-Semitism was notorious.

He realized the rear half of the calf still stood outside in the stiffening rain.

"Please, bring the calf in."

She led the calf past them gingerly. Tirzah eyed them over her shoulder as she did.

"And please, miss, could we impose upon you for some dinner?" he said after she had tied up the calf.

She hesitated. "If you can, could you please... pay us for it?" she said. "We can barely afford to feed ourselves."

Svetlana shot up from her bed of straw. Her face turned as red as her lips. She reached into her handbag with such a furious energy that MacKenzie wondered if she would withdraw money or a pistol.

"I should have expected as much! Here! Here's two-and-a-half rubles, as much as I paid for last night's dinner in marks. And don't think about trying any of your Jewish tricks to inveigle us out of any more. I know you all have noses big enough to smell our cash!"

MacKenzie's and Tirzah's jaws dropped. It would have been hard to say who had the more astonished countenance. MacKenzie wanted to say something, but he was too shocked to think of anything. The girl took the money with a trembling hand. Once she had it, she fled the barn.

"I say, Svetlana!" MacKenzie said once he could speak again. "Did you have to be so rude? She's our unwitting host. She owes us nothing."

"The Jews owe all of us Christians reparations for all the evil their kind has wrought," she said. "I only paid her so she has reason to conceal our existence. No doubt she thinks perhaps tomorrow we'll pay her for another meal—assuming she doesn't club us over the head as we sleep. Or poison our food."

"If she does, it's only because you were so hateful. If we pay a chef who provides us food for a living, how much more a peasant whom we just crashed in on and who barely has a living herself? We're the imposers here. She could have denied us refuge."

"Aye, that would be the typical Jewish response to Slavs in need. I'd have seen to it that she learned real poverty in Siberia if she had! And—bother it—the roof leaks!"

MacKenzie felt a cold splash on his head. Tirzah returned with a wooden plate of coarse bread and two cups of milk. She froze just inside the door, her wide eyes fixed on Svetlana. MacKenzie stepped between them.

"Thank you, Tirzah. This means more to me than you know. Goodnight."

The girl turned on her heels and practically ran back to the house. MacKenzie sat with a sigh beside Svetlana and handed her the bread. He tasted the stale bread, which seemed two days removed from growing mold.

Svetlana smacked her lips as she tasted hers. "She saved the finest for her guests!"

"It's better than what they had for us in South Africa sometimes. The kinds of things we ate out on the veldt would make an English lady's hair stand on end."

"And the things we ate in Siberia would make her faint!"

Still, they were so hungry that they devoured it. Svetlana had barely finished before she plopped back on the straw on folded hands and promptly fell asleep. Exhausted though he felt, MacKenzie could not join her. She had drifted off to slumber without a shred of guilt over her vicious words.

It haunted his heart that his hosts found themselves so destitute that they could barely eat while they had fed him. What they had was half-rotten anyway!

Finally, he drew himself up and crept out of the barn to their hovel. He shivered from the rain until he gained the respite of the overhanging roof. No one could accuse these people of neglecting their animals, for their house appeared just as dilapidated as their barn.

He rapped gently on the door. Tirzah opened it hesitantly. She looked like a frightened fawn. MacKenzie felt his stomach churn as he noticed her trembling ever so slightly.

He held up his hand. "Oh, no, miss, I mean you no harm! I just wanted to apologize for my wife's harsh remarks. Coming from the situation we did, your barn is the most luxurious accommodation I've ever enjoyed. It's worth something more like this to me."

He fished out two sovereigns from his pocket and held them out to her.

"I'm sure you'll be able to find somewhere that accepts these coins and feast for some time on them," he said.

Tirzah's eyes narrowed.

"And our accommodation is *all* you ask in return?"

MacKenzie's heart leaped in horror. He had not even considered that she would suspect him of ulterior motives. "I swear it."

She hesitantly took them.

"I'm sorry, sir. It's just that, we don't expect much unfeigned generosity from Christians."

She lowered her eyes to the coins, not looking at MacKenzie.

"Yes, well, there's much you don't know about your King, I would imagine," he said. "He wept over your city before it was destroyed."

She looked up with a sneer. "I'll bet He did!"

"Luke 19:41–44. Look it up if you don't believe me. And, while you're at it, read the Gospel of Matthew and see if *my* King doesn't fulfill the prophecies you've heard all your life about *your* King."

Tirzah looked back down at the gold sovereigns. "Very well, sir, I will."

MacKenzie had only heard trepidation or resignation in her voice thus far, but suddenly, he detected a spark of interest. She seemed awestruck by the gift of the gold coins and that MacKenzie had referred to Jesus as her King as well as his.

"And, by all means, pray to the God of Abraham that He would show you truly if Jesus is the Son of David," MacKenzie said.

"Very well," she said with a polite smile.

"Goodnight, Tirzah."

She gently closed the door. MacKenzie crept back through the rain into the barn and settled into the straw with a sigh. He hoped he had just put a dent in the wall of separation between Jews and Gentiles that God had torn down but which these Russians seemed determined to rebuild. At the very least, he knew that he had more fairly recompensed the family that had given him shelter when he had needed it most.

Hlidskjalf
May 29, 1905

The storm whipping its gust around the castle ramparts suited Tirpitz's mood perfectly as he perused the Kaiser's telegrams retrieved from the opera house. Darkness shrouded the spacious office, the lamp beam over the correspondence the only light.

His face reflected the intensity of his inner turmoil. Those enemy agents had made fools of the Order! They had killed three good men and escaped from three traps: the chloroform, the car chase, and the paint trail. He had finally given up on pursuing them and settled down to study the telegrams. Things did not look any better here either.

So, the Kaiser truly was paying court to the Tsar! That would thrill the Master. No doubt he expected Tirpitz to fix it. But what could he conjure to put between the Kaiser and his cousin? He could not manufacture a plot by "Dearest Nicky;" everyone knew the Tsar was too ingenuous, if not downright stupid. If anyone was plotting, it was the Kaiser. And how could he talk the Kaiser out of it without revealing that he had read his personal telegrams? The Master was so dead-set on a war that would put Germany over everything else that he couldn't stand back and let the Kaiser rule as he saw fit.

He inhaled sharply. He had to be strong—and resourceful. He prayed to Odin for a share of the god's wisdom.

"Herr Hauptmann, I beg to report," Heinrich said as he knocked on the closed door.

Tirpitz stashed the telegrams in his desk drawer with a smooth, quiet hand.

"Enter."

Heinrich opened the door and saluted. Tirpitz returned the salute. He released his gritted teeth to see his beloved friend.

"Ja?" he said amiably, trying to hide his exasperation.

"Herr Hauptmann, the English agents have left the country for Russia. The army stopped them on a train bound for Warsaw, but they escaped on foot. By now they are probably back on their way to Warsaw. They're long gone."

"Then we must tighten security around the Kaiser. Request that the Master let on of an anarchist plot and have myself and five other agents assigned to his protection. And arrange to replace his telegrapher with a trustworthy Order man who will keep me informed of the Kaiser's plans so we can stay one step ahead of these English pests."

He would know the woman again if he saw her. He thought of her lustrous blue eyes, like two rare sapphires. They were the only ones he'd seen bluer than Hilda's...

"What of Hauptmann Gibson?" Heinrich asked.

Tirpitz had not given him a second thought. What, indeed? He teased his mustache. Much as he disliked torture, he might make an exception here, given that the Order and the gods' reputation lay at stake. "Ja, we have his company to console us for missing our other English guests. I think I should like to have a nice, cozy chat with him—see what he knows about them. A chance to vent our spleen, eh?"

CHAPTER 12: THINK OF UKRAINE

The dawn's chorus of songbirds proved an excellent alarm clock for MacKenzie. Either that, or the chill in his bones became too much for him. He felt drenched, and all around, he smelled the stench of wet hay. Still, the birds seemed grateful to have survived the night's storm, so he felt he should be as well.

He looked over at Svetlana. Even with her hair as disheveled as a mustang's mane, she remained beautiful. The cast of her face, her luscious lips, and her dark, graceful brows—there was a part of him that wished he could wake up to that sight beside him forever.

But then, what of her viciousness toward the Jewish girl? She had no compassion for the poor or the spiritually lost. She was a typical Tsarist elitist—all he would expect in a duplicitous, cruel Okhrana agent. How many anarchists had she had shipped off to frozen wastes in Siberia? If he didn't need her now that Field and Gibson were gone and he was in Russia, he'd be glad never to see her again.

"Sveta," he whispered.

Svetlana opened her eyes. In an instant, she hugged her arms to her chest. "Och, brrr! I haven't been this cold in years."

"We have an auld Highland saying: 'What can't be helped, must be borne.'"

She glared at him. "And I have a new Ukrainian saying: 'This is nothing compared to Siberia!'"

"You were the one making the observation."

"I'm the only one here who's truly qualified to judge what's cold, Ranald."

"Sveta, we shouldn't be arguing. I think Tirzah would be happiest if we left as soon as possible."

"I certainly would be happiest getting out of a Jew's barn as soon as possible too!"

"Someone woke up on the wrong side of the straw this morning. Anyway, this is your country; what do you suggest we do now?"

"The first thing is to skip breakfast. I'll have to be a lot closer to starvation before I swallow any more of that rubbish. I think I can get us something much finer for dinner along with our next lead."

"Aye?"

"Have you heard of Monsieur Ivan Alexandrovich Beletsky?"

"The oil magnate?"

"Aye, but he has so many other businesses besides oil. He's richer than Croesus and has his finger in the pies of every country in Europe. He collects secrets like his wife collects pearls, they say, and he pays informers of a network so extensive it puts the Okhrana to shame."

"And what does he do with that information?"

"Makes business decisions, mostly. That's the reason he's so wealthy; he kens about every whiff of change and every hint of a breeze in the global market. If anyone else has heard about the Kaiser's negotiations with the Tsar, he has. He has one of his summer villas in the country outside Vilnius. If he's there, we can get there by train in time for dinner tomorrow. Of course, you can't be Scottish any longer. From this moment onward, you are the Okhrana agent Peter Ivanovich Kutuzov."

"Och! 'My only love sprung from my only hate!'" MacKenzie said.

Svetlana scoffed and shoved him ever so slightly.

June 1, 1905

The sun had turned onto its downward course by the time they arrived at the Beletsky villa. *The man must be passionately fond of colorful onion domes like those of St. Basil's Cathedral*, MacKenzie thought. His villa was arrayed with them. They rose like swirls of cream topped with golden crosses.

The villa walls were made from a wood with a reddish finish. The layout, however, reminded MacKenzie of a Roman villa, with buildings rising around a courtyard with a fountain in the center.

They made their way along a pavement of whitewashed stone to the largest building, adjusting their wrinkled attire to better match the grandeur of the place. At the mahogany door, a footman dressed in pine-green velvet bowed to them.

"We must see your master at once," Svetlana said. "Government business."

"I will see if the master is accepting visitors at this time," he said with a tone of disinterestedness that MacKenzie thought untoward in response to a member of the imperial government. "His guests are not set to arrive for another hour."

The footman bowed and entered the house. MacKenzie scratched a mosquito bite on his wrist. The footman returned and opened the door with another bow before escorting them to the drawing room. The drawing room walls dripped with color, from the watercolors of Russian palaces and mythological scenes to the Pompeian red paint.

Monsieur Beletsky sat in his chair like a king on a throne. His corpulent mass barely fit between the two armrests, and MacKenzie wondered how it fit in his black silken suit. A thin black beard lined his jaw above his collection of chins, and he was reading a report on yellow paper with lordly indifference.

Madame Beletsky sat beside him. She had a wonderfully apportioned figure, ample where it was desirable for a woman to be and slender where it was not. She wore a silk gown of pine green. MacKenzie could see what Svetlana had meant about the pearls. She had graced her neck with five rows of the finest pearls he had ever seen, but then, he was not much of a connoisseur in that regard.

The tycoon smiled as broadly as his puffy cheeks would permit.

"Welcome to my home, Monsieur and Madame," he said. "I expect you two are the agents that caused such a ruckus at the German border two nights ago."

Svetlana nodded. "Just so."

"How do you know about that?" MacKenzie asked.

"One of my—ahem—employees was aboard that train. After all the fuss, he eavesdropped on the guards and learned that they were after two English spies. He obtained your luggage before they could confiscate it, though I hope it wasn't at the risk of his life."

"The guns were unloaded," MacKenzie said.

Monsieur Beletsky stroked his beard. "Very wise. I can have them sent to your lodgings, then."

"You act like you've been expecting us," Svetlana said.

He nodded slightly. "I have, I have. A spy who has business in Germany and Russia will inevitably end up at my door. No one knows more about these two countries than my network. I'm like an old man who gathers every cat in the neighborhood by putting out food for them. The difference is, I have a price for my food."

"And what would that be?"

His eyes twinkled. "We can discuss that later, but I charge a hefty price for what I give to English agents."

"We're not English," Svetlana said. "We're both with the Okhrana."

His eyes widened as much as his folds of fat would allow. "The Okhrana?"

"That's right," Svetlana said.

His eyes narrowed into a suspicious stare. "And is it Okhrana policy to create diplomatic incidents with foreign countries?"

He leaned forward like a wolf eyeing its prey. MacKenzie felt as though those emerald eyes were boring through him. Surely, he would recognize the truth. He was already half-right about them being British spies.

He leaned back in his chair. It creaked under his shifting weight. "I understood Okhrana policy was to foster goodwill with foreign governments," he said. "You'll quickly find yourself in serious trouble if you lie to me!"

"If it wasn't true, would I invent such an outrageous thing as my cover story?" Svetlana said.

"I think anything would be preferable to being known as a British agent in Russia. We're as close to war as you can get without anyone being killed."

MacKenzie had to stop himself from pointing out the fishermen the Baltic Fleet had fired on and killed. For the moment, he was Russian, and Britain was his sworn enemy.

Svetlana stepped forward and assumed her foxy grin. "Are you familiar with Okhrana secrets, Monsieur Beletsky?" she asked coyly. "I know them all. You can test me in anything you desire. I am very close to Monsieur Rachkovsky."

He stroked his beard as he glanced upwards in thought.

"Anything at all," Svetlana said.

His gaze returned to them with a leer. "Who is Monsieur Rachkovsky's most trusted agent?"

The smile dropped from Svetlana's lips. "You might be asking too much there, Monsieur Beletsky. That is a state secret kept with the utmost discretion."

Now Monsieur Beletsky grinned. "You said, 'anything.'"

She began to turn red. "You're taking a serious risk here, Monsieur Beletsky, defying the Okhrana! You seem so comfortable on that chair; I'd hate to see you huddled on a rickety sledge in Siberia. At least you'd have all that blubber to keep you warm—until they worked it off you."

The man's eyes blazed with anger rather than fear. He looked like a boar cornered by a pack of hunting dogs and ready to gore them with his tusks. MacKenzie brushed Svetlana's arm, hoping she would take the hint.

"I'm not going to fear any second-string Okhrana agent who isn't any closer to Rachkovsky than to know that," Beletsky said.

"How do I know you would recognize the answer if I gave it to you?" Svetlana said, "How do I know you aren't milking me for the most precious secret of the secret police?"

"How do *you* know I won't have you both arrested as British spies in Japanese pay if you don't answer?" he said. "I know the answer to this question; answer wrong, and I will. We can gather a mob to hang you both by the neck, or, if you insist upon formalities, I can pay a court to do it for you!"

He snapped his fingers. Two bulky young men in dark-blue suits appeared from the hallway. MacKenzie could not think of anything to say. He would in all probability be hanged if he kept silent, but at least as bad a fate would await Rachkovsky's most trusted agent if he revealed her identity. Svetlana had started this game, and he could only hold his breath as he awaited her move. She seemed to have overplayed her hand. She glared at the young men at the entryway.

"Get them out of here!" she said.

Beletsky waved his hand, and the two men stepped out.

Svetlana sighed. She had lost whatever advantage she had thought she had had by revealing her Okhrana status.

"*I* am Monsieur Rachkovsky's most trusted agent. I am Svetlana Petrovna Rachkovskaya."

Beletsky snapped back in shock. Now his eyes looked like a startled rabbit's. "Truly, you are Svetlana Petrovna Rachkovskaya, for no ordinary agent knows that secret!"

"Now that you know we're not English, I expect you to share everything you know to the empire's secret police regarding this matter," Svetlana said.

In another moment, Beletsky recovered from his shock and leaned forward hungrily like a wolf again. Now MacKenzie had no idea why. He had already gotten what he wanted, had he not?

"I don't bandy about others' secrets free of charge—not even to the Okhrana," Beletsky said.

"Do you want to be arrested?" Svetlana asked.

"There's no jury with a price too high for me to afford," Beletsky said. "Or judge, for that matter. And as for your father, well, is there anything he wouldn't do for the right price? I understand kickbacks are your family's main source of income."

Svetlana's eyes flashed, and MacKenzie's heart sank. He had forgotten all about Peter Ivanovich Rachkovsky's infamous venality as he had enjoyed sharing in the luxuries it had provided Svetlana. Could he ever delight in them again?

Evidently, part of her felt shame as well, for she regarded Monsieur Beletsky with an air of badly wounded pride. She looked rather like she had at the German soldiers who had mocked her Little Father, the Tsar.

Monsieur Beletsky settled triumphantly in his chair. "We can discuss it over dinner. I'm having a pleasant little dinner party, and you shall be my honored guests. Trust me, what I know will prove most interesting to the Okhrana, Mademoiselle Rachkovskaya. If you'll excuse me, I must dress for dinner."

He rose from the chair, which groaned under his weight, and departed the room, accompanied by his valet.

"Sveta, that was most unprofessional of you," MacKenzie whispered in Gaelic. "You really infuriated the old man by threatening him with the force of the Okhrana."

"Against anyone else in this empire, it would've worked. But I'll never forgive him for the position he put me in. I'll have the fat slob sent to Siberia someday, on that you may rely!"

"You offered. 'Anything,' you said."

"I didn't ken he would ask that! I didn't think he was that familiar with our operations. I figured anything he would ask about would be simple and routine. How else would he ken if I told him the truth?"

"Have a care next time. There's an auld Highland saying, 'The tongue may cast a knot, which the teeth cannot untie.'"

She rolled her eyes. "Thanks, *Father*. Wait here, and I'll go arrange the delivery of our luggage to the hotel."

That evening, Beletsky's dinner guests filtered into the courtyard in the center of the villa wearing evening gowns and black silk suits with tails. Here and there, a green army dress uniform with varicolored medals mixed in the crowd like drops of food coloring. A string quartet had arrived and began with a number by Tchaikovsky. Tchaikovsky sounded all the more moving when played by Russians, MacKenzie decided. They didn't ken the first thing about government, but they kent music, to be sure.

The air grew bluer and darker as the evening progressed, until the servants lit up the electric lights lining the courtyard, where the guests had taken their seats at the tables.

MacKenzie and Svetlana found themselves seated across from the host and hostess. The host's voluptuous stomach partly rested on the table with his chair tucked under it. As the servants brought by the caviar, MacKenzie hesitated. Svetlana nudged him, and he forced himself to partake of some on a cracker. His stomach turned as he ate.

The servants served the dinner, fittingly, à la russe, each course brought sequentially. MacKenzie recovered control of his stomach in time to enjoy the rest of the food, particularly the duck. He could not even guess what the chef had wrapped it in, though. His and Svetlana's stomachs felt so empty that they scarcely said a word to Monsieur and Madame Beletsky until they had filled them.

Svetlana finally dabbed the corners of her mouth with her bleached napkin. "That was a fine meal, Monsieur Beletsky. However, my stomach will not feel truly settled until I know what you know about the Kaiser's negotiations with the Tsar."

Beletsky snapped back in surprise. "What negotiations?"

"Did you not know the Kaiser is trying to sign an alliance with the Tsar?"

Beletsky beamed. "Is he? Dear me, that is good news. I'm much obliged to you, Mademoiselle Rachkovskaya. Ever since the League of the Three Emperors fell through, I've been having to insure my assets against war between Germany and Russia. That will be a relief not to have to worry about! And my French assets?"

Svetlana scowled like a gargoyle. "What do *you* think?"

"I expect the Kaiser will keep them safe too. The only assets I have to worry about now, I imagine, are my English ones, and I don't have too many of them. Can't do much business with perfidious Albion."

MacKenzie wanted to remonstrate about that epithet, but Svetlana beat him to it. "Perfidious *Albion?*" she said. "What about you? I gave you the most confidential secret in Russia to earn your trust, and now I've given you another for free! What do I get?"

"What would it be worth to an Okhrana agent to know of an anarchist agent poised in a trusted position to kill the Little Father? One who's sure to succeed?"

Svetlana's face went blank. "Sure to succeed? What are you talking about?"

"Something like that might have come up to one of my agents. I believe I can direct you to the meeting where the details will be worked out."

"Which organization is it? Where will they meet? When?"

He leered like an eel. "You know, Mademoiselle Rachkovskaya, my memory is a funny thing. I find I remember things better after I sleep on them, and I sleep better when someone is beside me. Would you care to refresh my memory?"

MacKenzie leaped from the table, pounding his fists on it. Suddenly his face was the one to flush. "Do you mean what I think you do?"

Monsieur Beletsky leaned back and regarded him with amusement, stroking his beard. "That depends on what you think I mean."

"And you would say this in front of your wife?"

Svetlana placed her hand lightly on MacKenzie's fist. "It's all right, Peter," she said sweetly. "There are many things I would do for the Motherland, and fortunately, some are more pleasurable than others."

Beletsky leaned even further back as he laughed. If he had not gripped the table with one hand, he might have fallen and broken his neck. "So the tigress is really a lovebird? 'More pleasurable than others,' eh? You've been flushed at me all evening. I hardly think this offer will make you *more* favorably inclined toward me."

Svetlana shrugged. "More pleasurable, less pleasurable; it's all the same to me. What matters is the safety of the Tsar. I always do my utmost for that."

"Sveta!" MacKenzie said.

"Hush, Peter Ivanovich," she said softly. She reached up and laid a hand on MacKenzie's shoulder to pull him back to his seat. "You of all people should know, as any Okhrana agent must, that there are higher purposes than honor. But I want certain assurances!"

"Such as?"

"I want a deposition from you first thing tomorrow morning. If there is no plot, I want it on record that you misled an Okhrana agent deliberately. I'll see you ruined for it! What would Her Majesty say if she found out about this?"

The Tsaritsa, Alexandra, was known for her strait-laced morals, much like her grandmother, Queen Victoria.

"I have no fears on that account," Monsieur Beletsky said.

"Very well. I accept your terms," she said.

"Then, my dear Mademoiselle Rachkovskaya, after you."

He swept his arm to what MacKenzie presumed was the man's boudoir.

Svetlana rose from the table and, in his sight, cast a rather catty glance at Beletsky's wife. To MacKenzie's astonishment, the lady did not return any ire towards her. She seemed downright nonchalant about an adulterous liaison being bargained in front of her. MacKenzie stared at the table until they reached the stairs.

"I'm so sorry, Madame," he said as they disappeared. "I had no idea she would do that to you."

Madame Beletsky scoffed. "What's more amazing is that *she* would do that to *him*. He's fat and repulsive and not half as good in bed as he thinks. Better her than me."

Her eyes shifted toward the quartet with insouciance. "It'd almost be worth the stigma to divorce him." She sighed without shifting her eyes from the strings. "But then, I'd also miss his millions."

Suddenly, she turned and smiled warmly into MacKenzie's eyes. "His dalliances do serve a purpose. That way, he doesn't know if *I* spend the night with someone else. It appears that Svetlana offended you with what she's doing?"

"Yes, Madame," MacKenzie said nervously. His hand fumbled with his watch in his coat pocket. He did not like where this was going.

"Then I can think of the perfect way for us to get revenge on them both, and I promise, there will be more sweetness in it for us than just the juice of revenge."

She placed her hand lightly on MacKenzie's.

MacKenzie swallowed hard. The heat under his collar shamed him. His body certainly wanted to do something his conscience refused to countenance. He could not deny the woman's exquisiteness.

There was only one thing to do. He slid his hand out from under hers and cleared his throat. "I must admit, the beauty of your features attracts me, Madame Beletsky, but there's something on your hand that repels me."

Madame Beletsky scowled, then suddenly slapped his cheek. Not satisfied, she made to strike him again, but this time, MacKenzie caught her wrist.

"I only turned you down once. That should merit only one slap."

She leaped from the table. "You have made a serious mistake, my friend!" she cried. "My husband's not the only one who knows things about the revolutionaries. I know the password to this meeting, and now I'll never tell! I hope they find you out and hang you up in a meat locker!"

The guests in the courtyard fell silent. All eyes turned to Madame Beletsky.

MacKenzie blushed at the scene she was making. "That hardly seems called for," he said quietly. "I refused out of honor, not spite."

"Well, spite means more to me than honor!" she cried and stormed off.

MacKenzie, for one second, thought he might have made the wrong decision. His conscience flung the thought from his mind in an instant. Maybe the revolutionaries would find them out, but he could go to God with an unstained conscience.

All the same, he stared blankly at the table. The guests resumed their chatter, mostly about Madame Beletsky's behavior, but MacKenzie did not join their conversation. With Svetlana off making love to the tycoon and the tycoon's wife furious at him, he felt downright lonely. He took a little comfort when the butler came and stood beside his chair.

"She's more stunned than angry," the butler said. "She's just unaccustomed to being rebuffed, and she doesn't take well to new things. You're a good man, sir."

"I hope I imitate Christ," MacKenzie said, surprised.

"You're also a smart one. She takes men and wraps their hearts around her finger, and then, once she knows they're in love, she casts them off with all the cruelty she can muster. I think she does it to avenge herself on mankind after the way her husband treats her. With them, it's hard to tell whose turn it is to avenge themselves of whom. You have succeeded where so many have failed and paid the price"—He looked down at the ground—"including myself. She won't let me quit. She likes knowing what she's doing to me. She's threatened that she'll reveal our affair to Monsieur Beletsky if I try to leave."

MacKenzie looked at him like he would a half-starved dog he encountered in the street.

"So that an honorable man shall not perish for being honorable, I'll tell you what she wouldn't," the butler continued. "I overheard her discussing it with her own undercover agent. He's her current lover, so she convinced him to keep it secret from Monsieur Beletsky. It's, 'lean and hungry.'"

"What's the organization?"

The butler smiled sheepishly. "That's all I heard; I promise."

"Well, I thank you, sir."

The butler left him, and he was alone again. The quartet had started back up again after Madame Beletsky's eruption had shocked them into silence. He listened to it play a piece he thought belonged to Mussorgsky, but he felt badly shaken. Monsieur and Madame Beletsky were bad enough, but for Svetlana to do something like that... Did she have any redeeming features?

After an excruciating wait, he saw the door opening slowly at the top of the stairs, and Svetlana appeared. As soon as she had quietly shut the door, she rushed down the stairs and seized MacKenzie's wrist on the way out.

She said nothing in the carriage that brought them to the hotel in Vilnius, the finest in the city, courtesy of her father's kickbacks. After they reached their room, she went straightaway into the water closet.

A cloud of steam wafted through the doorjamb as Svetlana's shower dragged on. Their luggage had arrived true to Beletsky's word, so MacKenzie decided to go through it. He found everything out of his careful order.

As he suspected! Of course they had gone through it. But was that Archie's seasickness cure? Providence always did work good out of evil. MacKenzie checked to make sure the ammunition remained in its place. Satisfied, he lay back on the bed.

His mind could not let go of what she had done. Neither could Svetlana's, apparently, for she seemed not to feel cleansed until she had poured the whole Viliya River over herself. Finally, she shut the water off, and MacKenzie surmised that the hot water had run out.

After a while, she emerged in her scarlet kimono amid a cloud of steam, with darkened hair damp and clinging to her. Her skin was still flushed from the heat of the water. With a sigh, she sat down on the bed opposite MacKenzie and brushed her hair. MacKenzie could not part his eyes from her. He felt a mix of enchantment and revulsion as he looked at her.

Svetlana continued to brush her hair long after she had removed any tangles. Feeling MacKenzie's eyes on her, she abruptly stopped and looked back at him.

"You ken, Ranald, I didn't enjoy it at all."

"No, I wouldn't expect that you did."

"I wish I could say I was thinking of you or something more pleasant, but with that monstrous tub of lard, the comparison was impossible. Russian slob—sorry to be repetitive! I'm reminded of your own countrywoman's words. You ken how one of your matrons advised your young ladies to, 'Lie back and think of England'? I was thinking of Ukraine!"

MacKenzie shifted his gaze to the wall.

"You're judging me, aren't you, Ranald?" she said.

"Aye."

She leaped to her feet. "And have you considered what would ensue if these rebels succeeded in assassinating the Tsar and replacing his government? It wouldn't just be one murder, even one as hideous as a treasonous murder of God's anointed. Have you considered the millions dead in the inevitable civil war, the millions starving and dying of pestilence in the aftermath, the millions of their opponents worked to death in the freezing cold of Siberia? Vengeful peasants, a new reign of terror, another murderous Robespierre or Napoleon."

She put her hands on her hips. "And that's just the start, for once they had Russia, they'd wish to do the same all across the world. Unfathomable numbers of dead and miserable! The Ukrainian wheatfields gone to the blazes! Now, no Okhrana agent can run that risk for some personal little scruple of honor! There are higher purposes than honor, you ken."

"No, I dinna ken!" MacKenzie cried. "I turned Madame Beletsky down when she made a similar proposition to me. One of the servants, a victim of hers, was so impressed that he told me the anarchists' password. It's my understanding even *you* didn't have access to that."

"No, I was planning to use my reputation in anarchist circles."

"Och, weel, in case that fails, it's, 'lean and hungry.'"

Svetlana rolled her eyes. "Doubtless comparing themselves to yond Cassius. If they keep it up, they'll get a dictator-for-life of their own, and he won't be kent for his clemency like Caesar."

"No doubt, but notice that *I* didn't compromise *my* honor."

"No, but you *did* get lucky! I can't depend on something like that every time *I* have a revolutionary secret to pry into."

MacKenzie gasped. "You've done this before?"

Svetlana burst into a mischievous laugh. "You ken what, Ranald? I do believe you're jealous!"

MacKenzie opened his mouth but shut it just as quickly. He knew better than to try to contest that point.

Svetlana draped herself over the bed and brought her lips close to his. "Dinna be jealous, Ranald; you can have me too. It'd be like a first time for me, since it would be the first time it actually meant anything."

MacKenzie gazed into her eyes. Once again, he had that reciprocating engine in his chest, but for the first time, it was not about that day. Madame Beletsky had made him feel feverish; Svetlana made him feel like he was burning at the stake. Her lips neared his teasingly.

He leaped off the bed. "Dinna tempt me, Sveta! How do I ken you're not toying with me like you do the anarchists?"

Her eyes gleamed. "Ranald, we're on the same side—for the moment, anyway. I assure you, I dinna treat you like I do anarchists."

"Then I'll tell you what Joseph told Potiphar's wife: 'How then can I do this great wickedness and sin against God?'"

Svetlana scowled. "Surely, God wouldn't begrudge two condemned souls like ours a little pleasure before we go to our deaths."

"And what utilitarian casuistry would you use to justify it before Him? I dinna have any secrets the world depends upon your getting."

Svetlana smirked. "Weel, no, I would have no justification for us, but I can give you some casuistry about the others. You told me you justify your lying as a spy because the ten commandments are in order of importance and the commands to honor the government and preserve life come before the command not to lie, did you not?"

"Aye."

"They also come before the command not to commit adultery."

MacKenzie stared blankly into her eyes, which gleamed as lively as a vixen's. He wondered how many revolutionaries she had snared with that grin.

He sighed. "I dinna have an answer for that right now, but there must be one. What you did just can't be right."

She laughed triumphantly. "Weel, you just chew on that for now, Ranald. In the meantime, we've got to use the information *I* gleaned to save the world."

CHAPTER 13: THE PLOTS THICKEN

Hlidskjalf
June 21, 1905

Tirpitz snatched the report from the typewriter. He licked his lips and went over it one more time.

Perfect. To almost anyone, it would appear as a report from an agent of the Order in St. Petersburg, notifying the Master of a memorandum signed by the Tsar and the Russian cabinet. If Tirpitz had not known better, he would have believed Count Witte, who everyone knew had as his mission the modernization of Russia, had convinced the Tsar to bury the hatchet with England and enter a triple entente.

In return for England abandoning its treaty with Japan, the memorandum ran, Russia would transfer troops from Central Asia to her border with Germany and support massive investments from English and French firms, especially in Caucasus oil. He had included French firms just to make it believable; his mention of England would really get the Kaiser's attention.

"Dearest Nicky" conspiring would be incredible; the Kaiser himself thought Nicky would put his talents to best use by raising turnips. Count Witte doing so, on the other hand, made perfect sense. And, of course, he had simply taken the ingenuous Tsar in with it! He was the last man to have spoken with the Tsar and thus the most powerful man in Russia.

Tirpitz would deliver the report to the Master, who would prove only too thrilled to forward it to the Kaiser, who would believe the Tsar had betrayed him, however unintentionally. He would break off his negotiations with "Dearest Nicky" for certain!

Tirpitz had typed the report so his handwriting would not appear on it. He placed the report on his desk and appended a pseudonym with his left hand instead of his dominant one. If it ever came out that one of his own agents had deceived the Kaiser, no one could trace it to Tirpitz. Yet he had fulfilled the Master's wish! Even if he had had misgivings about the assignment, he could take satisfaction in a job well done.

He was getting up from his chair as Heinrich entered and saluted.

"Ach, Heinrich!" he said quickly, exuberant with his feeling of success. "Is the Master in his office?"

"Nein, Herr Hauptmann. He left about an hour ago."

The corners of Tirpitz's mouth turned almost imperceptibly downward. The completion of his triumph would have to wait until the morning. He stashed the document in his top desk drawer and locked it. Heinrich knew better than to ask about it.

"It's about time to close up for the night, Heinrich," Tirpitz said. "Care for a drink with me?"

"Jawohl, Herr Hauptmann!"

"Brandy? Only the best!"

"Jawohl, Herr Hauptmann."

Tirpitz rose from his desk and walked across the broad office to the decanter. "What did you come in here for, Heinrich?"

Heinrich took his glass of brandy. "I feel I should remind you that the Kaiser's annual yachting cruise is coming up. Do you wish for me to reserve room for our men with the anarchist plot afoot?"

Tirpitz clinked Heinrich's glass. "Jawohl! *Prost!*"

The yachting cruise! What a perfect way to meet the Tsar in secret. A state visit either to or from St. Petersburg would require careful arrangements. This was a recurring event that no one would think anything of that would get him out of Potsdam.

The Kaiser would bring the treaty along and get the Tsar to sign, and Tirpitz could not get the report to him in time. The Kaiser would soon become too focused on preparing the details of his trip to read about the memorandum. Then, once he returned with the signed treaty, would he believe Tirpitz's news? This was a calamity!

To Heinrich, he remained businesslike. "Naturally, we shall need our most trustworthy men and best shots," he said perfunctorily. "Disguise them as sailors, but of course, inform the captain that it's for the Kaiser's safety."

They sipped their brandy and chatted of other things. Tirpitz did not let on that he felt that his life depended on his stopping that treaty. If he didn't, the Master in his anger might inform the Kaiser about that day. But how to do it?

His heart pounded, but he let nothing on to Heinrich as they slowly made their way to the bottom of their glasses. Finally, Heinrich finished and left his glass on the desk.

"By the bye, Heinrich, we'll need the closest cabin to the Kaiser's you can arrange."

"Jawohl!" Heinrich said. He gave the Order's salute, then spun sharply on the balls of his feet and marched out.

Tirpitz sighed. He hated keeping secrets from his bosom friend and comrade. Normally, he could unburden his soul only to Heinrich. If he kept secrets from his closest acquaintances, what distinguished him from the Old Scoundrel keeping secrets from his longsuffering mother? The Old Scoundrel had thought he was clever—oh, so clever—and that she had suspected nothing. And to his dying day, that day when he had finally overwhelmed his liver, he had never known that she had always known. She had always smiled in his face.

Every now and then, Tirpitz actually believed he had had the right parents. They had made him miserable to the days they had died, but how he had learned from them! His father had taught him the motivating power of pain and the value of that magical compound, alcohol, the knowledge of which things complemented each other in his on-duty and off-duty moments. His mother had taught him dissembling. His smiles in the faces of his victims could match anything the Old Woman had managed. An endless number of times, he had earned their trust, and then...

Well, I have no time to think on that.

Outside St. Petersburg
July 14, 1905

If anyone knew how to smile in the faces of her victims, it was Svetlana Petrovna Rachkovskaya.

The news of an imminent plot against the Tsar had diverted her completely from the treaty once she had Beletsky's deposition. Stating that she would never forgive herself if anything happened to the royal family, she had spent weeks crisscrossing Russia and looking up her contacts in the anarchist movement, all under her revolutionary pseudonym Svetlana Petrovna Kutuzov. She had dragged MacKenzie along with the undercover name Peter Ivanovich Kutuzov, posing as her cousin.

The plot was proceeding with the utmost secrecy, for Svetlana and MacKenzie's efforts uncovered nothing. They had learned from Beletsky that it would be discussed at the meeting of the People's Revenge on July 14. This particular political party was one of the more radical of the anarchists, devoted to violence against any aristocratic target or anyone in authority. It was whispered, "Heaven help the Okhrana agent who infiltrates them." Svetlana seemed determined to go anyway.

She and MacKenzie arrived at the villa where the People's Revenge would meet with hats pulled down and collars turned up. The party had scheduled the meeting for Bastille Day in commemoration of the French Revolution. She had learned from Monsieur Beletsky that the plot involved a bomb and the Tsar's yacht, but she had also admitted to MacKenzie that she had no idea how exactly the anarchists planned to employ it.

The anarchists had all manner of elaborate methods for delivering bombs: dropping them from bridges or chimneys, putting them in basements, throwing them into carriages stopped by roadblocks… To best combat the plot, she and MacKenzie would again appear as revolutionaries at this meeting to learn details.

In the days prior, Svetlana had made no secret of her disgust for Doctor Ivanov, the owner of the villa. He made a profitable living treating aristocrats' maladies while using the home he had built with those funds to host meetings for those who would do his patients in. His credentials as an associate of those aristocrats seemed reasonably sure to deflect suspicion, and if she could have had him arrested without blowing her cover, MacKenzie did not doubt she would've done it.

Inside the spacious yellow brick house, though, an orchestra of Russian instruments played loud enough to drown out the treasonous talk to anyone eavesdropping outside. The balalaika players particularly enjoyed themselves at the gathering. They played the rustic Russian folk songs of the peasants the People's Revenge wanted to base their communal society upon.

MacKenzie noticed the amiable greeting Svetlana gave the butler who waited at the door to the drawing room. No doubt she forced herself to smile at one she despised by imagining him shivering in rags up to his waist in freezing water mining for gold.

"Your name?"

"Svetlana Petrovna Kutuzov."

The butler gasped. "*The* Svetlana Petrovna! I almost feel ashamed to ask you the password, but this meeting is barred for anyone who does not know it."

Svetlana graciously waved her hand. "That's all right. We should all feel ashamed to live in comfort while the poor are so *lean and hungry*."

Dr. Ivanov's butler stretched out his arms. "Welcome, then!"

"This is my cousin, Peter Ivanovich Kutuzov," Svetlana said with a gesture to MacKenzie. "He is my escort for the evening. I trust you won't mind."

"Not at all. Anyone *you* trust is completely above suspicion."

Svetlana took MacKenzie by the hand and marched triumphantly in. A crowd of middle-class people dressed in suits and evening gowns chattered treason in the ballroom under the cover of the orchestra.

As Svetlana and MacKenzie approached the ballroom, a tall, lanky fellow with a mop of brown hair burst out of the crowd, laid his hands on Svetlana's cheeks, and kissed her mouth for what MacKenzie thought was far too long.

"Sveta! You're back in Russia!"

"Da, Alexander. Haven't seen you since London Bridge! Are you still with our Progress Party, or have you transferred your affiliation to the People's Revenge?"

"Nyet, I haven't changed, but we're trying to work out an alliance with them. You simply must tell them about your Siberian exile! That will win them over for sure! Let me go speak to the committee to prepare a spot for you in the lineup."

He dashed off with dance-like steps.

"Dinna let on your disapproval, Ranald," Svetlana muttered in Gaelic. "They believe in free love here, you ken."

Before long, Svetlana had attracted a swarm of revolutionaries like bees to heather. She had a celebrity's reputation among them after her London Bridge plot and escape from Siberia. Soon, no place remained beside her for MacKenzie.

Reasoning that he would take advantage of his anonymity, MacKenzie abandoned her to the press of the throng in the ballroom and explored the recesses of the villa.

Several hallways branched off from a central point like a starfish's arms. One in particular seemed darker than the others. MacKenzie could just make out the tapestries hanging from the walls. He made his way along the wall, as if descending into the underworld. The balalaikas grew fainter behind him.

Suddenly, the light from a threshold of a door just barely ajar caught his eye. Placing his feet carefully, he reached the slight opening and peered in.

A very young man in a sailor's uniform sat on a stool. He had auburn hair and a pale complexion. His bulky frame meant that he would be a match for MacKenzie if things turned violent. His hands, bulging with veins, looked like they could throttle the life out of someone much stronger than MacKenzie.

Another man in a black suit and blue spectacles stood in front of him, holding a large chunk of coal and a sizable tube in his hands.

"So, Pavel, the bomb is inserted like so," he whispered as he placed the tube inside the lump. "Cover it up again with this plug. It's a perfect fit—I worked on it all night. You simply throw it into the boiler, and the whole yacht will go up in smoke. The council gives you full discretion as to when you do it on the next voyage the Tsar takes, except that it must be far enough out to sea that no one can come to his rescue. When his vessel doesn't return after a reasonable amount of time, we'll make a proclamation that we destroyed him. You must maintain absolute secrecy; only the council and you will know of this plot."

The sailor reached out to accept the deadly device, but MacKenzie noticed his hands trembled.

The bomb-maker frowned. "Are you afraid, Pavel Arkadievich?"

"Nyet!"

"Your arms don't shake because there's no strength in them."

"Forgive me, sir."

He laid his hand on Pavel's right shoulder. "Pavel, it's only natural," he said with fatherly gentleness. "But you have to think of what will happen. Your death will be instantaneous since you'll be right next to the boiler. You won't suffer a bit. Oh, you'll go to the oblivion that awaits us all after death, to be sure, but you would have wound up there sooner or later. It's better than Siberia, believe me."

He raised his arm for a grandiose gesture. "In return, the people of Russia will sing hymns to your memory. There will be paintings of you all over the party's headquarters and statues in squares! Think, my boy! We'll tear down the statue of that false messiah Alexander II and put Pavel Arkadievich up to preside over Kiev for all time. Surely that's more lasting and worth more than a meaningless death, is it not?"

Pavel nodded. "Da, Professor. I see now."

"Stash the lot in your coat, and let's return to our comrades. Mademoiselle Olga would love the chance to give you a hero's send-off, I'm sure. A warm thought to protect you against a late-night chill at sea! Just remember not to let on the details of the plot. All she knows is you are on a mission of some kind."

MacKenzie darted behind a tapestry as Pavel rose from the stool. They exited the room and passed him by. As they did, a notion seized MacKenzie's mind. He knew who the Tsar's prospective assassin was, and he would likely be the only one to know now outside of the council and the assassin himself.

How had Beletsky known? Maybe his agency had pieced everything together—bomb materials going to a terrorist organization that had a known operative on the Tsar's yacht. On the other hand, maybe he had offered a member of the council more than he could refuse.

But it wasn't Beletsky's knowing that MacKenzie now wondered about. What if, instead of revealing Pavel to Svetlana, he protected him from her? Surely, if the Tsar perished, there would be no treaty and no world war. How better could he protect his chums in the mess of the Black Watch from another day like that day? Surely God would approve of that just as much as Samson pulling down the temple of Dagon onto the Philistines.

But did he have the heart to make himself an accessory to murder? Or did it even count as murder, given that he would serve his king and comrades? The Tsar posed even more of a threat to the empire than the Boers, and

MacKenzie had slain the Boers as enemy combatants. Not that he had relished killing them—quite the contrary—but he had no reason to plague his conscience over it when he remembered his oath. That was what all soldiers signed on to do. And in this case, he would only be fulfilling his oath to protect Great Britain. And, besides, would it not be honorable retribution upon the Russian people for his brother's death?

Somehow, he did not feel fully convinced. The knot in his stomach told him he had not completely won his heart over to that position. With no declaration of war, could he consider the Tsar an enemy combatant? But if he waited until Russia declared war, might it not be too late?

Then there arose the whole debate about preemptive strikes and whether hitting back first justified an aggressive act. He felt that it should, for a government tasked with protecting its people should do everything in its power to fulfill that charge, which stood out as its most fundamental duty. If it knew of a threat and simply proved more efficient than its opponent, thus saving more of its own people's lives, what was wrong with that? If he saw a cobra in his way, should he let it rise up to strike before he shot it? But when *he* plotted the preemptive strike, it somehow seemed less honorable...

"The stone that meets not with their foot, will not hurt them," the auld Highland saying would say about his messmates. *But—och—what good is a proverb when, "The Devil can cite Scripture for his purpose"?*

His stomach churned. Whatever was going on in his brain, he could not impose it on his heart. He did not need to make the decision right that instant; he had however long until the Tsar's next voyage to decide. Of course, tarrying in identifying the assassin might make it eventually too late to do anything. Maybe he did need to decide right now.

Of course, even if he stopped the bomb, he might die anyway. The Germans no doubt would watch closely after they had failed to catch the spies who had tried to abscond with the Kaiser's telegrams.

He considered the worst possible outcome—himself dying and the Kaiser and Tsar both living. World war would become certain at that point, and the Black Watch would relive that day with the entire Royal Army. Did he have it in him to prevent such a ghastly outcome?

He withdrew his handkerchief and wiped the sweat from his brow and his palms. Would he panic again? If he panicked at the thought of going through with his mission, would he panic when he actually did have to go through with it?

Och, that Connally had sent someone else! I told him to.

He had to do something; he just wished he knew what. He had to stop the bomb and get the treaty or otherwise mislead Svetlana until he let himself be blown to kingdom come. Which to do? Stopping the bomb meant the treaty might go through, and not stopping it meant he might make himself an accomplice to mass murder. He swallowed. For now, he would go aboard the yacht and try to figure something out.

He staggered through the pitch-black hallway and reentered the lively ballroom. The conspirators had sat down in rows of folded chairs, and the lecturers had begun to preach anarchism from a podium set up beside the orchestra. Their voices boomed threats to the Tsar and all government, augmented by the acoustics of the ballroom along with the orchestra until it sounded like a powerful demon talking temptation from the otherworld amid a fiendish orchestra. The well-dressed lecturers told the well-dressed congregants how they should feel ashamed that others dressed better and more dressed worse than they. Everyone should dress the same.

For MacKenzie, though, the rest of the meeting seemed a blur to him. He had no thought for anything but his dilemma. One thing struck him as certain—Svetlana probably would not find out anything for herself.

He sat down next to Svetlana and quickly concluded she would have no chance to investigate for herself. She had to sit through the lectures, and in between the hellish sermons, the revolutionaries mobbed her, asking question after question.

"Mademoiselle Rachkovskaya, do you really think you had enough gelignite to destroy London Bridge?"

"Where were you planning to place the bombs?"

"How did you procure the explosives?"

"Who do you think betrayed you?"

Svetlana answered each question, including the last one, to everyone's satisfaction, but that only made them more eager to plumb the depths of her wisdom. No one seemed to consider, as she had told MacKenzie that she hoped they would not, that no bomb plot of Svetlana Petrovna Kutuzov's had actually succeeded, and that a high proportion of her comrades in those plots had wound up in Siberia or on the gibbet. After all, she had wound up in Siberia with them, loyal to the end.

As it was, she had little time to catch her breath, let alone make any inquiries for herself. The subtle questions MacKenzie heard her ask did not receive anything revealing in reply. After all, only the People's Revenge's council knew the full details. Even if they did not suspect Svetlana, the council members were aware of the very real possibility of a police spy in their ranks.

MacKenzie and Svetlana sat through the long round of speeches in the drawing room. MacKenzie blanched at the way the speakers justified murder in the name of a higher good. But hadn't he just planned to do that himself? Surely, he could not make himself like them! He knew he should not do something he would find reprehensible in another person.

Finally, Alexander got up to introduce the last speaker.

"Comrades, I know we are past our scheduled closing, but I would feel remiss if I did not give you the chance to hear the testimony of Svetlana Petrovna Kutuzov. She has been with me through many a danger in Britain in the Progress Party. A truer friend you will never find, and I imposed upon her to give you her stirring account of her trials since she has graced us with her presence tonight. I invite you to stay just a little longer and receive fresh inspiration from her example. Sveta, please do come up here."

Svetlana rose from her seat as the room shook with a waterfall of applause, and she strode to the center of the room. She cleared her throat and spoke with a feigned conviction that would do any Shakespearean villain proud.

"Comrades, my true friend Alexander does me a greater honor than I feel I deserve, for I have done no more than my due part in our struggle against the oppression that undergirds all opulence and luxury. Certainly, others have done far more than I and paid a much higher price. Still, I will not deny to you the price that I have paid in the name of freedom, lest I encourage any of you to believe it is cheap. This scar you see I received from a brutal henchman of the Tsar after my arrest in Novgorod after the failed attempt to blow up London Bridge."

MacKenzie wondered if that was really what had caused the scar—had she even let the Okhrana torture her in her effort to deceive the revolutionaries? It looked rather small for that.

"The British are slow to extradite revolutionaries, but they are even slower to take their cause and are more than quick to oppress the Irish and their own workers. That plot was to punish them for their misplaced priorities. In truth, what government in existence can claim to have administered the justice that is its sacred responsibility under the social contract that it has done nothing but renege on after the people in good faith submitted their freedoms to it for that justice?"

The nodding heads irked MacKenzie, who thought his government, even though flawed, to be one of the most benevolent in the world.

"Nevertheless, because of some treacherous nark who will someday no doubt pay for his crimes against humanity, the plot failed, and those whom the Special Branch did not arrest in Britain, the Okhrana arrested upon our return to Russia. We hoped to find shelter with our friends, but we were betrayed."

A murmur ran through the crowd as people wondered if the traitor could be in their ranks at this moment.

"The Okhrana tortured me for the names of the others in the plot, but I will swear by all that you hold sacred that I provided no names to the secret police. They held me underwater for minutes at a time, disregarding the delicacy of a woman or their supposed gentlemanly manners, but still, I would say nothing. Finally, I left them with nothing to do but to send me to the vast frozen oubliette of Irkutsk, there to be forgotten for all time."

She clutched the podium as if she needed its support.

"The cold of Siberia is so great, as you know, that the mere depiction of it in words will freeze your own blood. You cannot move your arms from your chest, so close do you hold your limbs to yourself. The wind rips through you like you were a thin sheet blowing in the blizzards. To sustain the energy for your shivering, you receive a few crusts of bread and anything you can beg from the peasants. It's hardly enough to sustain every step, which must be made with chains around your ankles."

MacKenzie glanced down as he considered Svetlana enduring such an ordeal in the name of duty. Would he have done likewise for his regiment?

"The Tsar's accomplices in oppression did their best to destroy me, but miraculously, I survived. I seduced a guard, and when the fiend took me in his arms, I bashed his brains in with my own shackles. Then I stole the keys and released myself. I found myself alone in the windswept steppes, and by my wits and resourcefulness, I returned to rejoin my comrades."

The crowd broke into applause. MacKenzie forced himself to join in.

"Comrades, this is the system we live under! We do our best for justice and are given as our rewards torment and bestial cruelty. Is there any punishment severe enough for this repaying of good with evil? In faith, the Tsar must die, and I will personally pledge my full support to anyone who seeks assistance in the only just thing that can be done to the murderer of murderers! Ask me anything, and I will do it! It is the least I... I owe... the millions Nicholas the Bloody has cast into the squalor... of misery."

She wiped a tear from her eye. MacKenzie thought of the crocodiles that polluted every body of water in Africa.

"I'm sorry, comrades. Reliving this experience has momentarily... overwhelmed... my heart. By your favor, I shall conclude here."

The room erupted with applause a third time. For several minutes, anyone who had a mind to leave could not do so without shaking her hand or embracing her. Everyone wished to pay their respects before they exited back into the night.

As they rode in the carriage back to the hotel, MacKenzie decided to test if her efforts had proven fruitful or in vain. "Did anyone take you up on your offer to assassinate the Tsar?"

Svetlana laid her head on her hand and propped her arm on the door. "Nyet. I thought for sure I had them won over. Evidently, their plot is being matured in the highest secrecy. I'm beginning to think Monsieur Beletsky got the better end of that bargain—another devious Russian exploiting a loyal Ukrainian!"

She crossed her arms and looked out of the carriage window with a glare that could devastate the countryside. MacKenzie pitied her that she felt dirty with no return. She had traded her body for a hint of a secret she still could not pry into. He reasoned for the moment that he should maintain that secrecy—and hope that he would not also feel dirty for nothing in return!

Peterhof Palace, Russia
July 15, 1905

Svetlana felt a twinge of guilt as her carriage pulled up in front of the Peterhof. She had sent MacKenzie on a fool's errand and made her appointment in complete secrecy from him. She had no intention of ever revealing to him what she was about to do. Best, by far, for him to remain in the St. Petersburg hotel while she handled this part of the business.

As she looked up at the palace above her, however, she consoled her conscience. It looked like a chunk of the New Jerusalem had descended to the Old Earth. Between stands of dark green pines, whose aroma wafted around the palace grounds, lay a vast pool filled by fountains, like a spring-fed lake in the woods.

The fountains of gold on all sides of the pool poured streams of water that formed rainbows as Svetlana walked past. On both sides of the entrance, more fountains rose like a terraced water garden, with six levels of golden fountains spraying upward like geysers. The rippling and splashing made a tremendous but relaxing noise.

The palace itself awaited Svetlana as she climbed the steps to the left of the terraced fountains. It consisted of three stories marked by numberless arched windows with a marigold exterior. The central fountain seemed to spew as high as the roof when approaching it from the lowest level and looking up to the gold figures crowning the whole edifice.

This was what she risked her life and sacrificed her honor for! MacKenzie could never understand. The peasants and the proletariat needed an awe-inspiring, iron-handed autocrat at the helm, directing the Motherland to greater glory. Only in this way could she avert catastrophe; only in this way could Ukraine continue to nourish the world.

MacKenzie thought of honor above all else, but his nation had gone through its growth pains already. Countless English kings had fought civil wars as the nobles, and later Parliament, pushed back against them. Russia could not afford that. This nation, so vast and populated, would see a calamity the likes of which had never been. She would sacrifice everything to prevent that.

A French king, his army having been defeated and his person captured, had said, "All is lost save honor." Svetlana was not that naïve. For her, the report ran, "All is lost save order."

Svetlana made her way up the steps. Upon reaching the guards, she produced her Okhrana identification papers. The guards, dressed in green uniforms, came to attention and admitted her.

Still looking about every now and then like a bird watching for predators, she made her way to Peter the Great's study. Paneled oak, a delicate light brown, lined the wall with images of the learning and power the great Tsar had brought to Russia. If only he had been more kindly disposed to her own people...

Svetlana sat on a bench by one of the desks. The only sound in the room was the quiet tick of a clock. Before long, she heard a knock like the "Preobrazhensky March."

"Enter."

A young man in a black suit with a light-blue waistcoat entered. He had a long, olive face with black sideburns down his jaw and a black mustache over his lip. His eyes widened. Svetlana rose to greet him.

"Alexei Alexandrovich?" she asked.

He opened his mouth to speak but could not produce words. Instead, he nodded.

"You are the Tsar's personal telegrapher, are you not?" Svetlana said.

He cleared his throat. "Da, Mademoiselle. And you are the Okhrana agent who desired a secret meeting?"

Svetlana nodded. "My name is Svetlana Petrovna Rachkovskaya. Have you taken a look at your sister's bookshelf lately?"

"What?"

"I was there to investigate some remarks she had allegedly made. Very worrying what I found on her shelf. *The Conquest of Bread* and *Memoirs of a Revolutionary*, both by that renegade Kropotkin, for a start."

The man's olive skin began to flush. "My sister is loyal! Anything you find there was planted by the Okhrana!"

Svetlana chuckled. "That is a real problem nowadays, isn't it? Hard to tell the genuine evidence from the planted, the actual denunciations from the spiteful. It seems to me our policy has become to send all the accused to Siberia and let God preserve the innocent. Normally, I prosecute my duty to the Tsar with the utmost diligence, but I think I can turn a blind eye to this small matter in exchange for something more important to the empire's safety."

Now thoroughly provoked, the telegrapher stammered his response. "My-my-my telegrams!"

"Precisely. Specifically, the ones from the Kaiser."

The telegrapher's eyes narrowed to thin slits. "I happen to know that by law, the only correspondence the Okhrana cannot read is either the Tsar's or the minister of the interior's. You have no legal authority to request those."

Svetlana examined her fingernails. "Perhaps, but I do have the legal authority to send your sister to Siberia. I spent four months there myself, and believe me, she wouldn't survive. And if she tried to use her frostbite as an excuse not to mine the salt, she'd be flogged until bloody icicles hung down her back."

The telegrapher pounded a fist on the desk beside him. "I know when I'm being set up and blackmailed!"

"Good. Then you must also know when you have no choice."

He crossed his arms. His eyes now blazed like a musk ox daring a wolf to brave its horns. "We have a proven history of loyalty, and I am a vetted servant of the Tsar, whereas I know the Tsar loathes your father. Who do you think he will believe?"

Svetlana matched him anger for anger. "Not you, obviously! My father has enough of a reputation that he's now master of the entire Okhrana. He has the full support of Count Witte and has been granted his rightful place at the highest levels of government in St. Petersburg."

She pointed a fierce finger at him. "Your family history means nothing. Prince Kropotkin, the leading anarchist rogue, was descended from the Tsars himself. I assure you, there's nothing to keep me from sending even *you* to Siberia! I can have the books ready to plant in your quarters at any time. Perhaps you two can keep each other warm in the gold mines."

The telegrapher's lips parted as his arms uncrossed. She could sense him wavering. Taking on Rachkovsky would have taken guts aplenty, but an influential politician like Count Witte was over the top for someone threatened with Siberia if he failed.

Svetlana approached gently. Suddenly, her countenance, which had befitted any icy queen of winter, softened into sweetness befitting a spring maiden. "But if you help me, I can promise you my complete discretion. I am aware how damaging it would be to me if it were leaked that I had disseminated the Tsar's personal telegrams." She ran her hand along his arm. "And, if it makes you feel any better, this is all to protect the Little Father from a very real and dangerous plot. I can't give the details, but I swear to you, it's only for the Tsar's personal safety."

Alexei Alexandrovich groaned. "Very well. I'll forward the telegrams to you."

"Splendid. Send them to Fontanka 16, care of Baba Yaga. That's all for now."

He turned and fled the room. Svetlana smiled. Ranald would have long since fainted by now, she snickered. He was smart enough to be a spy, but he did not have a killer instinct. He could not do what was necessary. He had no stomach for dirty work.

Unlike me! She sighed. *Unlike me.*

In fairness to Ranald, they had both taken oaths, but she felt certain that his oath to the Crown was nothing like the oath she had taken after that day. Soldier's oaths were nothing like her oath to her father, how she would never be a friend to a revolutionary. And, even if she abided by that oath until her dying day, she would still not feel she had recompensed the scoundrels for what they had done to her and her family. Whatever ill MacKenzie might have thought he had endured as a soldier, she felt she could match him with her civilian life.

Her hand swept unconsciously over the burn on her cheek. And, of course, what if that little conversation had led Ranald to realize that the Okhrana had broken all the amateurish British diplomatic ciphers? Surely, a spy like him would catch the porter at the British Embassy they had bribed for its papers.

She chuckled. And then what? Ranald would sit the man down and give him a stern talking-to, no doubt! He could never understand the oath she had taken. It had been the most solemn of oaths, and she was prepared to do anything to keep it.

Svetlana returned to the room at Hotel Europa to find MacKenzie seated at the table, with lidded plates on its snowy white tablecloth. He crossed his arms beneath a grim scowl.

"Where have you been?" he demanded.

"Attending to my duty."

"I ordered the food two hours ago thinking you would be back any minute. Now it's stone cold, no doubt."

"You've had hamelier fare in South Africa, I'm sure. I ken I did in Siberia."

"Just what were you up to?"

"Ranald, I was ensuring we would have access to telegrams from the Kaiser to the Little Father. Surely you can't object."

"And why was I not brought along? You snuck out of here."

"I didn't think it was something you had the heart for. Dinna worry. I didn't betray you."

"And what do I have to go off of on that score?"

"You still won't believe me that we're on the same side. Weel, you will when the telegrams arrive. I've just made a little arrangement. Now we won't be dependent on anarchist scum or the unfortunate Captain Gibson. Can't tell you about it, though. I was sworn to secrecy."

She removed the lid over the food. Her eyes lit up. "Och, Ranald, you remembered! Beef stroganoff and zakuska—my favorites!"

She looked up into his eyes, but no words escaped from her lips. Her eyes flitted to the watercolors on the wall as she searched for something to say. She had deceived someone who had spent that time in thoughtfulness toward her...

"Weel done, Ranald. You've made me speechless. It's not often I'm at a loss for words—I can't be in my line."

MacKenzie looked away. "Shall I say a blessing?" he said impatiently.

"Of course."

MacKenzie bowed his head and said a Gaelic blessing.

"Dinna worry about the zakuska, at least, Ranald—it's supposed to be cold," she said as she raised one of the hors d'oeuvres to her lips.

That was so thoughtful of him—and I treated him like an anarchist! Svetlana felt so defiled by her little trick that she scarcely noticed the cold food. Apparently, MacKenzie was still irked. They ate in silence. They barely spoke a word before climbing into bed with a "goodnight" and settling under the silken sheets.

St. Petersburg
July 20, 1905

A rhythmic knock came at the door. It tapped out the "Preobrazhensky March." Another message from Fontanka 16. Svetlana strode to the door and opened it slightly. As usual, someone pushed a thin envelope through the small aperture and mumbled something, but MacKenzie could not make it out. Svetlana tore the envelope open and snatched the telegram. She leaped back like she had just spotted a coiled serpent.

"The game's afoot, Ranald! This from the Kaiser from north of Stockholm: 'I shall shortly be on my return journey and cannot pass across entrance of the Finnish Sea without sending you best love and wishes. Should it give you any pleasure to see me—either on shore or on your yacht—of course am always at your disposal. I would come as simple tourist, without any fetes.' Simple tourist, indeed! A magician, more like, offering, 'New treaties for old ones.'"

MacKenzie recognized the reference to the story of Aladdin and the "new lamps for old ones." "Sounds like our best chance to see the blasted thing, though. We'll have to get it to France before it's ratified."

"It's our only hope. You said you had something for us to listen in to their meeting?"

"Aye."

"I'll try to forget the treasonous aspect to that."

For a moment, silence reigned. Both of them were thinking, and from the narrow-eyed glances they exchanged, they were thinking the same thing.

"Ranald, forgive me, but I must ask. Can I rely upon your full support in thwarting the People's Revenge's plot?"

"Why do you ask?"

She slammed the telegram on the writing desk. "Dinna insult my intelligence, Ranald! I ken where your true loyalties lie. You're most concerned with the threat to Britain, and if the Kaiser and the Tsar both get killed by an anarchist, that would seem to me to take care of your problem."

Does she ken? "I can't argue with that."

"So, will you go aboard with me and try to thwart the plot? You'd be risking your own life for your two greatest enemies, you realize."

"I realize."

She put her hands on her hips like a lecturing schoolmarm. "Ranald, you can't imagine what kind of horrors a revolution could unleash! I assure you that more people will die than if we had a general European war. Is it more honorable to let millions of Russian peasants die than a few thousand British soldiers?"

MacKenzie bit his lip. All his fellows from the mess of the Black Watch flashed before him. Saving the two sovereigns meant risking each of their lives. It would mean sending all of them back there to that day. He could not do that any more than Svetlana could risk putting her people through a revolution. The Kaiser and Tsar would deserve what they got! They were willing to do the same to him and countless other Scots. They had already done it to his brother.

"Those few thousand British soldiers are my comrades," he said.

Svetlana relaxed her arms and softened her glare. "All right. Think of one life. You ken that without you, there's a good chance that I might die. Have I not been your comrade too? I'm willing to risk my life alongside yours to stop the war. What was that you swore to me—'I will not be one day for you, and another against you'?"

MacKenzie hesitated.

Her stare hardened again. "Or has some hierarchical consideration caused you to renege?"

MacKenzie's stomach grew sick. He had never faced a decision this difficult in his life. She asked her last question so spitefully he questioned his position. No alternative seemed attractive. Despite his distaste for Svetlana's lack of scruples, he had to admit that he owed her his life, and he prided himself that there was no kindness he didn't try to repay, to say nothing of his oath to her. But he had an oath to Britain as well. He had to ask what honor demanded in this situation. Do what seemed best for himself and his chums or maintain order in a foreign country? Which oath to keep? For he could not keep both.

Did he not have a duty to love and protect even his enemies from harm? If God had commanded him to give Willy and Nicky water when they were thirsty or food when they were hungry, did He not also command him to guard their persons? But would it not be justice for two such blood-stained monarchs to be blown to kingdom come? Something in him almost blurted out that he knew who the assassin was!

He looked away from Svetlana. He could not let her cloud his judgment at this moment. His mind quickly ran through the events that might ensue if he saved Willy and Nicky.

His Majesty and Monsieur le Président did not want war with each other, and Russia had become downright exhausted from fighting Japan. That left enough room for him to doubt that this treaty meant war if he let it go ahead. He would just have to inform the king before the Kaiser and Tsar strong-armed France.

And what of Sveta's life? She would not survive a bomb any more than he would. And he had sworn an oath to her. But then, she certainly would have found him and King Edward most disposable if *her* country faced this kind of peril. He still could not commit.

"I'll go," he said.

"Swear to me anew that you'll help me, Ranald. I want to ken you won't back out."

He could not perjure himself. "I won't. This time *you'll* be the one with the questionable ally."

Svetlana, much to his surprise, gave her foxy smile. "I'm certain, Ranald MacKenzie, that you'll do the right thing when the chips are down. Now, something I'm sure you'll approve of is that we pray now because the stakes are so deucedly high. Will you pray with me?"

"Not with an icon, and not to a saint!"

"Och, Ranald! You Presbyterians cheat yourselves of so much."

"The Holy Spirit can make up for whatever we lose out on by obeying His command."

She rolled her eyes but then closed them and bowed her head. "Holy Father, who did decree by the hands of angels to honor those in authority over us, be they parents or magistrates, and who did annex a promise of blessing that those who do so would live long in their land, please be with Ranald and me as we seek to obey that command. Please watch over us in the valley of the shadow of death and grant that we survive to see our cups overflowing as we celebrate Thy deliverance. Help us to do our duty, and protect my sovereign, Your minister to me for good.

"Please be with these misguided fools who oppose us. In their quest for justice and betterment, they do not follow the example of David, who would not lift so much as a finger against Your Anointed. Open their eyes, lest we should have to open their veins. Establish peace with justice in Russia and throughout the world."

She paused to allow MacKenzie to add his prayers, but he did not have a word to add. Such a Biblically informed prayer, dripping with Scripture, was the last thing he had expected from her.

"Establish peace with justice"—his very own words in his own prayers. Had some of her Scottish Presbyterian persona actually seeped through to her heart? Even a prayer for the repentance of her enemies so that she would not have to kill them! And he almost ready to see the Tsar and Kaiser and their courts blown to kingdom come!

He almost confessed everything again, but that day flashed over his mind. What if that prayer had all been a ploy to cause him to spill any secrets he might be harboring? He had seen enough actions in her to contradict her words.

They could have heard a mouse's footfall.

"Ranald, would you like to say something?" she said at length.

"I dinna think I can add anything to that."

"Then—this we pray in the name of the Father and of the Son and of the Holy Spirit. Amen."

"Amen."

If only he knew if she was being sincere!

MacKenzie was shaving early the next morning when the rhythmic knock came at the door again. Svetlana again opened the door only wide enough to receive the envelope and promptly ripped into it. She put her hand to her cheek.

"Och, Ranald, we have to leave at once! This from the Little Father: 'Delighted with your proposition. Would it suit you to meet at Bjoerkesund, near Viborg, a pleasant, quiet place, living on board our yachts? In these serious times, I cannot go far from the capital. Of course, our meeting will be quite simple and homely. Looking forward with intense pleasure to see you.'"

MacKenzie did not realize he had cut himself with the razor until he saw the red streak down his throat.

"He's taken the bait, all right," he said. "Now we've got days to stop world war."

CHAPTER 14:
THE SECRET MEETING

St. Petersburg
July 22, 1905

"Hm, sailor or nobleman?" Svetlana muttered.

"Beg pardon?" MacKenzie said.

"Obviously, we will present ourselves to the captain as two Okhrana agents tracking a plot against the Tsar, but we need a cover story to fool the others as well. While I can pass myself off as a maid, we'll need some sort of disguise for you. My father can procure a uniform for either a sailor or a visiting nobleman. I doubt you have the skills of a sailor, and I'm sure you dinna ken the etiquette of a nobleman."

"Gey and true, I'm afraid."

"Then we'll tell the captain you're an Okhrana agent coming on board disguised as a sailor and ask him to give you nothing of any importance to do."

MacKenzie wondered if he would do anything at all to stop the bomb.

"I'll wear this wig and bring make-up to change my complexion, and I've sent to my father for a false beard for you," Svetlana said.

Now disguised as ordinary crewpersons, Svetlana and MacKenzie appeared at the berth of the *Polar Star*, the Tsar's yacht. For such a name, the yacht appeared inappropriately dark. It sported a black hull. Two closely spaced funnels of yellow and black let off steam. It had three masts, atop which fluttered the white flag with blue saltire of the Russian navy.

Seeing the waves lazily lapping and slopping at the hull, MacKenzie felt grateful to God that Monsieur Beletsky's men had uncovered his seasickness cure.

The ship's whistle blew a raspy hiss. They met the captain as he gave orders to the crew to make haste. The crew chattered or sang as they loaded and made ready. The sailors, scurrying with loads like ants, wore dark sailor uniforms exactly like Pavel Arkadievich's. MacKenzie would have to come right up to him to identify him, assuming he wanted to. He was still seriously contemplating shielding Pavel from Svetlana.

The captain himself wore a dark blue uniform with gold braid that marked him out as the senior officer. Svetlana got his attention over the noise and curtsied.

"You are the captain of His Majesty's yacht?"

"Da, Madame."

"I am Svetlana Petrovna Rachkovskaya, and this is Peter Ivanovich Kutuzov with the Okhrana. We will be joining your yacht for its upcoming cruise with the Tsar."

The captain's eyebrows arched. "How do you know about that? Not even the ministers were informed."

"Never mind how we know! What's important is that the Okhrana also knows of an imminent plot against the Tsar by one of your crew. I must insist that Gendarmes search everyone who boards. The devils are busy on Mount Triglav, to be sure."

The captain's eyes went blank.

"That's just something I say when the anarchist fiends are up to something," Svetlana said.

The captain nodded. MacKenzie knew the reference related to the Russian orchestral masterpiece, "Night on Bald Mountain."

"I shall be a maid for this voyage, and Peter Ivanovich shall be one of your crew, though I trust you will not entrust too many duties to us that would distract us from our true duties to the empire."

"But of course."

Before anyone could board, two gendarmes in blue uniforms arrived, dispatched by Svetlana's father. Both had blue peaked caps, but one had a bushy, steel-gray mustache, and the other a flowing brown beard. They looked as cheerless as mourners, but they had the bulk to contend with Pavel Arkadievich. The two gendarmes and the sailor epitomized the Russian bear. MacKenzie and Svetlana stepped forward to see them first.

"Good morning, Baba Yaga," one of them whispered. "We brought a female operative to handle *your* search."

"Baba Yaga?" MacKenzie whispered. "Your codename?"

"Da."

"Hardly seems fitting."

"Och, aye, indeed. I'm a magician like her. I enchant revolutionaries' hearts and make them disappear."

"But, as I recall, she was hideously ugly. You strike me more like *La Belle Dame sans Merci*."

"Thank you, and you're a regular John Wellington Wells," she said with a smile as she pulled her hair over her right shoulder.

MacKenzie heart sped up.

Just the same, neither the men nor the woman uncovered anything. MacKenzie watched them search Pavel Arkadievich, and nothing happened. He betrayed no sign of treachery that Svetlana might pick up on. The bomb must have already been loaded in the coal bunker. MacKenzie kept his lips closed.

Last of all, the Tsar came on board. He was clad in a blue naval uniform with insignia on his shoulders. He had a full mustache like the Kaiser's, but unlike him, he had grown a beard with a neat point. He had a kindly air, much too kindly for a government that massacred its citizens when they tried to present petitions and persecuted its poorer classes of Jews.

His peaked cap almost hid a scar that MacKenzie remembered he had received from a Japanese policeman who had tried to assassinate him with a saber. MacKenzie knew he could not have brought himself to attack royalty up close with a bladed weapon like that, so could he allow a bomb to go off instead?

His Majesty looked rather like the Prince of Wales, his cousin. Seeing him in that light, as his future sovereign's cousin, made MacKenzie pause. He would easily give his life for the Prince of Wales, so would he not defend his relative by blood? But then, it was rather a dysfunctional family. Blood ties meant nothing between the Kaiser and King Edward, who prepared for war in mutual distrust.

Archimedes' medicine aside, MacKenzie felt almost seasick with the nerves in his stomach as the yacht cast off. Every second he delayed, he ran a risk, but he still had no answer to his dilemma. MacKenzie tugged on his sleeves and the legs of the pants. The confounded uniform was too snug. Hopefully, no one noticed.

Off the Coast of Finland
July 23, 1905

The yacht had reached Bjorko Sound, nestled between a beautiful Baltic island and the mainland of Europe. The island sported its green summer growth. The waters in this sheltered part of the sea were so gentle that MacKenzie wondered if he had even needed the seasickness cure.

The telephone in the bridge rang. One of the officers strode to answer it, but MacKenzie knew what the person on the other end was going to say already.

The officer reported to the captain with gaping eyes. "Sir, the *SMY Hohenzollern* is steaming in from the west. Does the Tsar know his cousin is coming for a visit?"

"Da, he does."

The wide eyes narrowed. "Was that the purpose of this voyage?"

The captain put his hands behind him. "I cannot confirm or deny that. Please inform His Majesty."

"Very good, sir." The officer saluted but almost stomped off toward the Tsar's quarters.

MacKenzie looked to the west. The sun appeared blood red as it sank below a canopy of clouds streaked with scarlet. It would have been a beautiful sunset under any other circumstance, but MacKenzie did not want to glimpse red at that point.

When the sun rises again, will it appear above a world at war?

His thoughts ran far too darkly for the Sabbath.

Svetlana appeared on the bridge and curtsied to the captain like a properly submissive maid. She marched over, grabbed MacKenzie's arm, and dragged him to an unoccupied corner of the bridge.

"I've searched the whole ship!" she hissed. "Nothing suspicious."

Now MacKenzie had to decide whether to hinder Svetlana. If he did nothing about the bomb, would he stand aside and leave it up to her whether it went off or not?

"Perhaps the Okhrana search scared the anarchist off."

"They didn't find anything. The criminal got his bomb on board, I'm sure."

MacKenzie's jaw muscles opened and shut in a move so subtle that anyone but Svetlana would have missed it.

"You have something to say, Peter Ivanovich?" she said.

MacKenzie sighed. "Nyet. The Kaiser's yacht is coming up."

"Maybe the fiend was waiting for something like that. I dinna ken how he'd ken, though. Maybe he was just guessing it took something important to take the Tsar from Peterhof at a time like this."

"Maybe," MacKenzie said, and nothing more.

Seeing the sunset had convinced him for a moment. The Kaiser and the Tsar could not sign that treaty! He hoped his resolve would hold; he was practically already committing himself because the bomb could go off any moment.

Was he ready to die? Of course! It was as much laying down his life for his country as he had sworn to. More than that, his soul was ready to go before God. Or was it?

He desperately wished he knew what God would say on this matter. He hoped he could live with His words for all eternity. Why was he even on board if it was just to die? Did he intend to aid Pavel Arkadievich?

The officer sent to inform the Tsar reappeared. "The Tsar will have dinner with the Kaiser tomorrow evening. He said to find out if the Kaiser would like to meet him aboard his yacht or aboard this one."

Of course! The anarchist will wait until they're both aboard this vessel if he can!

The Kaiser's yacht appeared over the horizon to the officers and crew aboard the bridge. It cut a most dashing figure as it steamed closer, smoke puffing out of two golden, wide-spaced funnels. Its three masts sloped at a jaunty angle like a rake's hat.

Had any other passenger stood aboard, the ship would have harbingered peace and comfort. As it was, this hateful vessel was more dangerous to Britain than any of its naval counterparts in Kiel, no matter how many guns they boasted in their turrets. MacKenzie wished the confounded thing would just sink!

MacKenzie excused himself to go below. He glanced around as he reached the door to Svetlana's cabin. Seeing that no one was using the passageway, he swiftly admitted himself. She sat on the bed built into the side of the small, sterile room with her arms crossed. A sudden image of her disfigured body thrashing in water that consumed and drowned her flashed across his mind. He shuddered. He might not like her, but that was too much for him.

"I suppose the crook is waiting for the sovereigns to both be aboard before he blows us all to kingdom come," she said.

"Assuming we thwart him, we still need the bug in the sovereigns' conference," MacKenzie said. "Which of us will do *that?*"

"I'll handle that. If they go aboard the Kaiser's yacht, I'll be less conspicuous as a maid than a Russian sailor will. If the Kaiser comes aboard here, I'll still be less conspicuous. Just say I'm cleaning up. May I have the bug?"

MacKenzie fished it out of his pocket. He held it out to her but suddenly retracted his hand as she reached out for it.

"Ranald, what on earth are you doing? How could I possibly reverse-engineer that thing here?"

"I'm sorry, Sveta—just the thought of top-secret British technology in Russian hands..."

"I give you my word I'll do no more than place it onboard whichever yacht it takes."

"Like you gave your word to help the anarchists kill the Tsar?" he demanded.

Svetlana shot up from her seat. "A little louder, if you please, Ranald," she hissed. "As if my loyalties as a penetration agent aren't suspicious enough."

"I'm sorry, Sveta."

"And while we're on the subject of giving one's word, it seems to me that the one of us who hasn't sworn to protect the Tsar's life is the one it'll be left to to stop the bomb once I'm occupied with the bug. How safe do you think I feel?"

MacKenzie raised his hand solemnly. "I swear I'll try to do the right thing."

Svetlana shook her head.

"I just wish I kent what you thought was right."

So do I.

***

The Honorable Spy

MacKenzie awoke in his own cramped cabin with surprise. He had not awoken in the Baltic Sea amid burning wreckage. He was at a loss. He felt that reflected a slight on his abilities as a spy. A spy should never be at a loss. Certainly, Svetlana never seemed at a loss.

He dressed in his borrowed uniform and went up to the bridge.

"Ah, Peter Ivanovich!" the captain said. "The Tsar will dine aboard the Kaiser's yacht this evening. I trust the Okhrana will see to his safety as he does."

"I will do my duty, captain."

The captain nodded. "Splendid," he said.

MacKenzie was glad the captain didn't press as to who his duty was to.

Perhaps the anarchist would abort the plot when he found out the Kaiser and the Tsar would meet aboard the other yacht. Or maybe he would decide to blow up just the Tsar while he could. MacKenzie could only make sure by waiting in the engine room until the anarchist decided to strike. But then, how could he do his duty to listen in with the steam and pipes whining and pumping in his ears? At least, that was what he told himself. It was a weak argument, he knew.

He found Svetlana. "They'll be meeting this evening aboard the Kaiser's yacht."

"I'll see to the bug," she said. "You see to the bomb."

***

Tirpitz finished off his roasted leg of veal and started into his roasted vegetables. He drummed "Der Coburger" on the maple table.

Heinrich and his off-duty men sat in the embroidered couches lining the walls of the Kaiser's dining saloon, awaiting their orders. The midday light beamed in behind them in the windows, giving them an aura like the Aesir. Today they would have to act with the wisdom and foresight of Odin, but Tirpitz had a tough choice to make.

How much to reveal? The Order had sworn to support the Kaiser. Would he order them to spy on him? Everyone knew subconsciously that they had their unspoken first duty to the Master and to the gods he served, but no one would say that aloud. Certainly, Tirpitz would not.

Still, if he could confirm what the Kaiser and Tsar said in secret, he could get to Chancellor Bülow and turn him against the treaty before the Kaiser could get him to ratify it. Or, better yet, if he knew the precise terms of the treaty, he could forge another report that would indicate the Russians had already broken it.

"*Kameraden*, today is a most important day. Those two spies who escaped us after trying to steal the Kaiser's personal correspondence with the Tsar could be afoot, trying to listen in to the Kaiser and Tsar's meeting. No doubt something is going on that attracts their attention. These two busy little bees must not be allowed near our dearest cornflower. Vet everyone who comes on board. I want a man posted outside the saloon as the Kaiser and Tsar meet to keep any of these pests at bay. It wouldn't be amiss if I could report to the Master what it was that they are so interested in so we can gauge what our foes know of German diplomacy. Anything you can report on their conversation would be helpful. Dismissed."

His men rose and saluted. Tirpitz reciprocated. When they had left, he drew his handkerchief from his pocket and wiped his forehead. Hopefully, they had not noticed his perspiration. Otherwise, he thought he had handled it very well.

* * *

MacKenzie tried to put it out of his mind that the deck beneath him might send him hurtling skyward and into the sea at any moment. Of course, that nagging thought had a way of staying foremost in his brain. At least he would be in heaven, free from the torments of his memories of that day forever. Or would he after he had made himself an accessory to murder?

He glanced at the *Hohenzollern's* promenade deck under the lifeboats and caught sight of the Kaiser strutting along the length of his ship. The Kaiser gestured with his right hand, but his left held a cane. As MacKenzie caught sight of his shriveled arm, he felt a pang of pity in his heart. He even prayed for the Kaiser. To be in the public eye of the second most powerful nation in the world with such a deformity... Then he remembered that this trickster called his uncle the Arch-Troublemaker of Europe as he plotted world war.

The Kaiser wore a naval uniform, dark blue with gold braid and a white peaked cap. His brown mustache, waxed to turn up at the tips, stood out as his most distinguishing feature. MacKenzie tried to put the thought out of his mind of that face disfigured and burned.

He looked at his watch. The Kaiser and Tsar would meet in a few hours.

***

Tirpitz had patrolled the ship since he had finished his lunch. He and Heinrich walked past the saloon with two guards from the Order. The luxurious hair of the maid caught his attention. She had her back to him as she crawled on the floor, but her hair at least was ravishing. Suddenly, though, he noticed a small mark at her jawline. Something about that seemed familiar...

"You, there!" he barked. "What are you doing here?"

The woman drew herself up with a grace more befitting an aristocrat than a maid and replied in German without turning around. "Just tidying up, Mein Herr. The Kaiser wants everything immaculate for his cousin."

"Show your face!"

She turned around. Those vibrant blue eyes were like rare sapphires.

"I know you! You were one of the three spies in the opera house that night! Heinrich, arrest this woman!"

"I wouldn't advise that," she said coolly. "Why do you think I'm here? There's a plot to blow up the Tsar and the Kaiser. I was looking for the bomb. If you don't let me go, your sovereign is at risk as much as mine, to say nothing of yourself."

"*Your* sovereign? You're not English?"

"I'm with the Okhrana. The Little Father's safety is of the utmost importance to me, as is the Kaiser's—for the moment, anyway."

"So you're not Catriona Cameron?"

"I see Captain Gibson spilled what he thought the beans to be."

"Ja, he talked of his own free will—after we finished torturing him."

"I ask you," the maid said, "what would an Okhrana agent care about the Kaiser unless she were trying to protect the Tsar?"

"I could almost believe you—if only I hadn't caught you trying to abscond with the Kaiser's personal telegrams."

"Just following up on the anarchist conspiracy. You know that an anarchist was behind that leak, do you not?"

Tirpitz's lips twisted. "Maybe what you say is true. Still, I'm going to detain you until we can sort this out ashore. But, if you care about your sovereign like you say you do, you'll tell my men what to look for in this bomb."

"Gelignite. It's a clockwork detonator."

"Thank you. Heinrich, take her below."

***

MacKenzie paced the deck with swift strides. He clasped his hands behind his back. He knew it would make him conspicuous to anyone who happened to be nearby, but he felt too distressed to do otherwise.

Svetlana had planted the bug, for he had heard it coming through on his ring, but he also knew the Germans had seized her. He could not go across and rescue her, for the mission depended on him listening to the Kaiser and the Tsar's meeting—if the bomb did not cut it short.

That matter, of course, remained the most pressing. No doubt the explosion was imminent. Pavel could have no better moment, a certainty of getting the Tsar and possibly a chance to wipe out two emperors for the price of one.

MacKenzie still felt chained to the deck by indecision. In this case, indecision became a tacit decision to help the anarchists. His death day had come. He had survived his wound on that day only to be blown to pieces.

He wanted to pray but did not know what to say. Surely, a prayer in his final moments was appropriate, but what to say when he was allowing scores of people to blow up or to be drowned? Like Samson, he could say, "O Lord God, remember me, I pray thee, and strengthen me, I pray thee, only this once, O God, that I may be at once avenged of the Russians for my brother." No, that seemed too vindictive. He had to think of the souls in khaki he would save.

He went to look for Pavel. Maybe his instincts would kick in if he saw the plot unfolding. *It is not known what sword is in the sheath, until it be drawn.* He stopped. He could not condemn any of his friends to that day. No one should have to go through that! If he had to die to save them, then that was truly the noble thing!

He glanced around and caught sight of a chubby young lass, about four years old. She was spinning a top with glee, and her blue eyes lit up as she watched it whirl. She paused and pulled her strawberry-blonde locks out of her face.

Surely nothing could be right that involved her being blown up!

MacKenzie raced below deck toward the engine room. Suddenly, his prayers became that he would not be too late. The pipes and valves ran through the structure like the ship's bowels. The hot air pressed him all over. He snatched up his Webley as he caught sight of the engine room.

He heard a sigh through the door.

"I won't go to heaven, but I shall bring heaven to earth."

MacKenzie burst through the door with his pistol ready.

"Drop it, or I'll blow your head off! And, nyet, I don't expect you will be going to heaven. Hell, more like."

Pavel dropped the coal and raised his hands.

"I just meant there is no heaven, nor hell, either."

"When the courts have finished with you, I expect you'll find out. I urge you to repent before they execute you. Come up on deck."

MacKenzie noticed several crewmen lying unconscious on the deck. They seemed to have struggled with Pavel Arkadievich but had proven no match for his brute strength. MacKenzie needed to wipe the sweat from his brow with his handkerchief after that sprint into the hottest part of the ship, but he made sure he kept his eye on him.

He picked up the bomb and followed the anarchist up to the deck. To MacKenzie's astonishment, they found Svetlana just coming on board from a boat that had ferried servants to the *Hohenzollern*.

"Sveta! How did you escape?"

"I think the story would horrify you, Ranald."

MacKenzie did not press her. He felt horrified enough at himself. "This is the saboteur," he said wearily. "Please put him under arrest. He snuck a bomb disguised as coal and was about to put it in the boiler."

Svetlana glowered, though why, MacKenzie had no idea. He noticed the blood stain on her dress. The dress itself remained intact; the blood did not seem to have come from any injury to her person.

She sighed. "Ranald, I'm afraid this won't do. *You* don't have the authority to arrest anyone, and I did not catch him red-handed. Bring him down to the engine room, and I can say I arrested him in the act. Quick, someone's coming!"

They descended back to the engine room. Suddenly, Svetlana snatched the bomb and the Webley out of MacKenzie's hands and shoved him off balance. He slammed into a steel pipe and dropped, stunned, to the deck. She tossed the lump of coal to Pavel.

"Now's our chance!" she said. "Blow us all to kingdom come, for the people!"

Pavel leaped toward the boiler. He took three great strides as MacKenzie watched helplessly. What was happening? Had Svetlana been working for the revolutionaries all along? Had it all been an act, the only true words she had spoken to him being the speech she had made at Doctor Ivanov's? He tried to rise, but he was still stunned.

Svetlana raised the Webley, and the shot echoed in the cramped room. Pavel collapsed with a spurt of blood out of his back. He crumpled to the floor, and Svetlana swiftly retrieved the bomb. She held out her other hand to MacKenzie. After a few moments, he took it, and she helped him rise to his feet.

"Sorry, Ranald," she said. "Cruel necessity."

"What on earth is wrong with you?" MacKenzie said. "You had only to take him into custody!"

Her eyes burned like bonfires. "It's your fault, Ranald! You revealed to him that I was an agent provocateur, so I acted like one and set him up. Do you think I wanted him blabbing to all his associates that I am an Okhrana spy?"

The captain came running down the passageway into the room.

"What's going on?"

"We have stopped the saboteur," Svetlana said. "Here is the bomb he was about to put in your boiler. Impound this, and we'll have it analyzed when we get ashore."

"I'm afraid he assaulted some of your crewmen, Captain," MacKenzie said. "You'll need to find someone to tend to them and replace them on the watch."

They went back on the deck to find everyone astir. Whispers flew from worried lips to anxious ears. Had an anarchist fired that shot? Had someone been assassinated? Were these nobles next?

The captain raised his hand reassuringly.

"It's all right, everyone. Just a little backfire from the engines. Everything's in order now. You may all go back to your socializing."

***

Tirpitz heard the shot too from on deck. He found the sentry from the Order.

"Where did that shot come from?"

"The Tsar's yacht, Herr Hauptmann."

"Then they must have more Okhrana agents aboard! I'm going to have a word with our prisoner—see how many more of her ilk are hanging around here."

Tirpitz descended into the hold and gasped. Heinrich lay in a pool of blood, a savage puncture wound in his heart. Tirpitz knelt down and examined the hole, cradling Heinrich's head in his right hand.

"Heinrich, what happened?"

His friend coughed. "She had a stiletto."

"How? She didn't have any weapons on her when we seized her."

"Hidden in her skirts?"

Heinrich coughed again. In an instant, his head became dead weight in Tirpitz's hand. His pupils widened into a glazed stare at the deck above. Tirpitz had to wipe a tear from his eyes. He tenderly closed Heinrich's eyes. In an instant, tears cascaded down his cheeks to the deck. He had to restrain himself from sobbing, lest anyone hear him.

He looked up and raised his hand. "I shall avenge you, my comrade. By Odin's spear, the murder of this divine Baldur shall not go unrecompensed!"

For several minutes, Tirpitz struggled with his tears. When he finally rose to his feet, there were no tears, only fists and a clenched jaw. The Okhrana agent surely would not return aboard if she had made it off this ship. Somehow, he had to meet her ashore.

And then what? What would suitably avenge the loss of his comrade? If Heinrich was like Baldur, surely, the Okhrana agent deserved to be tied down under a serpent dripping venom into her eyes like Loki, who had killed Baldur. If Heinrich was like Patroclus, Tirpitz had a duty to kill her and parade the corpse for all to see. Surely, she had forfeited all claim upon leniency from feminine delicacy. Neither of those punishments seemed practical, of course, but if anyone could suitably avenge Heinrich with appropriate levels of pain, Leopold Tirpitz could.

***

MacKenzie shut the door to Svetlana's cabin and rotated the ruby in his ring to activate the receiver. Crystal-clear silence, not static—a good sign.

He sat down on the bed. The threads of his uniform strained to hold him in. A hushed knock with the rhythm of the "Preobrazhensky March" rapped at the cabin door.

"Hurry, Sveta!"

Svetlana slipped into the room and sat down on the bed beside him. They did not have to wait long before they heard the Kaiser and Tsar enter the stateroom through the ring. The plates and silverware clinked as the men sat down to dinner.

MacKenzie knew a trusted servant was cutting the Kaiser's food; he could not do it himself. For the longest time, the two sovereigns exchanged small talk as if the Kaiser only had in mind a simple family reunion.

"How is Alix?" the Kaiser said.

"She's feeling the strain of these serious times, I'm afraid," the Tsar said.

"Well, send her my best wishes."

"Thank you. And how is Dona?"

As dinner concluded, the Kaiser settled down to business. MacKenzie knew he could not restrain himself for long.

"Nicky, it's wonderful to see you holding up so well after all that you've been through. What an appalling shame about your fleet! If only France had acted like the ally or England like the neutral they pretend to be. You know how Germany has done everything we can within the constraints of neutrality. I dare say, we've been better allies to you as a neutral than France as a treaty-partner. Her eye is roving for Uncle Bertie, I'm afraid. In addition to being a lusty *touche-à-tout*, which one could excuse in a king, he is the Arch-Troublemaker and trickiest deceiver in Europe!"

The Tsar groaned. "Yes, it truly is an outrage. France let me down, and England did her best to humiliate me after the Dogger Bank incident."

MacKenzie wondered how much more a nation could be humiliated after its fleet had opened fire on civilian fishing vessels.

"When France refused to support me—me, her ally of fourteen years—after England whipped the whole thing up, that can only mean that Uncle Bertie is trying to turn her against me," the Tsar said. "You know, he cozied up to her without breathing a word of it to her ally, who must surely be as concerned in this matter as she!"

"Uncle Bertie loves making his little understandings with every nation in the world."

A thump like a fist on the table boomed in the ring's receiver. "I can promise you he'll never trick me into one, and certainly not against Germany!"

"Perhaps it is time you made a little agreement with your true friend. Remember that treaty we drafted last year?"

"Yes, but I can't recall what it said."

"What a happy accident that I have another copy."

"Accident, my eye!" Svetlana hissed.

"Certainly, let me see it!" the Tsar said.

The spies made out the crinkling of paper in the receiver. MacKenzie could also hear the Kaiser whispering some kind of prayer. MacKenzie prayed in the opposite direction and hoped he had more influence with the Lord.

"This is superb!" the Tsar said. "I couldn't agree more."

Svetlana muttered a Ukrainian oath. MacKenzie thought a Gaelic one.

"You'll note the new clause I inserted delays the activation of the alliance until the end of the war with Japan," the Kaiser said. "We'll let you get your house in order before we get involved in any European fracases."

How magnanimous of the scoundrel! Let Russia recover her strength before he sics her on us! Still, it is a reprieve.

"You can note also how these clauses as I have amended them will be taken as less threatening to England than the drafts we worked on," the Kaiser continued. "But we all know this agreement will put an end to Uncle Bertie's arrogance, if not to his perfidy. We can't control that, I fear, since it's in his devilish nature. We'll protect each other from it instead, to be sure. Should you like to sign?"

"Most assuredly."

"I have a pen handy. I'll have my man from the Foreign Ministry, von Tschirsky, witness our signatures. Have you anyone to witness?"

"Yes. I shall have Admiral Bireleff, my naval minister. He's aboard."

"Let us call them at once."

MacKenzie became conscious of trickles of sweat down his temples and his spine as the ministers presented themselves. He could almost see the scene of that day before him again in all its bloody detail.

With such an alliance, the Kaiser could not resist the urge to provoke Britain into a war he would then surely win. The Tommies MacKenzie would be ordered to lead would fight valiantly and be slaughtered with all the gallantry a Mauser would permit them.

MacKenzie heard the clink of the Kaiser's pen in the inkwell and the scratching of the Tsar's signature. It was a death-warrant for Scotland.

The Kaiser scratched his own signature, which he might as well have signed in British blood. Suddenly, MacKenzie heard the Tsar beginning to weep.

"You are the only trustworthy friend I have," the Tsar choked.

"Herr von Tschirsky, will you witness this august pact?" the Kaiser asked.

More scratching of that infernal pen!

"Admiral, as you have witnessed my signature, please affix your name as well," the Tsar said.

"No, don't read it!" the Kaiser said. "Its contents are the utmost secret."

Another scratch and the document was confirmed. Svetlana groaned at the Kaiser's unreasonable instructions to Bireleff, but MacKenzie clasped his hands and bowed his head.

**

The Tsar and Kaiser finished their treacherous tête-à-tête. Not only did they threaten Scotland, but they made plans against Denmark, no more than a pawn in their struggle with Britain.

MacKenzie rotated his ruby to turn the receiver off as the Tsar came back on board his yacht. He and Svetlana went on deck for fresh air. MacKenzie gripped the railing and stared at the Kaiser's yacht. His eyes sparkled with forming tears.

Svetlana laid a tender hand on his shoulder. "Ranald, I ken I was harsh with you earlier, but I really do appreciate the service you've rendered to the Russian Empire. You dinna ken how much it means to me!"

MacKenzie's heart leaped into his throat. He feared how she might react, but he had to tell her the truth. "I did a service to the lassie over there. Is that Anastasia?"

"Aye."

MacKenzie fixed his eyes on the Baltic. "Truth be told, Sveta, I was going to let us all be blown to kingdom come. I reasoned that if the Kaiser and the Tsar were no more, my chums would be safe. I was willing to lay down my life for them. It seemed a fair solution until I saw her. She... she reminded me of my sister when she was a lass."

By now, he was choking on tears. He looked back fearfully to see Svetlana beaming.

She laughed. "Your sense of honor, indeed! I kent I could count on you in a pinch. You dinna have the ruthlessness of a spy, Ranald. Here you are, faced with a coalition of all Europe against your empire, with millions of Mausers, Mosin-Nagants, and Lebels pointed at your pitiful little band of Lee-Enfields, and you rolled the dice on it to save a four-year-old girl!"

"If our positions had been reversed, you would have let the bomb go off?"

"Ranald, we're on the verge of revolution, and if I could solve it with a simple explosion, it would take a lot more than one four-year-old to stay my hand."

MacKenzie looked away again with tears running down his cheeks.

"Ranald, what's wrong now?" she demanded. "You stopped mass murder! You recovered your precious sense of honor in time."

MacKenzie glanced at his hands on the rail. "Time is something we dinna have. The treaty's been signed. Now it's just a countdown to a general war."

She gripped his shoulder, tighter this time. "Heaven forbid, Ranald! All is not lost. Our Council of Ministers must still ratify it. I think Grand Duke Nicholas, who is the Tsar's uncle, and Count Lamsdorf, the foreign minister, will be against it. We need to get the treaty before it's ratified. I'll pass the terms to them, and you will give them to King Edward."

She stroked his arm. "Forewarned is forearmed, they say, and we'll get the French and the council to annul it. We'll have a conference of nations convened long before the treaty goes into effect! If President Roosevelt is so keen on establishing peace between my country and Japan, what do you think he'll say about the peace of all Europe? We just need an opportunity to rummage through the Tsar's correspondence. I'm a trusted police agent, so I'm sure we can cook up some kind of story, you and I."

MacKenzie sighed.

***

Svetlana and MacKenzie waited for the passengers to retire and made their way casually to the Tsar's quarters. A guard waited at the door.

"Halt!" the guard hissed. "What business do you have in the Tsar's quarters this time of night?"

"We need to do a security check for anarchist devices, Sergeant," Svetlana whispered. "Please let us pass."

"The captain's instituted extreme measures in light of this afternoon's incident. The Tsar's quarters are under lockdown, and no one is permitted in."

Svetlana's eyes flared. "Do you know who you are talking to? I'm Svetlana Petrovna Rachkovskaya! The Tsar's safety is dearer to no one than me."

"If an agent of Monsieur Rachkovsky's is involved, no wonder the captain wants to ensure complete privacy for the Tsar."

Svetlana put her hands on her hips. "And what's that supposed to mean?"

"Could an agent provocateur aim higher than the Tsar?"

Svetlana flushed. "I stopped the plot earlier!"

"The way I heard it, the man was stopped within three steps of the engines with the bomb. Better leave the Tsar's safety to me, Mademoiselle."

Svetlana shook her fist in his face. "You'll be sorry for this, Sergeant!" She huffed and stormed off along the deck.

MacKenzie meekly followed. "Not as sorry as we're going to be if we dinna get that treaty," he said.

"This is just a setback, Ranald, not a defeat. We'll get it ashore somehow. We still have time before it goes to our council and then France. The Motherland has some serious problems to take care of here before she can be led into any more wars. You heard the Kaiser; it's not to take effect until the end of our war with Japan. There's still time to report it to the cabinet or even for a conference. But first things first. I have a very sensitive duty to attend to ashore, and I'll need your help and utmost discretion."

CHAPTER 15: MONSIEUR BELETSKY'S BALL

St. Petersburg
July 26, 1905

Svetlana's fingers fluttered over the typewriter keys like she was tapping out Morse code. Every now and then, she would pause and stare up into space.

"One can't be too diplomatic with a report like this," she said. "You'll notice it's not in my handwriting, and I have no intention of signing it. My enemies will jump at this chance to ruin me."

"I thought none of your enemies kent you were their foe," MacKenzie said. "Aren't you too good an agent provocateur for them to find that out?"

Svetlana laughed. "Dear me, Ranald! You dinna think I have enemies in the Okhrana? I've never seen such a factional bunch. Or are you Brits so harmonious among yourselves you can't conceive of intragovernmental strife?"

"Och, you should have seen the officers in South Africa. The African school and Indian school went after each other like *they* were the enemy combatants."

"And which were you?"

"I had just started my career when I came to South Africa. Didn't have time to build any partiality."

She ripped the paper from the typewriter. "That's a luxury I can't afford. Now, you will deliver this to Fontanka 16 for me."

"Me? Why?"

"It has to go directly to my father, but as a penetration agent, I'm not allowed to deliver reports there. If I came by in person, I would be reprimanded, and my enemies within and without the Okhrana would ken something was up for sure. If you give it to a guard and tell him to deliver it to *le Général Russe*, it'll get where it needs to go. Be sure to tell him le Général Russe is expecting it. That way he'll be less inclined to intercept it."

"What does it say?"

"Just a little update for my father at headquarters on the progress of the mission—letting him ken about the meeting, the treaty being signed, and so forth."

She put the report in an envelope and sealed it with her tongue before handing it to MacKenzie. The envelope bore no postage, address, or sender of any kind. MacKenzie noticed a small stroke of ink in the corner.

He pointed to it. "Think this will be enough to tell him who the sender is?" he said.

Svetlana laughed again. "Poor, naïve Ranald MacKenzie! You thought that was a signature? No, my dear, that is what we in this line call a 'fly.' You ken that the Okhrana has agents who read correspondence as it passes through the post office. When one of them finishes with a letter, he makes a mark to show other agents not to waste their time, but he makes it inconspicuous enough that any regular chap who receives it will not suspect it's been opened. That's just a precaution so that my enemies dinna open it."

MacKenzie hoped no one would ever find out he had gone by Fontanka 16. The headquarters of Russia's secret police had such notoriety that he felt soiled just walking up to it on the pavement. The dust he was picking up on his boots did not help, though it should have made a man who worked in London feel right at home.

A horse-drawn carriage whipped past him. MacKenzie coughed out a dirty updraft of air. Flags hung from balconies in the second-story windows. They seemed to say that patriotism could absolve a government of all crimes. Certainly, Svetlana felt as though it did.

In the past few days, he had reevaluated his feelings for Svetlana. He couldn't agree with too much of what she did, of course, but he had to admire her devotion to her country. She was as dedicated to her homeland as he was to his, as unwilling for it to suffer calamity as he was to allow a repetition of that day. One day of bitter agony had wrecked his soul, but she had endured four months of one of the harshest places on earth and become all the stronger. She had willingly spent those four months of misery just to serve Ukraine, and serve it well she had on this mission.

She was quick-witted and quick-footed. He wasn't too comfortable with her wielding a pistol since the original Hebrew of Deuteronomy 22:5, his minister father had taught him, prohibited women from "bearing the arms of a warrior." All the same, he wouldn't have made it through all this without her, just as she wouldn't have without him.

Before, it had bothered him when his heart had fluttered at the sight of her; now, it seemed only natural. Even though she was Ukrainian and thus a Russian subject, he no longer viewed her the way he viewed her empire. They had risked their lives together, after all.

Waves rippled softly just on the other side of the embankment, reflecting the golden light from the setting sun. MacKenzie could not bear to look at it directly, even though he was avoiding eye contact with everyone. Working with Svetlana, he had reconciled to his conscience, but he still didn't like the place he was going.

Fontanka 16 shone pale yellow in the fading light. It had a regular array of rectangular windows over two stories, a tribute to the sense of order Svetlana was willing to do anything to protect.

MacKenzie came to the main entrance with a canopy over it. Two gendarmes, their uniforms and boots covered with a fine coating of dust, glared at him.

MacKenzie gave a salute.

"Missive for le Général Russe. He's expecting it."

The gendarme looked disapprovingly at MacKenzie. If MacKenzie had been an agent, what he was doing would have been completely unacceptable. Nevertheless, the gendarme took the envelope and stepped inside with it.

MacKenzie saluted again, right faced, and made his way off. He knew the odds were next to impossible that anyone who knew him would see him here, but he breathed a sigh of relief anyway. Just the same, he kept a keen eye out for any anarchist shadowing him.

Svetlana's face had lines when he returned to the hotel room.

"Everything go correctly?" she said.

"All Sir Garnet."

"You weren't followed?"

"Not at all."

Svetlana's lines now arose in her high cheeks from a smile. "Splendid! Maybe you have what it takes to make a spy after all, Ranald! Come with me tomorrow, and I'll show you some more technique."

***

The next day, Svetlana brought MacKenzie to the Peterhof, where he was again astounded. In 10,000 years, he never could have earned enough to afford any spot on these grounds. He understood the grievances of the peasants who lived in squalor, who approached another such palace with a petition, and who were fired on and slaughtered by the hundreds. No doubt Svetlana approved of such assertions of order.

He found himself with Svetlana where, unbeknownst to him, she had been nearly two weeks earlier, in Peter the Great's study.

She placed her hand on his. "Leave the talking to me, Ranald, but listen closely. You may learn something."

A knock like the "Preobrazhensky March" sounded at the door.

"Enter," Svetlana said sweetly.

A young man with olive skin and copious black hair entered and shut the door as quickly as he could. His eyes looked like a startled rabbit's, and when he glimpsed MacKenzie, he froze.

"It's all right, Alexei Alexandrovich," Svetlana said with her most soothing, silky intonation. "Monsieur Kutuzov here is as indebted to you for the Little Father's telegrams as I."

"Why did you wish to see me? I had hoped that last telegram before the Tsar met the Kaiser would have satisfied you. Are you not now up-to-date on everything?"

"It was most helpful, Alexei Alexandrovich, to be sure. You did well. However, the Tsar and Kaiser discussed something on the yacht of great importance and great secrecy. I thought you might feel you had discharged your duty to the Okhrana, so I came here to ask for your help once more. I still need anything the Kaiser and Tsar exchange. I thank you for your assistance, Alexei Alexandrovich. I do appreciate this, and you have done a great service to the Motherland."

Alexei Alexandrovich's eyes shifted from wall to wall. "As a matter of fact, Mademoiselle Rachkovskaya," he said hesitantly, "the Kaiser sent the Tsar a telegram saying something about their meeting. It made no sense to me, but perhaps you shall benefit from it. I could not sneak a copy away, however. Perhaps I can bring it to Monsieur Beletsky's ball three nights from now."

A frown flashed over Svetlana's face. She leaned back in her chair and ran her hand over her hair. "Are you certain that's the most convenient place?"

"Yes, Mademoiselle! It's a crowd of people so thick no one would notice if I slipped it into Monsieur Kutuzov's hand with a handshake. I'm invited, and he's the biggest flower a social butterfly can visit, so no one would think anything of my presence there. I could have him invite you as well."

Svetlana waved her hand as if dismissing a servant. "Monsieur Beletsky and I have had our differences," she said. "I'm not sure you can procure an invitation."

"But if I do..."

"Very well, Alexei Alexandrovich. That is acceptable to me."

"Very well, Mademoiselle." He made a hasty escape.

Svetlana leaned over to MacKenzie. "You see how considerate I was, Ranald?" she whispered in his ear. "I had to pressure him to get the telegrams in the first place, so I was all peaches and cream to him today. I even swallowed my pride to give him his way over Monsieur Beletsky's ball. I dinna like the adulterous rogue, but I dinna see what harm he can do us, so it was a sacrifice I could afford to make."

St. Petersburg
July 30, 1905

The reciprocating engine pounded in MacKenzie's chest when he glimpsed Svetlana in her evening gown. She emerged from the water closet as radiant as a constellation. It was rose-colored with flowery embroidery and ruffled to the waist and at the elbow, trailing on the floor. To follow Queen Alexandra of Britain's fondness for collars while at the same time having a low cut to her gown, she had a bejeweled choker on her throat. She picked up her box of earrings and went over to a mirror to put them on.

"Let's try to enjoy ourselves, Ranald," she said as she did. "I ken Monsieur and Madame Beletsky repulse you, but with a large gathering in a large ballroom, we'll scarcely need to spend much time with them. Just pay our respects and go about our business."

MacKenzie was suddenly reminded of the disgust he had felt at what Svetlana had done. She seemed to think that God had given her the gift of beauty as a weapon she could use in any way she saw fit.

"A credit to your regiment!" she said when she saw him in his suit. "If only you could wear a scarlet dress uniform with a government kilt to this."

She held out her arm. For a moment, MacKenzie hesitated.

She cleared her throat.

"Och!" he mumbled.

He took her arm in his, and they made their way to the cab that would take them to Monsieur Beletsky's townhome.

The walls of the townhome, made of smooth-cut white stone with bunting in the arched windows and mahogany doors, had lights from beneath in white, blue, and red. Being comfortable and overly well-fed, Monsieur Beletsky could afford to be patriotic.

MacKenzie almost felt a pang of guilt for attending the ball. The whirlwind addiction to entertainment exhibited by the aristocrats and the wealthy of his homeland struck him as bad enough, but these Russians did the same and oppressed their poor to boot. Still, would it not be just for a mere captain of His Majesty's Royal Army to cost his nation's greatest enemy a little in hospitality to him? It would even the scales just a little. Besides, he had come on business.

A servant in pine-green livery and a white powdered wig opened the door and bowed. MacKenzie helped Svetlana out of the carriage, and she put up with it for appearances. They made their way along the immaculate pavement, over which had been rolled a thick red carpet, to the door of the house. MacKenzie handed their invitations to the doorman.

He opened them and gasped. "Mademoiselle Rachkovskaya and Monsieur Kutuzov!" he said. "My master insisted you see him upon your arrival. Igor, bring the mademoiselle and monsieur to the master immediately."

Igor, an imposing, broad-shouldered manservant, bowed to them and led them through the entry hall to the ballroom. They made their way through the crowd until they reached the Beletskys. Madame Beletsky looked ravishing in her evening gown and pearls, while Monsieur Beletsky seemed to burst the seams of his silken suit and top hat.

He took Svetlana's hand and drew it to his lips. "Mademoiselle Rachkovskaya! So good of you to attend. I hope you still have fond memories of our all-too-brief meeting at my villa."

Svetlana smiled. "I shall never forget you, Monsieur Beletsky. I owe you a debt I hope someday to repay in full."

Monsieur Beletsky showed his tobacco-stained teeth in a grin. Madame Beletsky glared at MacKenzie, her eyes like the muzzles of a double-barreled shotgun.

"And, Madame, with regards to your parting wishes, the revolutionaries send their compliments but say their meat lockers are so well-stocked they couldn't fit another thing in them," MacKenzie said.

"What's he talking about, my dearest?" Monsieur Beletsky asked his wife.

"Nothing, my darling," she said. Madame Beletsky laid her hand on her husband's. "He's just referring to the kind farewell I gave him when he left our dinner party."

MacKenzie laughed. "It seems such a shame to spoil such a sincere send-off by seeing you again."

Madame Beletsky's eyes bore down on MacKenzie as if to promise that if he said anything more about their conversation at the villa, she would claw his eyes out. MacKenzie decided not to press his victory any further. He had to remain here long enough to get the telegram.

"I trust you were with the Tsar on his recent cruise and found it enjoyable?" Monsieur Beletsky asked Svetlana.

"It was most interesting, Monsieur."

"We must talk about it someday."

"You will excuse me, sir. I should not wish to distract you too long from your other guests, but I agree we must talk it over someday…"

She pulled on MacKenzie's arm to draw him away from the couple. "… In Hades!" she hissed in his ear.

Svetlana swept her arm over the ballroom floor. "Shall we dance? I dinna see Alexei Alexandrovich, so we might as weel enjoy ourselves."

MacKenzie's heart fluttered at the thought. The orchestra was beginning to play one of his favorite compositions: Tchaikovsky's waltz from "Eugen Onegin."

The drums rumbled almost imperceptibly. The brass began an introduction in a succession of phrases echoed by the strings, growing in pitch to a grand opening. Then, MacKenzie knew, the strings would take over with a light-hearted, dainty waltz. It felt so authentic—MacKenzie thought he probably would never have another opportunity to dance with such a beautiful Slavic partner to a Slavic orchestra playing his favorite Slavic work.

The Russians dinna ken the first thing about government, but they do ken their music.

He took Svetlana's left hand in his right and wrapped his left arm around her waist. They now stood in a closeness MacKenzie would never have dared with Audrey, and away they went. The strings and brass took turns with each other, the drums keeping the time. The music was alternatively grandiose and sometimes merry as the brass answered the strings, the woodwinds providing a light descent.

MacKenzie one-two-three-ed around the dancefloor with the agility of a hummingbird. Svetlana's eyes widened with awe. She said nothing, though her lips parted slightly. She fixed her eyes on his.

MacKenzie spun her around as the music took a grandiose turn. Svetlana was laughing now. The strings took their dominant post back in a series of long, graceful phrases, capped by the woodwinds.

The music returned to a repeat of its opening antiphony, and the brasses signaled the beginning of a magnificent ending. MacKenzie whirled like a tornado. The brass signaled the concluding notes, which ended with the entire orchestra working together.

Svetlana was panting as the dance ended. "I say, Ranald, wherever did you learn to dance like that? Just how many balls have you been to?"

"Surely, you ken we Highlanders are splendid dancers. You've seen a sword-dance?"

"Aye."

"I'm very proficient at it."

Svetlana smiled. "Weel, the greatest ballets are Russian, not Scottish, you'll note."

MacKenzie smiled back. "I certainly didn't mean to denigrate the acrobatic feats your country achieves. It's just more motivating if missing a step costs you your foot."

"Aye, I grant you that—I can appreciate both my Slavic heritage and the Scottish culture I use as a cover."

"And I didn't think I could ever appreciate anything Slavic before..." He caught himself.

Svetlana's lips turned up in that foxlike grin. "Before you met me?"

MacKenzie felt the blood rush to his cheeks.

The orchestra began the march-like opening to the "*Kaiserwaltzer.*" A fitting opening for the Emperors of Austria and Germany together, the staccato, spritely steps of the strings led to overtones of brass and woodwind building up to a fanfare with drums.

It was all too much for him. His heart pounded such that he thought it would croak out, much as it had on that day. However, on that day, he had longed for an instantaneous end, but here, he wanted the euphoria to go on forever. He wished it were an elven dance that would last until he died. The beautiful music, the fun and grace of the fluid, whirling three-step, and, best of all, Svetlana's sapphire eyes on his.

He was in love. He did not want to be, but he was nonetheless. He could count so many reasons not to love, but their bond from sharing so many dangers was carrying the field. He felt beholden to her for her assistance to him on this mission and all the finer things he had enjoyed with her funds. She had a liveliness that ignited one in himself, a fire which he thought had been quenched forever after that day. Every time she pulled her hair over her shoulder, he almost dropped to his knees.

Audrey could never have danced like this with him. She never could have worn anything as beautiful as what Svetlana was wearing now. And she never would have wanted to. Svetlana had romantic passion, and for the moment, it seemed centered on MacKenzie. She, who could have anything in the world, wanted him…

On they danced through the night. They barely paused for breath or punch until forced to do so or they would drop. Svetlana was MacKenzie's world and all his joy. Suddenly, though, Svetlana halted. MacKenzie almost toppled over with his momentum. Svetlana pointed over his shoulder.

"Hello! There's our man at last!" she said.

MacKenzie turned to see Alexei Alexandrovich in front of a crowd at the punch table. He fumbled his hands nervously. As they hurried over, he ran a hand through his hair to push a lock out of his face.

Svetlana nodded as if to a longstanding friend. "Alexei Alexandrovich, it's good to see you."

MacKenzie held out his hand. Alexei Alexandrovich gripped it, and MacKenzie wrapped his fingers around the paper in his hand.

"You wanted this telegram from the Kaiser to the Tsar?" he said.

"Not so loud!" MacKenzie hissed.

Suddenly, the crowd behind Alexei Alexandrovich parted as two gendarmes forced their way through. MacKenzie drew his hands behind his back to conceal the telegram. The gendarmes glared in his face.

"Captain Ranald MacKenzie?" one asked.

MacKenzie cleared his throat to give himself a second to think. "Who? Gentlemen, I am Peter Ivanovich Kutuzov of the Okhrana," he said in Russian.

They scoffed. "Then do we arrest you as a British spy or as an Okhrana agent who is trying to steal the Tsar's personal correspondence?"

MacKenzie stepped back and tried to hand Svetlana the paper behind his back. The gendarmes scoffed again.

"That won't do you any good, sir. It's a blank piece of paper."

"Surely you can't arrest a man for carrying a blank piece of paper!" MacKenzie said.

The gendarmes stepped forward and seized MacKenzie's arms. "This is Russia, Captain MacKenzie," the first said.

"Mademoiselle Rachkovskaya, is this the British spy Ranald MacKenzie?" the second asked.

MacKenzie looked back desperately at Svetlana. She was a master of worming her way out of these situations. Surely, she could save him.

To his utmost astonishment, she nodded. "Da, this is the British spy. Take him away."

CHAPTER 16:
PETER AND PAUL FORTRESS

St. Petersburg
July 30, 1905

"Captain MacKenzie, I am talking to you!"

"Sorry, sir," MacKenzie said like a subaltern caught daydreaming.

"Got something on your mind, hmm? More pressing than life or death?"

His interrogator's leer was visible in the bright light over MacKenzie's head. All else remained darkness around the narrow, focused beam of light. MacKenzie remained too preoccupied by the pain in his heart over Svetlana's betrayal to even think of what the interrogator asked. The heartbreak *was* more pressing than life at that moment.

"I was saying, where are your orders from the Directorate of Military Operations?"

"Dinna have any, sir. Acted on my own initiative. My government does not countenance spying, unlike some I could name."

He did not know why he had added that last part. He regretted it when the colonel backhanded him across the jaw. His teeth banged together painfully.

"At least we're honest in this country about it," the colonel said. "Everyone knows we spy."

Then why is it called the secret *police?*

"If you acted on your own initiative, how was it you knew about the Tsar's secret rendezvous?" the colonel asked from the darkness.

Should he tell the truth? That would put Svetlana at risk, but surely, she deserved to be sold out with him. He had fallen head over heels in love with her just hours ago, but now he loathed her. He would stay as faithful to her as she had to him.

"I learned of it, sir, through Mademoiselle Svetlana Petrovna Rachkovskaya. I assume you ken her."

"And where did she get that information, pray tell?"

"The Tsar's telegrams."

"Those are off-limits to all Okhrana personnel! Who authorized her to read those?"

MacKenzie swallowed. He knew that if he answered truthfully, he would cut Svetlana's sole lifeline out of Siberia. Could he do that to her? Even if he loathed her, could he send her and her father both to Siberia? There'd be no escape for either of them then.

Hang both of the scoundrels!

"She told me, sir, that her father had tasked her with looking into the Tsar's negotiations with the Kaiser."

"Did he, indeed? Now, about this codebook..."

"Those are hieroglyphics from an archaeological dig, sir."

The colonel slapped MacKenzie from the other side of his face.

"Don't insult my intelligence!"

"Then dinna insult *my* loyalty to my country!" MacKenzie said. He crossed his arms. "I will tell you nothing that will hurt her. I have nothing left me but my duty to His Majesty."

The colonel chuckled like a hyena over a carcass. "I would say all you have left to you is the determination to prolong your demise." A piece of paper crinkled in his hand. "I have here a confession to your spying for Japan under War Office orders. If you sign, we will march you out in front of a firing squad and terminate your existence like a soldier."

"But that would be a violation of neutrality! It would mean war!"

"Perhaps, but if you don't sign, you'll be sent to the gold mines in Irkutsk for the remainder of your natural life. You'll still die, but it will be such a less comfortable passing."

MacKenzie remembered Svetlana's depiction of Siberia. That seemed the worst calamity that could befall a man. No, worse by far for his regiment to relive that day. He had sworn that he would do anything to prevent that day from happening again to the Royal Army. He just wished the alternative had not become the very next worst thing.

"I'll die, eventually, no matter what," he said. "Now I have the lives of my messmates to think of before my own."

"I think you will find that rather a foolish attitude in the end."

"Is foolish the Russian word for loyal, then?"

The colonel punched MacKenzie in the diaphragm. He doubled over, trying to suck in air. The colonel stood back and watched MacKenzie with a leer until he could stand again.

"That's naught, man. I've been shot there by a Mauser. No comparison."

"I don't want you to be rash, MacKenzie," the colonel said with mock concern in his voice. "Go back to your cell for a few days. Think about taking every step for the rest of your life in clanking chains. Think about your limbs freezing and falling off with frostbite. Think about gasping for air like that each morning as you plunge waist-deep in frigid water."

"I will, Colonel, and I want you to think about what awaits a man who persecutes the innocent when he goes before an almighty Judge. Think of a worm that doesn't die and a fire that isn't quenched."

"Bah!" the colonel said. "Siberia is worse; I don't think even God could tolerate it."

"Och, aye, He can!" MacKenzie shouted. "He made it in His wisdom for a reason, and He made some place far worse for those who die in their sin."

"The reason He made Siberia, my dear fellow, is to cut arrogant fools like you down to size. As soon as you go there, I swear there'll be no returning from it. Now, back to your cell!"

Two gendarmes seized MacKenzie's arms and dragged him out of the interrogation chamber.

A dripping sound echoed in the hallway. MacKenzie wondered if he would ever see daylight again. They had dragged him to the Peter and Paul Prison, infamously known as the Russian Bastille. A revolutionary could perhaps dream that someday his comrades would overthrow the masters of this fortress and release him, but a foreigner had no such hope. The revolutionaries, even if they emptied the rest of the prison, would want him there as much as the monarchists.

Opening a cell door, the gendarmes shoved him in.

MacKenzie sat on the bed and put his face in his hands. He had known better than to fall in love with Svetlana, and yet, now that she had betrayed him, nothing else seemed to matter. He wished he had never laid eyes on her! All he could do now was keep a diplomatic incident from occurring. If one did happen, the treaty might suck Germany and France into any war between Russia and Britain. He would deny that satisfaction to the Kaiser as far as it lay in his power.

Och, that Connally had sent someone else!

He had told him to. A more competent spy would have known not to trust Svetlana. Would Sidney Reilly have fallen for her friendly façade? Knowing him, he would have slept with her and *then* evaded her trap.

Confound her! Send her back to Siberia!

He shivered. If she had spitefully treated him, he had a duty to pray for her. MacKenzie folded his hands.

Lord, I...

He could not bring himself to pray for Svetlana. He wanted her to pay for her crime. Nothing seemed too harsh for her.

Lord, please...

She deserved anything but mercy! That prayer she had prayed about her enemies had been a ploy! She was a promiscuous, murderous hypocrite. Surely, God had no reason to forgive her.

But then, God had no reason to forgive MacKenzie either. Had it been up to just MacKenzie, He would not have. By nature, MacKenzie was a child of wrath, even as others. Left to himself, MacKenzie would have sneered at God's gift of His only Son, spitting and striking Him if he could have. Did he have anything God needed? Could he add anything to Christ's perfect righteousness?

MacKenzie sighed.

Lord, I resign the matter to Your judgment. Do what seems good to You to this woman. My formal petition is that you bring her to repentance—and that You help me to mean that.

He lay back on the bed. The rusty springs creaked as he fell back. He stared at the stone ceiling. There was a crack in the mortar. Moss spread overhead. He noticed its musty smell for the first time. Surely anything was better than this place! He thought of Svetlana's depiction of Siberia. It sounded like Niflheim, the ice-world where the inglorious dead went in Norse mythology. Was that what he was—inglorious?

Och, that I had perished on that day!

MacKenzie laid his arm over his eyes. He found sleep hard prey to catch that night, and when he did finally catch it, the dreams scarcely made the chase worth it.

***

The jangling of keys in the lock awakened him. Cold sweat made his clothes stick to him. He looked up to see Svetlana rushing into his cell. She sat down beside him and laid her hands on his cheeks. She looked about to kiss him. MacKenzie tore her hands from his face.

"Ranald, are you all right?" she whispered.

MacKenzie sneered. "No, but it's gey and kind of you to visit me. I didn't expect to see your face again."

Svetlana rose to her feet with solemn dignity. "You are ungrateful to use that tone with me, Ranald MacKenzie, or at least unwise. Do you not ken that I have the power to release you?"

"Have you come for that?" MacKenzie gasped. "I thought you'd fairly well left me to it. I thought..." MacKenzie choked on his words.

Svetlana's eyes softened. "You truly thought I had betrayed you, didn't you?"

MacKenzie looked away. "What else was I to think?"

"Ranald, I had no choice!" she said.

She sat back down beside him on the bed. She laid her hand on his.

"They had the right man, and they kent it," she said. "If I had tried to interfere, we'd both be here, and then who would have provided your release papers?"

"My release papers?"

"I have an order from the new chief of police for the Russian Empire, whose name I'm sure you can guess," she said.

"Your father attained that despite the Tsar's hatred of him?"

"Aye, fairly! He's too good to dismiss in dangerous times."

She held up and unfolded a piece of paper like a hunting trophy.

"'Monsieur Peter Ivanovich Kutuzov has been performing a sensitive penetration mission under the guise of a Scottish captain, Ranald MacKenzie,'" she read. "'He has been under the strictest orders of secrecy.

You are to release him from your custody forthwith and provide him with any assistance he may require.' I wrote it myself, and my father signed it."

I will not be one day for you, and another against you.

MacKenzie wiped a tear away. "You are more righteous than I! I was so certain you had betrayed me that I tried to get revenge by telling them how you and your father had read the Tsar's telegrams."

Svetlana went pale. "You *what?*"

"What was I supposed to think?"

She sighed and looked away. "Ranald MacKenzie, repaying evil for evil rather than giving place to God's wrath... Fine time to do something normal, Ranald."

"You must ken how wound-up I was! We had had the most delightful time, and the next thing I ken, I'm in the Russian Bastille, apparently with your connivance."

"No, you had every right to think as you did, even if you violated your Christian sense of honor. It's not the first time my acting has put me in a difficult position, and it won't be the last. Let's hope my father's excuse that you were under orders of secrecy leads them to discount everything you said."

She quickly rose from his bedside. "Now, if you're ready, we'll put that to the test. Guard!"

"Mademoiselle?"

"I think you should look at this piece of paper."

She handed him the order through the bars. He saluted and unlocked the door. Svetlana beckoned. "Come, Peter Ivanovich. Let us present ourselves to the commandant."

MacKenzie sprang to his feet and followed Svetlana through the stinking hallway. They made their way to the commandant's house within the fortification. Svetlana requested admittance. Once inside, they saluted to the general.

"General, I have an order to release the prisoner Peter Ivanovich Kutuzov," she said. "Of course, you will also restore the items he had on his person when you arrested him."

She handed the paper to him. He barely looked over it. MacKenzie thought he noticed a sinister cast to the man's smile as he folded the paper and laid it on his desk.

"Everything's in order, Mademoiselle *Rachkovskaya*. Take Monsieur Kutuzov wherever you wish. See the clerk about the items you want returned."

Something about the way he said her name had not sounded quite right.

***

MacKenzie could not bear the sight of Svetlana's scarlet kimono the next morning after what he had done. Now anything red reminded him of his crimson stain of vengefulness.

He shaded his eyes and let his head press on his hand as his elbow rested on the upholstered arm of the fauteuil. While he had awoken many times the night before, it was not because of any back pain from the goose down mattress, duck feather pillows, or silk sheets.

Svetlana washed the last of her buttered toast down with apple juice. "I think I'll go to the Foreign Ministry this afternoon and see if the Little Father has given them the treaty," she said. "I'll go alone so there's no question of British espionage."

A knock came at the door. There was no particular rhythm. MacKenzie dragged himself to his feet and opened the door. The young bellhop, barely out of his teens, craned his neck to look around MacKenzie at Svetlana.

"Excuse me, Mademoiselle Kutuzov, there's a Monsieur Pobedonostsev here to see you."

Svetlana clenched her fists and raised her hands to her clavicle as she looked heavenward.

"Blast that man. How'd he find me?" she groaned. "Hold on, Ranald—this could get bloody."

CHAPTER 17:
SUICIDE OR SIBERIA

MacKenzie felt the reciprocating engine starting in his chest. He and Svetlana had both violated Russian law, and he had even notified the authorities about it. Fine time for an unwelcome visitor.

"Show him in," Svetlana said as she waved her hand to the boy.

The boy stepped out and returned with a rather absurd-looking figure. The man had a short, wiry frame and wore a blue serge suit with sleeves almost covering his fingers. His oversized head and face appeared badly pockmarked and were overshadowed by a large, eagle-like nose. He had a grim smile as he entered, revealing crooked, tobacco-stained teeth.

"Peter, this is my—ha!—colleague in the Okhrana, Monsieur Sergei Petrovich Pobedonostsev," she said, gesturing from MacKenzie to the man. "Sergei Petrovich, this is Peter Ivanovich Kutuzov."

"Otherwise known as Captain Ranald MacKenzie, Black Watch," Sergei said.

A fleeting look of fear flashed over Svetlana's face, but she immediately regained her imperious demeanor. "As you can see, Ranald, *sometimes* he's more formidable than he looks."

"I've come to bargain," the man said with a rather nasal twang.

"Something I don't do often," Svetlana returned.

"Da, well, I've learned something urgent. Your father has such an awful lot of reading to do, I—unofficially of course—help him screen it."

Svetlana clenched her fists.

"You stole my report to him!"

"Indeed. At any rate, I found it most fascinating. So, the Tsar has signed a treaty with the Kaiser?"

Svetlana's face reddened. "You double-crossing son of a gun! You set me up! You had Alexei Alexandrovich lure me to the ball so you could seize Ranald and then get to me!"

Pobedonostsev leered like a hyena. "Exactly, my dear. The report that stated how you had read the Tsar's telegrams was not signed or in your handwriting. Now I have an order in your own hand asking for the release of an acknowledged British spy."

He drew himself back and sighed theatrically as he raised his hand to his brow. "You know, it troubles me greatly to keep secrets from the Little Father. I feel I should burst if I didn't reveal to him how Monsieur Rachkovsky, whom he suffers to be head of the Okhrana only because of the dire situation, sent his own daughter to spy on him. The Tsar and Tsaritsa have surely not forgotten the last time your father overstepped the mark in exposing a favorite of the Tsaritsa."

He laid the back of his hand on his forehead as if ill. "It almost ruptures my blood vessels not to reveal to him how you exceeded your authority by reading the Tsar's private telegrams, how you brought a British spy to the most secret of meetings between the Kaiser and the Tsar, and how you then undermined your own government's efforts to apprehend that spy. Is treason too strong a word for that? Do you think the climate in Siberia will agree with you and your father?"

Svetlana turned pale. MacKenzie had never seen her terrified before. But then, she knew Siberia's horrors and that, with her father apprehended, no one could rescue her.

Her eyes narrowed to slits. "Why are you telling me this? Are the gendarmes outside to arrest us?"

"No, my dear Sveta."

Svetlana exhaled, though whether it was a sigh of relief or a groan of disgust, MacKenzie could not tell. "All right, you little rat, what do you want?"

"I'm willing to offer you a bargain. I will take over the investigation in Russia, and you will return with Ranald MacKenzie here to Germany."

"You know from my report that would be suicide! The Huns know us by sight. They took me prisoner for a few moments and got a perfect look at me! Even disguised, I barely escaped with my life!"

Pobedonostsev held up a piece of paper with typewritten text on it. "I have my report on your treachery ready to submit, which I'm sure is your passport to Siberia."

Svetlana gnashed her teeth. "Very well! I'll return to Germany, but I want our agreement in writing. If you should utter a word to the Tsar later, I want it on record that you consented to withhold the truth from him."

He produced a second piece of paper from under the first. "I thought you might feel that way. You'll see that the terms are exactly as I explained."

Svetlana snatched the paper and perused it. Satisfied, she stormed to the table, slammed the paper on it, and put her signature to the contract. "Here's the bargain for my father's freedom! I'll lay down my life for him. You sneaky little runt, you wouldn't lay down your life for the Tsar himself. Good luck finding anything here in Russia, blast your eyes!"

Pobedonostsev grinned like a troll and signed the compact. Svetlana snatched up the contract so he could not leave with it. Pobedonostsev waltzed out of the room, humming and snapping his fingers.

"The devils are busy on Mount Triglav," Svetlana muttered to MacKenzie. "Now you ken how grateful Russians are for all we Ukrainians have done for them."

MacKenzie's chest felt like an empty barrel, empty of all but the reciprocating engine pounding at his ribs. "Sveta, this is all my fault!" he said. "If I hadn't been so eager to get revenge..."

Svetlana swept her hand nonchalantly. "Dinna blame yourself, Ranald," she said. "It was a brilliant trap. The man couldn't catch an anarchist with two broken legs, but people on his own side... I would have had to supply those orders from my father anyway once he had you arrested. I doubt anything you said furthered his plot."

"Just the same, I'll go with you to Germany," MacKenzie said. "I'll see you through this to the end! As we say in the Highlands, 'If one pass through the thorn for me, I'll pass through the briar for him.'"

With a start like this, though, he couldn't help thinking of a line from his favorite song: "Then second-sighted Sandie said we'd do no good at all."

Berlin
August 6, 1905

Svetlana slowly opened her eyes. She glanced around nervously. She was still safe, waking up her first morning back in Berlin. The plain accommodations they had chosen out of necessity did not measure up to her first trip here but would likely prove safer. Still, the bed felt awfully hard!

She heard MacKenzie's soft breathing and glanced over to see if he was still asleep. His eyes were closed, but he hardly looked tranquil with sweat plastering his hair to his forehead and darkening his collar. Should she wake him? Was bad sleep worse than no sleep at all? She did not actually know. Certainly, she'd had her share of sleepless nights and nightmares, but she had never decided which was worse.

Her mantra! Surely, she could not forget her mantra.

"Remember, O Svetlana, the anarchists," she muttered just loud enough that she could hear herself without disturbing MacKenzie.

She then repeated her oath, as solemn as a blood pact.

Having followed her daily custom, she looked back over at MacKenzie. She could not deny that under the sweat lay a handsome countenance. In fact, he looked rather like what she had always pictured Adonis in her mind. That thick head of golden hair, the muscular jaw, the well-apportioned nose, those gray eyes, resolute but still capable of shining with kindness...

But much as MacKenzie wrestled with loving someone so savage, Svetlana wrestled with loving someone so naïve. She wanted a Mars, not an Adonis. On this mission so far, she had done all the killing (as usual), and she wondered if MacKenzie had ever shot anyone in his life. Maybe Boers, but how long ago had that been?

Svetlana had to stifle her quickening heartbeat at the sight of MacKenzie as she watched him sleep. How could she bring a Briton home to her father as long as their countries engaged in the Great Game against each other? They had reached the brink of war now that the treaty had been signed. She wondered with a mix of pride and anxiety what would her father say about questionable loyalties in his best agent.

Mercifully, MacKenzie ended her musings by awakening. He shuddered as his eyes shot open.

"You're drenched," she said softly. "Nightmare?"

MacKenzie sighed. "Half-nightmare, half-recollection," he said. "That confounded treaty threatens me with another day like that day."

He seemed about to say something but hesitated. Svetlana felt pity seep into her heart for the first time in as long as she could remember. She reached out and stroked his arm.

"Would you like to tell me about it? Perhaps it would make you feel better to get it off your chest."

He bit his lip. "I've never told anyone but Colonel Connally."

"I promise I'll keep it as secret as my Okhrana identity, whatever it is."

MacKenzie sighed again. He looked into her eyes and said: "I was at Magersfontein in the South African War in 1899. The Boers were besieging Kimberley, and our job was to relieve it. We thought we'd pulverized the buggers with our artillery, but they had entrenched at the foot of the ridge rather than atop it where we had expected them. We were marching through the night in quarter column, drenched to our bones in a downpour."

His face glowered. "As we drew nearer, our guide recommended a more open order, but the general feared we'd get lost. It was one of those battles where we needed everything to go right, and instead, every blessed thing went wrong! Our compasses didn't work, there was no light, we staggered and stumbled our way forward with every conceivable obstacle..."

He glanced down. "As the dawn broke, the skulking ploughboys murdered us like targets at a range. The muzzle flashes were like one vast string of electric lights. We were packed like sardines in a can; they couldn't miss us. I could hear bones cracking amid the bangs of those cursed Mausers! There were fountains of blood everywhere. The Dumdums hurled men about like rag dolls and ripped them up like paper toys."

Svetlana shuddered at her own memories.

"It was the longest five minutes in history," MacKenzie said. "Then the whole brigade went to ground. We lay there for most of the day with the African sun scorching us, the Boers ready to shoot any man who so much as reached for his canteen. We got sunburns on our calves, but we couldn't move an inch. Every stirring would draw a hail of bullets as thick as a swarm of blowflies."

"Och, Ranald!" Svetlana cried.

"I had actually advanced somewhat in front of my company before I realized they had all thrown themselves down and I had done likewise. So there I was, several yards in front of my men, alone against the entire Boer army. I felt deserted by all the world. I thought surely every rifle must be pointed at me. I didn't move as insects crawled over me and bit me. It took Herculean courage just to breathe. You've heard of an iron maiden? The whole Highland brigade was trapped in one. We could be shot in the front if we advanced and shot in the back if we retreated."

Svetlana felt like the walls were closing in on her.

"My heart raced until I thought it would croak out. Every instant, I expected a bullet between my eyes. I prayed and prayed with all the fervency I could manage. Then I learned that there's a limit to everyone's courage, even a Highlander's. Suddenly, the moment came when the brigade rose like a flock and dashed for the rear. The Boers felt no compunction about shooting us through the back. As I looked back and saw my company dissolve, I felt ashamed not to do anything."

He rose slightly from the bed. "I said, 'Remember Culloden, laddies! Up and waur 'em all!' and started toward the Boer line. Amazingly, some of them turned and followed me. We didn't get far, though. A bullet flung me back and went clean through me, right below the ribs here."

MacKenzie pointed to his scar. "The men and I fired back—I from lying on my backside—as the Boers picked us off. By the time the generals had settled on a truce for us to retrieve our wounded, all of my brave little party had to be carried off the field."

He glanced down. "I destroyed all those who trusted me with their lives, and somehow, I got the Victoria Cross for it! I'd throw it right back at the king himself if I could go back and prevent the whole sorry mess."

He looked back up into Svetlana's eyes, his own blazing with a fire she had never seen in them before. "I do my work now so that no Tommy will ever endure such a day again! If I survived and my men didn't, I'll see to it no one else dies on my account."

Svetlana drew back and propped herself up on her elbow. She ran her hand over his arm.

"I ken, Ranald; I really do. I can sympathize, for a memory dogs my steps too. I told you I ken how to be in poverty. When I was fourteen, I was still living with my natural parents, simple peasants in the Ukrainian countryside near Poltava. That day, we were making an annual procession with an icon.

"You Presbyterians can't understand the power of an icon, Ranald, but I was euphoric at the sight of it, far to the back though I was. Even more powerfully, Grand Duke Ivan was in attendance, and in my girlish dreams, I hoped I might steal his heart and have him sweep me away to riches in St. Petersburg."

She inhaled sharply as she shuddered. "As I watched the processional in all its finery ahead of me, a... a revolutionary's bomb went off right in the middle of the gathering. My parents were torn... torn inside-out right... right before my eyes! Limbs were strewn everywhere, including the grand duke's, and they kept turning up in the coming days. Those butchers slaughtered my neighbors like cattle. I got off one of the luckiest with just this wee burn here on my cheek where I was hit by a tiny shred of burning cloth."

She was choking on tears and for a few seconds could say nothing. "I'm sorry, Ranald."

She inhaled again. "In the next few days, the Okhrana arrived to investigate. The man I now call my father was with them. He questioned me as a witness, and when the interview was over, he asked if I wanted revenge on the anarchists. I told him there was nothing I wouldn't part with if I could avenge myself of this scum of the earth. He said I could have anything my heart desired, for I would be his daughter, but that I would have to part with my sense of honor in return.

"I would have the beauty, he said, when I grew up to take me into the heart of the free-loving revolutionary movement, where I could do the most damage. He promised to train me in espionage and send me into the field if I proved an adept pupil. Then he took me out to the site of the explosion. He gathered up pieces of the icon and placed my hand upon them."

She laid her hand on her heart. "'Swear eternal enmity to the traitors and that you will never be a friend to a revolutionary,' he said.

"I swore, and I repeat that oath every morning when I awaken. You ken how the Persian King Darius, when the Athenians had raided and burned one of his cities, had a slave repeat in his ear every morning, 'Remember, O King, the Athenians'? That's my mantra. The Okhrana expects each penetration agent to do his work for no more than two years; I've done it for eleven! I started when I was fourteen, and I do it to this day.

"So now you ken why I serve the Russian Tsar so loyally when my country wants a ruler of its own. Someday, when that can be peacefully arranged,

I'll be the first to stand up for it, and then I'll serve it as loyally as I do the Tsar. But not by revolution! The revolutionaries would be a thousand times crueler to Ukraine than any Tsar bent on Russification. He is the only one strong enough to keep these rebels in check, and I'll fight them for him to the death!"

She felt the heat in her cheeks. Her fists were clenched, but she wished she had them around the throat of that revolutionary lowlife who had planted the bomb!

Nevertheless, something about telling him was cathartic. She could see in his gray eyes that it had been cathartic for him too. Like him, she had unburdened herself of this secret to no friend before, no matter how close. She hated appearing vulnerable almost as much as she hated the memory itself. Yet, without interrogation, they had bared their souls to one another openly.

Silence settled over them as they stared into each other's eyes. Was that empathy in her own, she wondered? Had she ever felt that emotion since that day?

Her face was set in the same expression toward MacKenzie as when she had looked on the remains of her father's face. MacKenzie's were increasingly becoming lost in her gaze, but she could see the sympathy in them. She would not have accepted that from anyone else on earth.

She sighed. "You ken that I got my riches after all as Rachkovsky's daughter, but like you, I'd cast them down at his feet for the chance to go back and change how things happened. It was a poor bargain."

MacKenzie's arms moved almost imperceptibly, but he checked them. Did he want to embrace her? She let her eyes fill with longing for him to kiss her. A few seconds more, and she would press the issue herself. She knew his confounded conscience was staying him.

Svetlana leaned in. He made himself look away.

"I could use a shower after all that," he said.

He leaped from the bed to make good his escape from temptation.

Svetlana stared at the empty, displaced covers and sighed. *Disappointing*.

Hlidskjalf
August 6, 1905

Tirpitz strode into the castle with the air of a triumphant conqueror. His uniform was freshly pressed and brushed, free of every speck of lint and every wrinkle. He smelled the beeswax coating his mustache. Every button gleamed with its recent polishing.

Today he would earn his freedom if he could get the Master to destroy that file. No more torturing, excepting of course the two spies who had humiliated the Order and murdered Heinrich. He almost salivated at his hunger for revenge like it were a steamy veal cutlet.

He gave his name to the aide-de-camp, who reported his entry to the Master. The Master's voice boomed a summons into his office. Tirpitz marched into the office and gave the Order's salute.

"What are you smiling about?" the Master demanded.

"Sorry, Herr Oberst."

Tirpitz had not been aware that he was smiling. He quickly asserted control over his facial muscles.

"You wish to report?" the Master asked.

"Jawohl, Herr Oberst. The Kaiser and the Tsar met on his cruise. They signed the treaty in absolute secrecy. Even the Russian admiral who signed it wasn't allowed to read it."

"But you have a copy, don't you?"

"Jawohl, Herr Oberst."

He handed the Master the photograph he had snuck off the yacht. The Master's eyes glided over the four short articles. Tirpitz controlled his face, but he could not keep his heart from skipping with joy. He knew what to expect from the Master.

"This is a calamity! Germany and Russia are allies once again, and, when she sees this, France will have to join too. Our war will be postponed indefinitely."

"With respect, Herr Oberst, I believe I may be able to turn this to our advantage."

The Master sneered. "Ach, really?"

"Jawohl, Herr Oberst. The obvious target of this alliance is England. Right now, she is our greatest enemy. If we can push this Quintuple Alliance into war soon, we can crush her. She'll put up a fight, as she always does, even with all of Europe against her, but who shall conduct that fight? Our navy is still under construction, and we have but few colonial theatres in which to combat her.

"The obvious answer, to me, sir, is that the French navy will have to do the fighting at sea and the Russian army the invasion of India. We'll do our fair share, of course, but who's to say that the fair share must be the lion's share?

"Once the French navy and the Royal Navy have decimated each other, our navy will be the most powerful in the world, and once Russia has fought herself to exhaustion in Asia, our army will be the largest in Europe. We can then crush the French and the Russians at will. The Kaiser wants to be friends with France and Russia only because he fears England. Once England is no more, will he still be so kindly disposed to his exhausted rivals?"

The Master leered. "Excellent plan, Hauptmann Tirpitz. Worthy of Machiavelli himself."

"I formulate my strategies as you have set an example for me, Herr Oberst. I trust you will want me discussing these arrangements with the General Staff."

"Good thinking."

Tirpitz gulped. He knew he was taking a chance, but if he did not try now, whenever would he have the opportunity again?

"Herr Oberst, it will be my pleasure to coordinate with the General Staff, but I fear I may be rather too distracted by something."

"And that is?"

"A certain criminal file I was looking at the other day from 1895."

The Master smiled. "I believe that file is out of date now. I give it to you as a gift. It's yours to do with as you please."

Tirpitz felt his heart flutter such that it would surely break. He was free! Without the Master having that leverage over him, he could renegotiate his role as interrogator. He would still serve the Order and its gods, but as a field agent. He wouldn't renegotiate before he had settled accounts with the spies, though.

"And, Herr Oberst, there is one other matter that does need resolving first."

"Ja?"

"There is a pair of spies still prowling about for a chance to peek at the treaty. One, at least, claims to be with the Okhrana. These, you will remember, escaped from Germany two months ago. We encountered them on the yacht. I'm certain they know the treaty has been signed, but I'm equally certain they haven't seen it. Surely, they will try to infiltrate the palace and photograph the treaty."

He kept himself from smiling. "I propose, Herr Oberst, that we change the positioning of the sentries such that there is to the spies an obvious point to sneak into. We shall then post further sentries within the palace to seize them on the other side of the wall. What follows, of course, will be according to the Order's policy. She's the one who murdered Heinrich, I should add."

For a moment, Tirpitz felt a leaden weight upon his otherwise giddy heart.

The Master leaned back in his chair with his fingertips pressed together. "By all means! The reputation of the Order is at stake, and Heinrich was too good a man to go unavenged. Set your trap, Hauptmann Tirpitz, or perhaps we shall be saying soon, *Major* Tirpitz. Dismissed."

"Herr Oberst!" Tirpitz gave the Order's salute again, about-faced smartly, and practically floated out of the office.

He would issue his orders and then retire to his favorite restaurant for a veal cutlet. He had the perfect trap for those snooping vermin! And what he would do to the woman who had murdered Heinrich...

CHAPTER 18: TIRPITZ TRIUMPHANT

August 7, 1905

Tirpitz hummed the march "Prinz Eugen" to himself as he paced the floor in the darkened Tamerlane room in the Kaiser's Neues Palais. As his humming grew louder, he had to check himself to avoid waking any members of the imperial family.

His entire body strained with anxiety. What if the two spies avoided his trap? They had evaded him twice before, and if he missed them again, the Master would be furious. That was to say nothing of the Kaiser's reaction if his secret treaty was leaked to France and Britain before he had prepared for them to learn of it.

Would the Master, in his enraged disappointment, spill the secrets about that day? Tirpitz had burned the file, of course, but the Master's denunciation would prove a sure precursor to being locked away and forgotten. Could the dungeon at Hlidskjalf be destined not for the two spies, but for Tirpitz? He had never passed a completely peaceful night after that day, and tonight would prove no exception, it seemed.

Tirpitz had stationed himself in the Tamerlane room to keep watch in case the spies did make it past his trap. The eponymous painting in the room left him wondering as he ran the torchlight over it. Even in the otherwise absolute darkness, he could make out the artwork's splendor.

In the painting, the army of Tamerlane, bright in festive garments, bore the Sultan Bajazeth, clad darkly in failure, in a cage to their ruthless lord. Which part would Tirpitz play tonight? Would he present the spies in a cage to his Master, or would *his* head wind up on the executioner's block?

He took it as a mixed blessing that Helmuth was taking his turn at watch at that moment. Helmuth enjoyed brutality more than anyone; he could watch

Tirpitz's method of torture with the gleeful grin of a child at Christmas. He lacked Heinrich's subtlety and savoir faire, however.

Ach, he would avenge Heinrich! Until he had his hands on his enemies, he had to worry that Helmuth would botch things and let it slip to the imperial family that Tirpitz had set a trap with the Kaiser's secret treaty as bait.

He had to think of something else. He checked the clock below the gilded mirror. 10:30 p.m. Plenty of time for the spies to still come tonight.

Helmuth suddenly appeared and saluted. He had the grin of a hungry man being served a delicious meal. "They came, Herr Hauptmann, and are in custody," he whispered.

"Are they... unspoiled?" Tirpitz said, searching for the right word.

Helmuth sighed. "I haven't touched them, Herr Hauptmann," he said.

Tirpitz leered and laid a hand on Helmuth's shoulder. "Don't worry, Helmuth. If they're as stubborn as I think they are, the blood will flow copiously before we break them. I have particular designs for the woman who murdered Heinrich. You can have the man if it becomes necessary; I want the woman."

Tirpitz took the torch and almost waltzed from the Tamerlane room. "Were they disguised?" he asked.

"Jawohl, Herr Hauptmann. The woman was dressed as a maid, which is what she claimed to be when we apprehended her, and the man was wearing a guard's uniform—that of a hauptmann, to be precise."

"In a German uniform? So no one will whine if anything happens to them since they can't be anything other than spies."

By the time Tirpitz reached the knot of guards around the two prisoners, they had already shackled them in iron chains. He felt fairly sure the woman was the one who had killed Heinrich. Her hair was a different color, but the eyes and the scar were precisely as he remembered them. If she had been German, she might have been worth pursuing and bedding, for he could not deny her beauty. She had Slavic blood, though, and he would not debase himself to be one flesh with one of those, at least not if it meant stooping for her consent in the matter.

However, at the moment, he certainly respected the woman more. She had the fierce scowl of a lassoed mustang, while the man looked nervously at the ground like a weary slave. He looked like the spy from the Royal Opera House, but now he had a beard.

"Take off those disguises!" Tirpitz ordered. "I want a better look."

The guards tore off the woman's wig and the man's false beard. Tirpitz scrutinized them. Definitely the spies from the Opera House.

"Well, well, well, we just can't seem to avoid each other, can we?" he said. "You know, if you wish to see the Kaiser so badly, you should put in for an appointment."

"Never mind the Kaiser," the woman said. "You know what we're interested in."

"I don't see why you need to be so impatient. The terms of that treaty will soon become common knowledge when the Quintuple Alliance declares war on Britain. We'll take them back to the castle so as not to disturb His Majesty. But first, search them for weapons."

"The man had this when we patted him down," Helmuth said. He produced a Webley.

"What about the woman?"

Helmuth shrugged. "Haven't touched her, sir."

"Well, get on with it!" Tirpitz said.

Helmuth stepped forward to frisk her, but the woman, despite the shackles, still managed to slap his face.

"How dare you presume to touch a lady like that?" she demanded.

Tirpitz scoffed. "Lady? What kind of a *lady* stabs a man in the heart? I think you are more a harridan murderess than a *lady*. We have to search you for that stiletto you used."

"One moment, and I'll get it for you myself."

"So you can keep a second one hidden? Do your duty, Helmuth."

The male spy almost exploded in anger as they groped the woman. His chains rattled as he tried to leap on Helmuth, but the guards restrained him by the shoulders. The man could not really argue, though, when Helmuth found a stiletto strapped to each of her thighs. The male spy turned away, blushing, as Helmuth relieved her of them, but Tirpitz looked on with a leer. The woman's face resembled a thundercloud with lightning in her eyes.

He gestured for the group to come along. "We'll talk at more length at the castle. Are a pistol and stiletto all that they were armed with?"

"He was carrying this," Helmuth said. He took a rifle from one of the soldiers standing by and handed it to Tirpitz.

Tirpitz clucked his tongue. "English weaponry on one and another who claims to be with the Okhrana. This shall make for a most interesting tale. I never would have thought of England and Russia cooperating."

For a moment, he wondered if the Kaiser was too late to turn Russia loose on Britain if their intelligence apparatuses were cooperating against Germany. Of course, spies often cooperated with other nations' agents as long as it served their purpose. He could not count how many nations Sydney Reilly had spied for. His brain remained preoccupied with the question as the group made its way to the palace doors.

"Halt!" a voice said. "Brünnhilde!"

Tirpitz jolted. He realized a sentry had challenged them. "You idiot! Who do you think we all are?"

"You ordered me to be on high alert, Hauptmann Tirpitz!" the soldier said.

Tirpitz groaned. "And her solo," he said.

"Pass, Meine Herren."

***

MacKenzie said nothing in the carriage on the way to the castle. He sat with his head hanging just barely above his clasped hands. He knew he should be planning his escape, but even if he could, he could not see what to do next. The guards had locked the carriage doors and covered its windows.

He could not let himself give up! He owed it to Svetlana to remain resolute at least as long as she did, and he knew she would last until Judgment Day. He had promised he would see her through it to the end.

He glanced over at her. Her eyes were wild like a wolf's in a cage. MacKenzie drew himself back up. He could not let the guard seated opposite them see a Scotsman with less fortitude than a Ukrainian mademoiselle. That would not do. He remembered the line from Gilbert and Sullivan's "The Mikado:" "When a man's afraid, a beautiful maid is a cheering sight to see. And it's oh, I'm glad that moment sad was soothed by sight of me!" Dignity, though, seemed a poor shield against what awaited them.

His heart trembled with shame even more than fear. The Germans had their hands on Archimedes' most important inventions. They had his wireless ring. Worse, they also had the codebook for it. He did not have just himself to worry about, but every agent supervised by MO3 who used that code. And all this after he had let Captain Gibson fall into their hands. This failure surely surpassed that day.

Somewhere out there in the night, an owl shrieked, and MacKenzie thought of the banshees of his ancestors' mythology.

The horses clattered to a halt, and the guards opened the doors in front of an outsized set of steps, flanked by even more exaggerated statues. The moonlight gleamed off the white stone enough to reveal to MacKenzie that these represented the heroes of Germanic lore.

God preserve us!

He thought it with more desperation than hope as he stepped out of the carriage. He was sending up the same kind of frantic prayers that he had on that day.

The Germans marched them into the main hall, where the rattling of their shackles echoed off the limestone walls. The room felt cold, damp, and void of life. Tirpitz flipped on the lights. For a moment, everyone squinted at the sudden brightness. They stood amid a circle of guards among a collection of desks lining the walls of the hall.

"We need to get better acquainted, you see," Tirpitz said amiably. "Let me see their identification."

The guards handed over their passports and wallets.

"Hm, Ranald MacKenzie. Looks genuine. No fake identification, eh? Ach, that's right, your government does not spy. Captain, Black Watch. That explains the Lee-Enfield. Yours is a fine regiment, Captain MacKenzie, but one more renowned for recklessness than good sense. Really, risking being scalped just so you could wear a striped blanket!"

MacKenzie perceived the insult. His ancestors had enlisted for the Seven Years War in America, in many cases, just to wear the tartan plaid forbidden to ordinary Highlanders by the British government.

"I dinna suppose a Hun would understand such matters of honor," he spat.

Tirpitz showed his teeth in a grim smile. "I have a sense of honor, drawn from the finest ethos of warrior Germania." He unconsciously stuck his tongue out as he flipped through the codebook. "This is a most peculiar codebook. Your author went so far as to write in a different alphabet... or whatever this is supposed to be. We must talk more about this, Captain

MacKenzie—if you can tell us anything your poor mate Captain Gibson didn't already confess after you left him to our tender mercies."

Tirpitz grinned from ear to ear while MacKenzie felt ready to throw up. Tirpitz thumbed through MacKenzie's cash but did not find any additional information.

"Very interesting reading, Captain MacKenzie, I must say, and a little commission for my services to the Reich," he said cheerily as he stuffed MacKenzie's bank notes into his own wallet. "Not enough to be worth reporting, eh? And now for the Ruskie's... Hm, Catriona MacKenzie. Not Catriona Cameron? Neither of those is a Russian name. What's your real name, my dear?"

"It's hard to keep track these days."

"What would your father call you?"

"My father is dead."

"Confound it, woman, I'm losing my patience! Do you want hot pincers anywhere near your pretty face? Don't lie!"

Svetlana sighed. "Svetlana Petrovna Rachkovskaya."

Tirpitz paused.

"It seems to me your father isn't as dead as you claim. The daughter of Peter Ivanovich Rachkovsky, I presume?"

"By adoption. My biological father died long ago."

He licked his lips. "I suppose I should be honored that Mother Russia has graced us with her finest."

"You should."

Tirpitz handed the documents to the soldier on his right. "So much for the pleasantries. I want code phrases, contacts, and so forth. First, the code phrases."

MacKenzie and Svetlana exchanged tight-lipped glances.

"You'd better talk, you Jock and Cossack," Tirpitz said. "Do you know what your lives are worth to me? The two of yours together aren't worth a fly's spit. Let me tell you what happened on that day, the day my life changed forever. Guards, stand aside. I'll tell you when to come back."

The guards left them to go down the hall. Tirpitz spoke quietly as he told his tale.

"I started on my path to where I am now as a student at the University of Freiburg, Faculty of Medicine. I became a neurologist, but like many medical students, I had turned to anarchy. At the time, I felt the only way to improve the lot of my penurious, downtrodden patients was to remove the oppressive hierarchy that kept them in grinding poverty."

Svetlana scoffed quietly.

"You've heard of the anarchist motto of, 'Propaganda by deed'? Of course you have, Fräulein Rachkovskaya! My plan was to assassinate the local duke, Herr von something or other. I didn't know much about him other than his prominence. What his personal character truly was didn't matter; the fact that he was a noble did."

MacKenzie thought he saw regret in Tirpitz's eyes.

"I obtained a dagger and evaded the duke's retainers. The old man was in his library where I stabbed him to death. Ach, the look in his eyes! I spent the next three weeks creeping from hideout to hideout, scavenging from garbage to keep my strength up. I was in the process of boarding a steamer to Britain when my handler intercepted me."

Tirpitz inhaled sharply.

"He'd been shadowing me like a Fury since a few days after the murder and almost as closely as my conscience. He was most impressed that I had eluded both the duke's famously vigilant servants and the police all the way to the border, so he gave me a choice. I could work as his spy and put those skills to the service of the Kaiser and the Reich, or he would turn me in. What choice did I have? He knew I'd be his creature for the rest of my life if he kept my secret."

MacKenzie felt a pang of pity.

"As I spied for my handler, he introduced me to the pagan gods of old Germania. They are the true source of power in the universe, and now that I serve them, they make me powerful too. There's coming a day when their chosen race will dominate the globe, and I'm going to be on the right side of that war. It's a higher calling than anarchism, one that serves the Teutonic gods and their power and glory."

All of MacKenzie's pity evaporated as quickly as it had arisen.

"I put my neurology skills to use to perfect a technique for torture that's never failed yet. You can talk now or later—it's all the same to me. I don't usually relish it, but I'll make an exception for the one who murdered the best comrade I ever had and anyone who would protect her. Let me explain what will happen…"

Now his oily voice rose to sound positively demonic. With gruesome glee, he recounted the tortures he had inflicted on his former comrades—the anarchists—and foreign agents. MacKenzie looked away, but Svetlana stared him directly in the eyes as he went on with his discourse.

Tirpitz soon became visibly annoyed with Svetlana's imperturbability. First his voice rose even louder and quickened. Then his face flushed. He licked his lips between sentences. He gestured violently and horribly. Finally, by the time he got to the unfortunate victim's demises, he became frenzied. Still, Svetlana did not so much as shudder. Tirpitz regained his composure, straightening himself back up with a deep exhalation between his teeth.

"Guards!" he called.

They filed back in and seized the prisoners' arms.

"I can see Fräulein Rachkovskaya believes the Okhrana can match anything I can inflict," Tirpitz said. "I shall let her judge firsthand. I swore an oath to avenge my brother-in-arms, whom you murdered, Fräulein! Heinrich von Papen, his name was, and you are not fit to have kissed his boots, killing him the way you did. But I believe I can be talked out of that oath if I can replace it with something better. You, Captain MacKenzie, will explain this codebook and sign receipts to spy for Germany, or I'll do what I just described to Fräulein Rachkovskaya. Or at least as much as her body will endure. Then, if you don't, I see no reason why we shouldn't do the same to you."

MacKenzie's eyes lit with fire. "You'll gain nothing from your torments but an eternal torment in hell."

Tirpitz sneered. "Hell is where the sick and old go when they die, Captain. Perhaps if you die of torture resisting the enemy, you'll go to Valhalla, but if I were you, I should fear the eternal mists of Niflheim more."

When the Russians had captured him and he had felt betrayed by Svetlana, MacKenzie had thought himself worthy of such a fate. Now, though, with Svetlana to think of, his faith stirred him to courage. "I have nothing to fear from death. I'm a Christian."

Tirpitz smiled even more grimly. "So much the better. I've never had the chance to make a martyr yet—certainly not with the anarchists, who deny my gods as much as your weak excuse for one."

"He's not weak at all. He's omnipotent and eternal—in contrast to yours, whose fate, if I remember correctly, is to become dog food. He can outdo any pain you think you can manage, and where there's no end to the judge, there's no end to the punishment."

Tirpitz cackled. "If anyone's going to feel anything close to eternal torment, it won't be *me*. I think we'll have to update Herr Foxe's *Book of the Martyrs* when I'm through with you."

He leered and stroked Svetlana's cheek. "But it would be a shame for such beauty to go to waste. I think I'll enjoy it myself before I destroy it."

"You won't be the first," Svetlana said. "It's been enjoyed by better men than you, even if they *were* anarchists."

Tirpitz snapped back and drew himself to full height. He pointed a finger in the air. "Take them away!"

CHAPTER 19: THE ALARIC TOWER

"To the oubliette, Herr Hauptmann?" Helmuth said.

Tirpitz waved his hand. "Take them to the Alaric Tower cell with its moonlit window. I want Captain MacKenzie here to see Fräulein Rachkovskaya's face so he can imagine it disfigured by my torture. We'll commit him to the pitch-blackness of the oubliette to forget his senses until we reawaken his sense of pain if he won't talk after she's dead."

"Very good, Herr Hauptmann," Helmuth said.

He gave the salute of the Order.

The guards, a sergeant and an *unteroffizier*, seized MacKenzie and Svetlana by the arms and dragged them down the hall.

"Trust me, Captain MacKenzie. I have only yours and Fräulein Rachkovskaya's best interests at heart," Tirpitz called out as they left him. "I just want to save you a lot of unnecessary trouble."

As they led them away, MacKenzie marked the route they took. He glanced around and saw where his accouterments were left as the remaining party dispersed. They headed for a room far down the hallway with a door of bars. The next step brought him down a corridor whose wall blocked that room from view. Not that any of it mattered. He was shackled and was about to be locked away. There would be no escape. Memorizing his surroundings was simply a habit he had picked up in South Africa, now thoroughly useless.

They entered a round tower and ascended winding stairs, their chains rattling against each limestone step. They wound up an entire revolution when they came to a heavy iron door. A single flickering lightbulb provided illumination for the soldiers as their jangling keys turned in the lock. The door had a barred window through which they could watch the spies.

The door opened, revealing a set of steps leading down into a cramped cell. The only light came from a barred window set in the wall, which provided the moonlight that Tirpitz hoped would increase MacKenzie's anguish. As the door opened, a blast of foul odor swept around them and rushed into their nostrils. Svetlana coughed.

"We might have cleaned the place up if we'd known we'd be having guests," one of the guards laughed.

"I doubt that, you filthy pigs!" Svetlana managed to say between coughs.

"I wouldn't be too quick to call anyone else a pig, *Ruskie*."

"I'm Ukrainian!" she snapped. "Think about that tomorrow when you eat your bread grown in our fields!"

The guard shoved them into the cell. They nearly fell down the steps, but MacKenzie stopped himself and caught Svetlana at the edge of the landing. They made their way down the stairway to the narrow floor that comprised about a quarter of the tower's cross-section. The guard shut the panel in the door through which he could have viewed them, no doubt to block out the odor.

"Take post, Unteroffizier," they heard the sergeant say to the other guard. "And remember—if they escape, Hauptmann Tirpitz will do unto you as he would have done unto them."

MacKenzie and Svetlana made their way down to the damp floor of the cell. They looked for what might be the cleanest spot in the room. In the dark, it was mostly guesswork.

MacKenzie groaned as he sat.

Hauptmann Tirpitz was in earnest, he knew. Why else would he have told them about his own "that day"? Whatever was going on in that sick mind of his, it showed the stakes for which he played that he would bare that secret to them. It seemed unlikely that he would let them live to repeat it—not that anyone would have taken two enemy spies' word for it.

"Sveta, what am I to do?" MacKenzie said in Gaelic. "I can't spy for Germany or let on about the codebook, and yet I'll never forgive myself if I let him do that to you. On the other hand, if it came to a choice between me and letting the revolutionaries win, I ken which way you'd choose."

Svetlana looked into his eyes. Suddenly, she had all the plaintiveness of a starving animal in a cage. Her ice-hard exterior had melted into pools of tears streaming down her cheeks. MacKenzie would never have believed it of her.

"What are you going to do, Ranald? Surely you can't stand by and watch them do that to me!"

"Please dinna look at me that way, Sveta! I'd rather you look as you did to him—resolute and unshakeable."

"Can I keep that act up around you? You would see right through it to my fear, wouldn't you?"

MacKenzie's heart sank. Her voice faltered with desperation. He would rather Tirpitz torture him than see her tortured. The guilt alone after watching that would grind his heart into powder. His thoughts raced as he considered what he should do.

This felt even worse than his decision about the bomb on the Tsar's yacht. What was honorable? Certainly, a gentleman should do his best to protect a lady, but a spy should be willing to make the most ruthless sacrifices in the name of a higher good. But if he did that, what would distinguish him from Svetlana's amorality that horrified him so?

"What is honorable here?" he said.

"Aye, let me fall into the hands of your gallantry!" she said. "Surely, you will protect the weaker vessel, as your apostle says!"

"You've never cared a farthing for gallantry before."

"But does Christian honor look at the deserving of the object? Didn't St. Peter say to show honor unto all?"

That did it. MacKenzie sighed. "I guess I'll have to talk and sign the receipts and take my chances. Play for time. I'll try to retrieve the situation once you're safely away. And if they haul me up on treason charges, so be it."

"You'd... do that for me?" she said. "Risk your career and your life to save me?"

"Aye, I would."

Suddenly, Svetlana burst out laughing. MacKenzie looked at her blankly.

"How naïve you are, Ranald!" she said. "No, you're quite right. If it were between you and Ukraine, I'd choose Ukraine. And it's not like he's going to let me off the hook, not after I killed his precious Heinrich. I think I can get us out of here without your sacrificing anything."

In Russian, she called out, "Guard, guard! If you release us, you can have me for anything you want, please! I shall be your plaything in bed! Anything, I swear it!"

"Silence, you Slavic slut, or I'll come in there and knock you on your head!" the guard called in Russian.

"You see, Sveta, there's a limit to what even your beauty can achieve," MacKenzie said in Gaelic.

Svetlana tossed her head with another laugh. "I just wanted to ken if he could hear me and understand Russian. I can do my part to get us out of here if you do yours. You can get us out of these chains, can you not? I'm sure Archimedes wouldn't have left you empty-handed."

The acid! "Aye."

He undid the heel of his boot and produced the vial of purple acid Archimedes had prepared for him. He popped the stopper and poured a conservative amount into the lock on his left hand. It began to hiss.

Svetlana sang "MacPherson's Rant," the last words of a Highland outlaw on the eve of his hanging, to cover the noise.

"Sae rantingly, sae wantonly, sae dauntingly gaed he. He played a spring and danced it round below the gallows-tree," went the chorus.

The shackle broke open. MacKenzie unconsciously stuck his tongue out as he measured out the next doses for his three other locks. He had to save enough for Svetlana.

Finally, just as she reached the last verse, his last lock clinked open. She repeated the song as he moved on to her shackles. Having gotten the hang of it, he did not take as long to free Svetlana. The speed of the chemical reaction became his only limitation.

"Now go by the door quietly," she whispered. "Stay in the shadows."

MacKenzie crept up the steps and to beside the door while Svetlana slipped off her shoes. As MacKenzie watched in awe, she steadily pulled herself up the stones in the wall like a rock climber. The stench of the room meant that the guard could see nothing through the shut panel. MacKenzie knew that was Providence—God working good from evil, even something as foul as the stench of waste. She reached the window and grabbed the bars.

"Do you see any guards from down there?" Svetlana hissed just loudly enough in Russian. "Keep watch while I climb down."

MacKenzie stuck himself as close to the wall as possible as the guard slid the panel in the door back. With MacKenzie in the shadows behind the door and Svetlana at the window, he had every reason to believe MacKenzie had escaped from the cell and that Svetlana was following.

"Stay where you are there!" he shouted.

The keys jangled in the lock. As the guard burst in, MacKenzie struck him with his palm just below and behind the ear, dropping him to the floor. He grabbed the keys as Svetlana raced up the stairs and retrieved the fallen guard's Mauser and ammunition belt. She held them out to MacKenzie.

"I wouldn't be caught dead using a Mauser. I ken where they put my Lee-Enfield."

"I think we'll do better if I wear a uniform this time. Close the door and keep watch while I change."

Unlike Tirpitz, MacKenzie kept his back to her the whole time. Svetlana finally ascended back up the stairs. She had tucked her hair under the pickelhaube helmet. She smiled at his flushed face. All the gentility in the world could not conceal that.

"Let's go."

As she stepped off, MacKenzie grabbed her arm. "You ken, you could have told me you had a plan in the first place and eased my mind."

Svetlana smiled mischievously but said nothing. MacKenzie closed the dungeon's door and locked it. Now he felt irked, if not downright used. She had put him through several minutes of agony just for a boost to her own vanity.

See right through her indeed!

They took a few more steps. He grabbed her arm again. "Unteroffizier, don't you think that a hauptmann should precede his orderly? You're not a lady right now, you ken."

Svetlana fell in behind MacKenzie. "Begging your pardon, Herr Hauptmann!" she hissed.

"Just let me do the talking," MacKenzie said.

They descended the winding steps and reached the corridor on the main floor. They stopped at the threshold where the tower joined the rest of the castle and glanced around for any guards.

"I can't make out anyone in this darkness. Can you, Unteroffizier?"

"Nein, Herr Hauptmann. We'll just have to take our chances."

They marched down the corridor. MacKenzie followed the route he remembered to what he took to be the armory. They arrived at the barred door where a soldier waited. He saluted the Order's salute, which MacKenzie returned.

The Honorable Spy

"Soldat, Hauptmann Tirpitz desired me to analyze the English spy's accouterments for any violation of military law," MacKenzie said. "Dumdums for his Lee-Enfield and the like, the Kaiser's correspondence in his papers. Retrieve them for me."

"This time of night, Herr Hauptmann?"

"Urgent, Soldat! He wants any casus belli we can hang over the Englishman's head ready to confront him with when we interrogate him tomorrow. You know the English aren't as eager for war as we are. Don't be impertinent, or you'll be on report!"

The soldat squinted at him. MacKenzie froze his face in a stern expression.

"What, Herr Hauptmann, did Odin whisper in Baldur's ear at his funeral?"

"Soldat, no one knows that but Odin himself," MacKenzie said. "Not even wise Vafthrudnir."

The soldat nervously snapped to attention.

"My apologies, Herr Hauptmann!"

"I'll overlook your impertinence, Soldat, if you retrieve me the Englishman's accouterments promptly," MacKenzie said.

The soldat fumbled at the lock and practically leaped into the armory. MacKenzie and Svetlana exchanged furtive smiles. MacKenzie was glad he had pored over his books of Norse mythology as a boy, since his prompt response to the trivia question had wiped all doubt away in the soldat's mind that he was dealing with an authentic superior in the Order. The soldat returned with his arms full of everything the soldiers had stripped MacKenzie and Svetlana of.

"I brought the Ruskie's items too to be thorough, Herr Hauptmann, as well as Hauptmann Tirpitz's inventory of them so you'll see nothing is lacking," he said.

"Very good, Soldat."

"Now, if you would just show me Hauptmann Tirpitz's orders, I can hand them over to you."

MacKenzie went blank. Tirpitz had not left him with an article to his name, let alone anything close to resembling orders. His forged German identification papers Archie had provided as Wilhelm Kleber remained in the armload the soldat was carrying.

"I believe you entrusted those to me, Herr Hauptmann," Svetlana said in the lowest voice she could manage. "Here, Soldat."

She fished in her pocket for the unteroffizier's identification card. She held it out to the soldat. As he leaned in to look at it, she punched him in the throat. MacKenzie grabbed the Lee-Enfield before it could clank to the floor, and Svetlana dragged the choking soldat into the armory. MacKenzie snatched the belt from the soldat's waist.

"Tie him up with this. Gag him with a handkerchief."

As Svetlana did so, MacKenzie rifled around for anything that might prove useful. He spied papers lying on the orderly's desk with a letterhead of some pagan symbol. He snatched up all the papers on the desk without stopping to look them over. By now, Svetlana had finished rendering the soldat hors de combat.

Having recovered their articles and replenished MacKenzie's bank notes with the soldat's and the petty cash till of the armory, they marched out of the castle back into the night. Several vehicles lay parked in the cul-de-sac below. MacKenzie returned the salute of the guards as they lowered the drawbridge. He and Svetlana made their way down the steps and strode to the cars.

"Unteroffizier, can you drive?" MacKenzie whispered. "It wouldn't look good for a hauptmann to drive an unteroffizier."

"I'll manage, Herr Hauptmann."

A guard saluted as they approached the auto lot.

"Soldat, we need a vehicle to return to the Neues Palais," MacKenzie said. "And I'll need a map. Hauptmann Tirpitz wants a report on where the spies might have come from so we can trace any anarchists who might be abetting them."

"This time of night, Herr Hauptmann?"

"Urgent, Soldat! We want to present the English spy's confederates to him when we interrogate him in the morning so we can show him he has no hope of escape. Besides, the anarchists, if there are any, might escape if we wait until morning."

"And who is Siegfried's horse, Herr Hauptmann?"

"Are you trying to be impertinent, Soldat? Everyone knows it's Grani!"

"Sorry, Herr Hauptmann. Hauptmann Tirpitz said to be on high alert."

MacKenzie nodded. "Very well, Soldat. Next time, pick a harder question. Now, the car and the map."

"Jawohl, Herr Hauptmann."

The soldat retrieved the keys and the map and presented them to Svetlana. They loaded into the car, and Svetlana began to back out. She drove with a style so abrupt and jerky that MacKenzie feared the soldat would find something amiss. The soldat held his peace as they left, though, so he apparently remained cowed by MacKenzie's second Norse mythology reference. How fortunate the *Saga of the Volsungs* was one of his favorite books!

Once the castle had passed out of sight, MacKenzie touched Svetlana's arm. "Stop here for a moment." He handed her the map. "Can you make out the route, Sveta?"

"Aye. I'll have us there directly," she said.

"I guess this time we'll walk right in. With Hauptmann Tirpitz's inventory here as a model of his handwriting, I believe I can forge our orders to investigate the place."

MacKenzie carefully composed a pass on the order's paper authorizing himself in Hauptmann Tirpitz's hand to access the palace grounds. They drove toward the palace. Svetlana seemed cheerfully chatty, but a sudden gloominess overtook MacKenzie. He leaned his head on his hand, his arm propped up on the car door.

"Are you all right, Ranald?"

He sighed. "I was just pondering our motivations. What a lot we make! There's not an honorable driving impulse in the three of us. You're driven by hatred, he by bloodguilt, and I... I by fear."

"Spare me the psychoanalysis! I doubt you ken the first thing about Sigmund Freud's theories anyway. You'd probably faint if you read them."

Her face softened, and she continued in a gentler tone. "Ranald, guilt over past murders might be driving Tirpitz, but there is no hatred or fear in you or me tonight. We're here for our duty—you to your king, and I to the Motherland."

"You sound like how I hear your father writes his instructions—alternating harshness with smooth lies."

She grinned. "Thank you, Ranald. It seems to work well for him. You lie too when you have to."

"That reminds me: I've revised my position, and you're still wrong!"

"What about?"

"When you slept with Monsieur Beletsky for information. You've taught me not to pit one commandment against another, but I still believe I can lie to protect life."

"Oh?" she laughed. "And what pinpointed Presbyterian logic do you use to underpin that position?"

"I dinna ken the way to prove it with inescapable logic from a firm premise like I thought I had with the commandments being in order of precedence. It's just the most reasonable conclusion. Each of those examples I cited seem to have been motivated by faith, by heroes of faith.

"Before Elisha lies to the Syrians, he is full of faith. He fairly didn't lose his nerve *after* God had blinded them! He was, in fact, as much lying to save them as himself. Perhaps those who wish to use the truth for direly sinful purposes have forfeited their right to the truth. Does justice dictate that we owe the truth to those who wish to use it to kill someone? Then we would be abetting a sin rather than doing our best to prevent it."

"You could simply refuse to answer," Svetlana said.

"But in some circumstances, that's as good as an admission. If a burglar breaks into your home, has a knife on you, and asks if you have any children upstairs, refusing to answer obviously tells him that there is. You can try to deceive your way out of it, as many saints do in the Bible, or you can tell the truth and hope God makes him trip and break his neck on the way up the stairs. No one in Scripture opts for that approach, that I'm aware of. They will rather die than renounce God, but they lie their way out of other situations."

"Then, Ranald, we both went out on a scriptural limb; I just went further. While we're on the subject of what you will and won't do, can I ask you something personal?"

"What is it?"

"Can I rely on you to kill if it comes to that?"

"What makes you think I can't kill? I've done it before!"

She narrowed her eyes condescendingly. "But to treaty-breaking belligerents like Boers, I would imagine. You've been far too reluctant to go for the kill on this mission from my point of view."

"From your point of view, a leopard's too compassionate!"

"Ranald, our lives may depend on your shooting someone dead. Can I rely on you?"

"If absolutely necessary."

He noticed a mischievous twinkle in Svetlana's eye, but as usual, he had no idea what it meant.

CHAPTER 20: THE UNFORGIVING MINUTE

As the Mercedes approached the wrought iron gates at the entrance to the park and the Neues Palais, MacKenzie wondered wherever he had gotten this tenacity. He had stuck to this treaty like his terriers on a badger. He had risked his life several times and would again. Having escaped a trap that had promised nothing but horror, he was putting his head back in the noose. He did not panic now. God was upholding him, as he had prayed before starting. Just the same, he took a deep breath as they approached.

The guard at the gate stepped forward and saluted. MacKenzie held out his forged orders and identification. "We have orders from Hauptmann Tirpitz," he said. "He desires us to search the palace for anything disturbed by the spies and any traces of anarchists' assisting the spies."

The guard looked them over. MacKenzie locked the anxiety down in his stomach and did not let it show in his face. If Tirpitz was taking no chances, he would have alerted the guards to the true identity of Hauptmann Kleber.

The guard handed back the forgeries and saluted. "Open the gate!"

Evidently, Tirpitz had been so confident that no one could escape from the castle that he had not apprised the palace guards. Svetlana drove the Mercedes down the avenue of lime trees, their foliage lush and green from the summer days.

They came up on the side of the structure. Svetlana turned the vehicle into the driveway the Kaiser had had constructed for his own fleet of Mercedes limousines. This time, they would knock on the front door.

The gray driveway was flanked, like the avenue, with two rows of trees, in this case, manicured bays in large gray-green pots. The palace loomed dark over them against the night sky. MacKenzie remembered what it had looked like when they had scouted it in the daylight. It was symmetrical, with a massive, greened-copper dome crowning the center of the main palace. Two smaller domes, also of tarnished copper, presided over two wings that only consisted of one floor.

Between the two one-story wings stood the main palace. It sported red paint that imitated brickwork, when in reality, plaster lay under it. White sandstone pilasters, regular and symmetrical as Prussian guards on parade, interrupted the red, each matched with a sandstone sculpture in front and another above on the balustrade. The statues, regularly spaced and numerous, looked like an army that had glimpsed Medusa while in open formation.

The vehicle's white headlights reflected in the arched glass windows as Svetlana and MacKenzie stopped below the center dome. A guard stepped toward the car.

MacKenzie relayed his made-up instructions. "You will guide me to the Kaiser's study, bitte," he added. "Have to make sure the spies or their accomplices did not disturb anything of the Kaiser's correspondence."

The guard led them from the car into a hall that felt like an underwater cave. The room would have appeared dark even in the daylight, and MacKenzie felt a little claustrophobic. It had an opulence worthy of Poseidon.

MacKenzie glanced at Svetlana, whose jaw had dropped slightly open in awe. The checkered floor below them consisted of inlaid marble, and all around the walls and columns stood alternating marble and stone. Sea monsters looked down on the spies from the ceiling amid a painted collection of seashells. Classical statues towered over them along the wall.

Turning right, the guard preceded them into the Tamerlane room, where Tirpitz had awaited them earlier that night. Passing that, they entered into the Red Damask Chamber, named for the pattern on the wall. The floor featured a pattern of quartered octagons. Rich paintings lined the wall. Their varying sizes were the only part of the room that did not follow a pattern, though the decorator had arranged them in a pleasing manner.

Finally, the guard brought them through pastel room after pastel room, up a stairway, and to the Kaiser's personal study, the walls done in green damask. He saluted and took his leave.

MacKenzie waited until he had left and then darted the torchlight around, looking for a desk. Spotting what looked like the Kaiser's writing desk, they rushed over and began to pull at drawers. One resisted as though locked. That had to be it.

MacKenzie had just enough acid left to burn through the lock and open the drawer. At the top, inside the desk, lay a document in French, beginning, "Their Imperial Majesties, the Emperor of All the Russias and the Emperor of Germany..."

The Treaty of Bjorko! He snatched it out of the desk and laid it out.

"Hold the light on it," MacKenzie said. He handed Svetlana the torch and fished into his pocket for his flask.

"This is no time for a drink!" Svetlana hissed.

"Good, because I dinna want one. Archie rigged a camera at the bottom of this. I just line it up like so, and presto!"

"Take several shots, in case anything goes wrong."

"But naturally."

MacKenzie took exposure after exposure from different angles. One, at least, would surely come out readable. Just the same, he paused to read the terms of the treaty in case anything should happen to the camera. If either was attacked, Germany and Russia would assist each other with all their forces and refuse to conclude a separate peace. The treaty would come into effect at the conclusion of the war with Japan, and Russia would present it to France, urging her to join.

He read it, muttering to himself again and again to commit it to memory. Claiming to be a defensive alliance! The Kaiser had only to force Britain to declare war and then claim that they had started it. Napoleon had proven a master at provoking other powers into initiating hostilities. Would the Kaiser have dared to call it an "offensive alliance"?

"Shall we go?" MacKenzie said at length.

"Och, aye. Let's get out of here."

They retraced their steps through the palace back to the garden entrance in that magnificent underwater grotto. MacKenzie had memorized his surroundings, so they made a quick transit to their car. The guards saluted as they exited.

Just as they climbed into the car, the air came alive with alarmed voices. In the distance, they heard indistinct shouting.

"I believe our escape has been noticed back at the castle," MacKenzie hissed in Gaelic. "They're locking down the park. We can't leave by car now!"

"I think I'd like to explore the gardens," Svetlana said calmly.

So that the guards they had just left behind at the palace entrance would think nothing of it, MacKenzie and Svetlana made their way unhurriedly toward the garden. They gambled that they could escape out of sight before word reached the Neues Palais that spies were on the loose.

The shouting grew closer. MacKenzie could not make out what they said. He glanced back and saw squads of soldiers coming in from the park entrance and beginning to sweep the area.

Svetlana and he just had to make it to the railway station. They had already picked a train bound for Russia and stashed their trunks in one of the cars before setting out for the Neues Palais the first, unsuccessful time. If they could get aboard that train, the immediate danger would pass. But first, they had to get out of the park under the noses of predators on alert.

They reached a grove of lush trees and darted behind them. They heard the shouts back from the palace. The guards at the palace entrance had been alerted. MacKenzie snuck a glance toward the Neues Palais around an oak trunk. The guards were inspecting the car. A squad made its way toward the gardens.

"Stick to the paths," MacKenzie said. "If we trample the plants, they'll notice."

They ran hand-in-hand down the winding paths, their rifles slung from their shoulders. They could see nothing of what went on around them. Thick foliage blocked their view.

"We just came by this route," MacKenzie said. "Confounded circle. This time, take the fork right."

Retracing their steps, they corrected the error and made their way past a row of fruit trees. A shadow passed over them. MacKenzie looked up to spot an owl, a mouse dangling from its beak. As they ran, Svetlana's pickelhaube fell off, and her hair flowed down her back once more. They came to a three-way split in the path and halted.

"Which way?" Svetlana panted.

"For all we ken, one's as good as another."

They started toward different paths and almost lost hold of each other. Svetlana wanted to go left while MacKenzie went right, but she let him draw her down the right path. Suddenly, across a hedge, they heard German voices.

"Fan out around this part of the gardens. A torch for every pair of men. Hauptmann Tirpitz wants them taken alive. He'll decide when they die!"

Their blood now thoroughly chilled like wine in ice, MacKenzie and Svetlana darted back to the three-way split. Now they were going in the direction she had wanted to go. They saw an end to the trees. Along the path, however, stood a German sentry at the ready. They ducked behind a thick trunk.

"What now?" MacKenzie hissed. "We can't go forward; we can't go backward. Just like Magersfontein!"

He had called it by name rather than that day. Somehow, the name did not strike terror in his heart like it used to. Still, he hesitated. "I'd hate to shoot without a declaration of war," he muttered.

Before he could stop her, Svetlana raised her Mauser to her shoulder and fired off a shot. The sentry howled amid a spurt of blood and crumpled to the ground.

She grinned like an imp as she cranked her bolt back. "Now you have to shoot them, or they'll shoot you," she said.

"Why, you vicious little—"

A shot cut him off. Svetlana turned and fired again at the soldier who had spotted them. Before MacKenzie could unsling his rifle, she had downed the other one with the torch.

"The torch!" MacKenzie hissed. "If we look like a pair of them also searching, they'll be less likely to pursue us."

They dashed back for the torch, then turned and darted out of the garden toward the north boundary of the park. Between the fence and the woods, MacKenzie decried a red house. To the east and west, he saw torchlights making for the woods, the obvious place the spies should head. Shouts of German were too close behind them to head back that way.

He suddenly remembered Gibson's words at the opera house. "There's a two-story red brick house just north of the grounds of Neues Palais that's being used as an armory in case of an emergency at the palace," he had said.

"The house!" MacKenzie said, "It's a secret armory belonging to the Order. We can hide in there until they pass by. They'd never suspect it. Follow me."

Climbing the fence, they used the torchlight to appear like any other pair of soldiers hunting for the spies as they made for the house. It had an unwelcome if not downright unusual air.

It had only one window on its south wall on the second floor, presumably to keep watch on Neues Palais and only one on the west side as they passed it. MacKenzie glanced about to see if anyone was watching out of the western window. At the north side, they encountered an iron-reinforced oaken door. MacKenzie confirmed that the torches to the east and west had already reached the woods.

MacKenzie pounded on the door. "Open in the name of the Order!"

A small panel shifted in the door, and two green eyes peered at them from the other side.

"Spies on the loose, man!" MacKenzie said. "It's an emergency, and we need to activate the armory."

"Brünnhilde!" the sentry gave the password.

"And her solo!" Svetlana provided the countersign she remembered from earlier that night.

The guard hurriedly unlocked the door and admitted them with a salute.

"Everything in order, Soldat?" MacKenzie asked. "Anyone else here to help?"

"Just me, sir—as usual."

MacKenzie swung his palm into the man's neck behind the ear. He collapsed, and MacKenzie and Svetlana caught their breath as MacKenzie relocked the door.

"I suppose you intend just to wait here?" she asked.

"We'll wait here just until they stop searching the woods, but meanwhile, we'll prepare for the worst. Let's close the windows and see what kind of weapons they've stored here."

Taking the guard's keys, they closed the single windows on each side, then unlocked the cellar door and hauled it open. MacKenzie groped for a hanging light switch and turned it on. Wooden crates of munitions lay stacked up from the bottom of the cellar almost to the top.

"Enough for a battalion, I'd say," MacKenzie said. "Let's at least take a Maxim upstairs to the window with all the ammunition we can carry."

"MG 01" was written on one of the crates in bold red letters. MacKenzie pulled it down while Svetlana procured a crowbar. Prying off the lid revealed the German army's version of the Maxim machine gun. MacKenzie and Svetlana carried it out of the cellar and up the stairs together.

The house proved to be more of a blockhouse. It had wooden steps on the right that ran up to a second floor, and beneath the window sat a platform for weapons like the Maxim. Other than that, it remained barren of all furniture or furnishings.

MacKenzie and Svetlana returned for as many belts of ammunition as they could carry after draping them over their shoulders. Just as they reached the top, they heard pounding on the door.

"Open in the name of the Order!"

"We can't open up! They'll ken it's us!" Svetlana hissed in Gaelic. "Hide out in here? It's a death trap now."

MacKenzie felt his face flush hot. "Who would've thought they'd break open an emergency arsenal over two measly spies?"

The pounding became louder. "In the name of the Order!"

"What do we do now?"

MacKenzie sighed. "Fight to the death. We'll make them kill us quick so they can't torture us slowly."

"The spies are in the armory!" voices clamored from outside. "Call the others!"

"Weel, Ranald, let's finally see if you can kill," Svetlana muttered as they raced back upstairs.

They opened the southern window and knelt behind the firing platform, MacKenzie on the right and Svetlana on the left. Shrill whistles pierced the night air. A squad came up at the double from the park. The Germans were close enough that MacKenzie had to use the foresight. No sense wasting the Maxim ammunition on such a small group.

MacKenzie groaned. The time had come to kill again. He had never relished that task, and after South Africa, he had hoped he would never be called upon to perform it again. Three years in intelligence work behind a desk, striving to prevent world war, and now the last thing he would do on earth would be to kill as many German soldiers as he could. He slid the safety from behind the receiver and raised the Lee-Enfield to his shoulder. He had ten rounds in the magazine and one in the chamber. He pulled the trigger.

With no more than a muzzle flash, the bullet went on its way through the five grooves of the barrel and at the nearest German at lightning speed. The shot flung the man back, but before the Germans could go to ground, Svetlana's Mauser had downed another. The Germans knelt and opened fire. Shots struck the brick exterior, and the spies returned fire. They accounted for two more.

MacKenzie fired repeatedly, the smooth action of the bolt replacing the rounds after each shot. The ejected cartridge cases tinkled in a pile at his feet.

He kept mental note of each round. Meanwhile he had to keep his eyes open for any new foes. Svetlana had to reload twice as much as MacKenzie, her Mauser holding half the ammunition of his and using a slower bolt.

By the time he had used up all ten rounds, the German squad had vanished from the face of the earth. MacKenzie shoved two five-round chargers in the magazine and peered out the window. A Wolfhart car, its headlights like a warship's searchlight, sped in from the west with another squad trailing it. The car mounted an MG 01.

"Can't have that," MacKenzie muttered.

He leveled the Lee-Enfield and sent a shot that ripped into the front left tire. The car shrieked in a spin and tumbled over like a wounded horse, hurling the MG 01 into the darkness.

Svetlana gasped. "Splendid shooting, Ranald!"

The squad that had accompanied the car sped toward the house. Two more squads appeared with ladders. A quick burst, they surely reasoned, and they would subdue the spies in the blockhouse.

"So far, we've just been serving lead appetizers," Svetlana said. "What do you say we give them the main course?" She picked up an ammunition belt for the Maxim and dangled it from her hand.

"I'll aim it; you feed it," MacKenzie said. "Switch places!"

The three squads had united and were rushing the house with the ladders. MacKenzie rolled behind the platform to gain the left side, and Svetlana rolled to the right.

MacKenzie took a belt of ammunition and inserted it into the feed block from the right, then grabbed the belt from the other side of the block and pulled it through until the cartridge lined up properly. He cranked on the cocking handle twice. Taking aim, he pressed his thumbs into the trigger.

The gun recoiled severely, recovered, and began to rattle off bullets with a series of "tac's". The recoil from each round sent the casing flying out of the gun and pulled the next into the chamber. The cases clanked on the floor with each of the tac-tac-tac's.

As Svetlana minded the ammunition belt, MacKenzie swept the gun around, mowing the squads like a scythe on grain. Men simply dropped to the earth like leaves in autumn, and the ladders lay where they had fallen.

Svetlana laughed. "Whatever happens, we have got, the Maxim gun, and they have not!"

MacKenzie groaned. "Dinna remind me *your* army has these things too."

With the treaty they carried, MacKenzie's chums might very well have Russians do unto them as MacKenzie and Svetlana were doing to the Germans. MacKenzie saw no way of stopping it now. He could only fight for a quick, relatively merciful end.

Even now, he did not lack an auld Highland saying: "He who lived longest, died at last."

A gunshot rang out from behind them, and a bullet pinged into the wall just inches from Svetlana's head. She gasped, and they both spun to see the sentry, whom MacKenzie had downed at the door, leveling a Mauser at Svetlana. His battered condition had affected his aim, and as he cranked back his bolt, MacKenzie snatched up his Webley from his holster and fired into the man's heart. The man shrieked as the shot blew him backward onto the stairs. His body thumped on his way to the bottom.

Svetlana exhaled sharply. "My thanks, Ranald."

"I thank God he didn't think to open the door to the others."

"He was probably still dazed after you thumped his skull."

MacKenzie slid his Webley back in his holster and surveyed the scene outside. More Germans, spread apart like acacias on the savanna, were arriving.

"I think they've learned not to rush us," MacKenzie said. "I guess now they'll want to shoot it out. They're too far apart for a Maxim."

Both sides readied their rifles, and the shooting contest began. The rifles thumped in antiphonal chorus, MacKenzie and Svetlana two soloists and the Germans a hellish choir of basses.

The Germans worked in pairs. As one fired lying down, the other advanced a few paces, and so on as they made their way forward. Even so, they suffered terribly under the two rifles of the spies. A few stray trees stood on either side of the house, and the Germans halted as they gained the cover from them.

A voice in German roared above the din. Suddenly, the guns facing MacKenzie and Svetlana fell silent. They could hear German orders, but they could not make out what was being said through the ringing in their ears. The German soldiers all went to ground and lay still. MacKenzie and Svetlana ducked back behind the wall on either side of the window.

"I imagine our respite is only temporary," Svetlana said.

MacKenzie nodded. "I think we stand about as much chance as the *Thunder Child* against the heat ray." He wanted to upbraid her for her impetuosity in opening fire, but he did not want his last words to her to be harsh. Besides, *he* had gotten them into this trap at the blockhouse.

"Ranald, in case we dinna make it out, I just want you to ken that I..." Svetlana began before catching herself. "That is, you're the finest human being I've ever kent. There's certainly no one like you in the Okhrana."

Tell her how you feel!

MacKenzie almost blurted out that he loved her. They were both about to die—what would it hurt?

"And if you had been with us in South Africa, the war would've ended much sooner," he said instead.

Some things never change, do they, laddie?

Svetlana smiled and drew her hair over her shoulder one last time. She clearly interpreted what he had said as a compliment of the highest order. She knew he loved her, MacKenzie realized. She delighted in that as much as, if not more than, any of her other conquests. She had messed with her hair to see the enchantment in his eyes as a final pleasant memory. As always, this tigress was toying with him. At the moment, he could not begrudge her.

The Mausers opened up simultaneously. MacKenzie and Svetlana rose up to return fire. A German dropped from the tree he had been hiding in. As he cranked the bolt, MacKenzie saw another leap up to throw a grenade. The man hurled it before MacKenzie could shoot him, so MacKenzie shot the grenade out of the air instead. It exploded.

"Nice shot, Ranald!" Svetlana said.

"No harder than pheasant."

A pounding sound came at the door downstairs. It was a boom of wood on wood, like an almighty bass drum.

"They're breaking the door down!" Svetlana said. "They'll be upon us in seconds."

MacKenzie's heart lightened. Escape *was* possible! "Or, if we can eliminate the party behind us, we can dash out the door and escape while the others think they have us caught."

The door pounded again.

Svetlana looked into his eyes. "Can we do that?" she asked.

Finally, MacKenzie had a chance to smile while leaving Svetlana in the dark. He relished it. As the ram thundered again and again on the door, MacKenzie emptied his clip into three more Germans and inserted two new ones. He drew back behind the wall.

"Keep them busy on this side and leave the rest to me."

"I'll try, sir," she said. It was the standard response of a soldier ordered to do something necessary but impossible.

MacKenzie nodded before he rolled under the windowsill and crept for the head of the stairs. They could hear indistinct shouts of German through the battered door. Svetlana could not use the Maxim without MacKenzie, but she left it there as a deterrent as she fired on with the Mauser.

MacKenzie lay down to use the floor to shield him. A crack appeared in the door as the Germans rammed it again. MacKenzie wanted to say some kind of prayer.

"Lord, please grant me just sixty seconds," he whispered under his breath as a boom heralded the appearance of three cracks in the door.

Another boom. The door burst open at the foot of the stairs in a shattering of splinters.

"*Tullach ard!*" MacKenzie shouted his clan's slogan as he shot the first soldier through the threshold: "The high hill!"

Before the German hit the wooden floor, MacKenzie likewise gunned down the man behind him. The third raised his Mauser to take aim, but MacKenzie put a .303 round in his chest before he could.

MacKenzie cranked his bolt back faster than they could aim, using his thumb and first finger and pulling the trigger with his second. The trusty weapon thumped and clinked as MacKenzie took shot after shot in a matter of seconds. The Germans rushed forward, but one dropped every two seconds.

He hoped Svetlana could spare a glance to see him now, blazing away with a ferocity like a shark in a feeding frenzy. Rather than a mindless franticness, however, his marksmanship proved quite deliberate. His thumb and finger remained fixed to the bolt just as his left arm fixed the butt to his shoulder. He did not linger over any target. He fired, trusted that the shot had struck home, and moved on to the next one.

No German could enter the house without being greeted by a bullet. There was a respite from the relentless stream of bullets only when MacKenzie had to reload, which took him barely seconds. During those seconds, the press of soldiers shoved the pile of the fallen clear from the doorway. The unscathed threw themselves down to take cover behind them, but MacKenzie just shot them through the crowns of their skulls.

A Mauser shot through the doorway in a belated reply. The bullet hissed within centimeters of his ear, whipping him with a gust as it went past. In a split second, MacKenzie had replied with a bullet of his own. This one did not miss. Others opened fire through the doorway, but none could hit MacKenzie's slim silhouette lying atop the stairs. His replies, on the other hand, were infallible.

MacKenzie cranked back his bolt and shoved in another two clips just in time to drop four more. He readied another shot, but no target presented itself. In less than sixty seconds, he had downed as many enemies as a Maxim might have.

He leaped to his feet. "Come on!" he called in Gaelic.

Svetlana fired one more shot and jumped back to join him.

"What on earth was that?" Svetlana asked.

"Do you not have Mad Minutes in your army?" he said as they raced down the stairs, referring to the Royal Army drill he had just put into practice.

"Ranald, you're a killing machine!" she squealed. "I'm thoroughly impressed!"

They trampled over the German bodies and burst out the door with rifles ready. Not a foe stood against them, though thirty-seven lay sprawled at the door. MacKenzie thought he noticed Hauptmann Tirpitz lying bleeding at their feet, but he could spare no more than a glance.

MacKenzie and Svetlana dashed toward the woods to the north of the blockhouse. Every moment, they expected a bullet in their backs, but they allowed nothing to impede their steps. MacKenzie's codename wasn't Cheetah for nothing.

Behind them, all had fallen quiet. The soldiers who had shot at the window had doubtless become confused, MacKenzie concluded. They had expected their overwhelming force at the door to have dealt with their opponents inside and had surmised from the cessation of the shooting that MacKenzie and Svetlana were dead or captured. They waited in vain for an, "all clear!" from their comrades.

With one final sprint, MacKenzie and Svetlana burst through the tree line. They kept running deep into the forest, holding hands to keep from breaking up as they dashed around trunks and under branches.

"Make a sharp right!" MacKenzie said in Gaelic.

Before long, they had emerged from the trees on the other side of the forest. Finally, they paused to catch their breaths.

"They've figured out by now that we've gone, but we're out of the gravest danger," MacKenzie said between gasps. "We'll simply march back to the train. Remember to bear yourself like a soldier."

"Please, Ranald! If I can dance in high heels, I think I can manage whatever you soldiers do."

Still breathing rapidly, they made their way to the train where they had deposited their baggage. They recognized the painted writing on the rusty cars and the navy-blue engine. In a few minutes, the train would set off for Russia to pick up the grain on which the Germans had recently placed exorbitant tariffs. By the time they reached it, the railway workers were making the final preparations for its departure. They waited nonchalantly at a respectful distance as the men closed the cars and moved on.

With one final sprint, they reached one of the middle cars. As the train's whistle shrieked, MacKenzie thrust open the door and climbed inside. They had chosen the right car; their trunks with their effects lay hidden in the darkness of the corner.

MacKenzie held out his hand to help Svetlana up. Her feet lifted off the ground just as the car began moving. They shut the door.

MacKenzie fumbled in the darkness for the trunk and produced one of Archimedes' miniature lanterns. The faint orange glow left most of the car in shadowy darkness, but they could at least see each other. MacKenzie sighed and put his safety on. He rubbed his right shoulder, which had been thumped by recoil more times than he could count.

"That's going to hurt tomorrow."

Svetlana beamed, her smile brightening the darkness. "Weel done, Ranald."

He glared at her.

"I said, 'Weel done,'" she repeated.

"You really ken how to cause trouble, don't you? You savage little *Oprichnika!*" Now he could afford to be harsh.

She grinned. Russia's first secret police, Ivan the Terrible's *Oprichniki*, had used dog heads as one of their emblems. She fished in her pocket and produced her necklace with its howling dog.

"So you recognize the reference in it. A symbol of three and a half centuries of order over the unruly peasant. I just wanted to make sure you'd be willing to shoot if we were caught."

"It would have been no wonder if we had been with you provoking a noisy firefight like that! Sneaking by would have been the more prudent choice."

"And whose idea was it to head for the blockhouse instead of the trees?"

They glared at each other for an instant, but Svetlana soon smiled her sly fox's grin. "But Ranald, we're safe, and we have the treaty. What more could you ask for? We make a very good team, actually." She stroked his arm.

MacKenzie released his clenched teeth with a sigh of relief. "Aye, we do."

He could not deny that he would have found it hard to shoot Germans without Svetlana forcing his hand.

Svetlana gasped and pointed to the corner. "What's that?"

MacKenzie turned to look where she was pointing. Almost immediately, he heard her bolt mechanism lock. He spun back to ask what the matter was. To his astonishment, he found Svetlana's Mauser gaping inches from his own chest.

CHAPTER 21: THE RITUAL

"Sveta! What the deuce do you think you're doing?"

Her face, half-covered in shadow, half-lit by orange light, looked like a tiger in ambuscade.

"The camera, if you please," she said.

"It's British property! I'll not give it to a Russian!"

"I thought you'd feel that way. That's why I'm not asking nicely."

"Is this Russian gratitude after I saved your life?"

She cocked her head. "It's more like Ukrainian determination. It's nothing personal; I have a mission to accomplish. The camera."

MacKenzie crossed his arms.

"I will have that treaty whether you're dead or alive," she said. "Why would you die when it will do no good?"

"What happened to the very good team we made?"

"Only one person can have that camera now."

Her firm jaw underpinned a deadly scowl. MacKenzie recognized the same coldness in her eyes he had seen when she had gunned down the revolutionary. She had every indication of being serious. She was actually betraying him this time! Sighing with chagrin, he fished the flask out of his pocket and handed it to Svetlana. She stashed it in her trunk and locked it. She put her own safety on and laid the rifle on the floor.

She grinned like a goblin. "You really thought I was going to shoot you, didn't you?"

"With you, I never ken. You're like confounded quicksilver."

"In faith, there's only one weapon of mine I want to use against you..."

To MacKenzie's surprise, Svetlana threw her arms around his neck, drew him to her, and pressed her lips to his. He was less surprised that he found himself kissing her back and stroking her luxuriant hair. The rivalry between their two nations, the fact that in that camera was a document that would set them at war, meant absolutely nothing at that moment.

MacKenzie felt the reciprocating engine pounding against his ribs. His whole body felt aflame. He never would have guessed his heart and his lips could contain such passion. Svetlana drew him down to the floor of the railway car and began to undo his top buttons.

MacKenzie broke her embrace and suddenly leaped back up, his entire face flushed. "Och, Sveta, dinna! I can't do such a thing!"

Svetlana laughed, remaining where she was. "Dinna stop on account of *my* reputation, Ranald. It'd be the first time I made love with someone I respect."

He fell back further. "I stop on God's account. Maybe you wouldn't feel badly, but I assure you, I'd hate myself in the morning."

Svetlana groaned and drew herself back up. "You and your self-denial, Ranald. You make yourself so miserable and guilty."

"That may be, but at least I didn't make myself one flesh with an anarchist."

Svetlana gasped and swung her hand to slap his face, but MacKenzie caught her wrist.

"Why are you angry if it was the moral thing to do, as you said before?"

She snatched her hand back. For once, she had no answer.

"I have another question," he said. "Why, after all we've been through, did you kiss me now? Why, after you just betrayed me?"

"I told you it was nothing personal! You really impressed me, Ranald, with that Mad Minute. Up until then, I thought of you as smart and decent but weak. Now I see you're a predator like me! We're two alpha wolves, Ranald, you and I."

"I pray God I'm not like you, Sveta."

"You sound pious now, but in sixty seconds, you killed more enemies than I did on the entire mission. You just need a little provocation."

"I need a *duty* to kill..." MacKenzie glanced down. He didn't want to consider it anything shameful to be a soldier, but when she put it like that...

Suddenly, he brightened and lifted his head. "Och, I feel I should advise you. Only Archie kens how to access the film in that camera. You'd better return it to me if it's to be developed. I promise I'll give you a copy."

"We'll find a way ourselves, thank you."

"I must warn you, if you make a mistake and expose that film, the past three months will be for naught. It's rigged to expose the film if not handled just right in case it should ever fall into the wrong hands—like now."

Svetlana sighed and went back to the trunk. She withdrew the camera but held it just out of MacKenzie's reach.

"And you swear to me you'll let me have a copy of the treaty?"

"Aye. What possible reason would I have for not giving it to you?"

She sighed again and handed the camera over.

London
August 20, 1905

Once the train had passed into Russia, getting back to Britain proved no challenge. MacKenzie had not expected any, as long as Svetlana needed the treaty from him.

Explaining their presence when the Russians opened the car door was a little awkward, but Svetlana's Okhrana identification silenced all questions. After reaching St. Petersburg, they sailed across the Baltic and the North Seas and arrived back in London.

At a loss for what else to do, MacKenzie brought Svetlana to his living quarters at Finsbury. He was not about to take her to Vittoria House now that he knew she was a Russian subject.

"This is my flat. You can wait here while I report to headquarters with the camera. I'm certain they'll be willing to provide you a copy when they hear what you plan to do with it."

Svetlana's wide eyes flitted about. "Ranald! I wouldn't keep a dog in this hellhole!"

"It's nothing compared to what you've shown me over the past three months, but I'd wager it's better than what you had before you met Rachkovsky."

"All right, you have me there."

"Make yourself at home, and I'll bring you your copy of the treaty when Archie's got it developed."

"Make it quick. Dear me, look at this place!"

Svetlana's remarks about his quarters barely dampened MacKenzie's enthusiasm as he danced away to Vittoria House. He marched down the steps and into the headquarters with the air of a Roman general in his chariot at a triumph.

"Blimey, Captain Ranald MacKenzie! Bless my soul, you're alive!"

Audrey leaped from her desk, embraced MacKenzie's arm, and kissed his cheek. Once, MacKenzie would have given that arm for a kiss from her, but now he did not feel so sure.

"What a loss about Captain Gibson!" Audrey continued. "Until this moment, I feared they got you too. I didn't know if I could believe your radio report that you'd succeeded. Those treacherous Huns! Do you have it?"

He withdrew the camera with a grin and held it like a trophy. "I wouldn't have returned without it."

"Go straight to Archie. He's instructed to make five copies: one for His Majesty, one for the cabinet, one for the Foreign Office, one for the colonel, and one for the War Department."

"Make that six. I have a contact who will present a copy to the members of the Russian cabinet most likely to object."

"Ow, Ranald! That's blooming fantastic!"

Archimedes lost no time disappearing into his darkroom and developing the film from the camera. To MacKenzie's relief, the words came out quite clearly, and anyone could see the signatures matched the Kaiser and the Tsar's handwriting. As he returned to Finsbury, it felt like he was on a celestial road among the clouds.

"We both got what we wanted," MacKenzie said as he handed Svetlana the photograph.

She cocked her head with a coquettish gaze. "You got *all* you wanted?" she said coyly.

"Everything I was assigned to get. My superiors were silent on the subject of finding a girlfriend."

She smiled her fox's grin. "So you have leeway in that area?"

"Lassie, think of what our superiors would say! A Briton and a Russian subject! Our countries have been rivals for years. You just went to war with our ally and fired on our fishing vessels. This very piece of paper is as good as a declaration of war! It would be career suicide."

She dropped her chin and looked deeply into his eyes. "Ranald, I love only three men in this world. One's my adoptive father, another's the Little Father, and... you're the third."

Her eyes glistened with forming tears.

MacKenzie sighed. "If only I could trust those eyes."

She inhaled sharply. "Ooh, Ranald, you wound me! Crocodile tears at a time like this? The mission's over; I'm not hiding anything from you."

"It doesn't change facts, Sveta."

She grasped his shoulders in supplication. "Ranald, do you think me loveless? Do you think me hard as nails? Aye, I am, but not with you! Would you send me off to shiver alone in a prison of cold-heartedness?"

It's better than the prison of cold frost you send your enemies to.

MacKenzie almost put a voice to that thought, but he realized he could not bear to be cruel to her. "Sveta, we have to face reality," he whispered instead. "What would your father say to the two of us?"

Svetlana drew her mouth nearer to his. "Kiss me before you ask that," she whispered back.

She drew her hair back and over one shoulder. MacKenzie felt like he might drop to his knees. He realized he was sweating when he felt a trickle run down his temple.

He gently edged her back. "Lana, there's more in the world for me to think of than your lips—or hair."

"But you ken you love me!"

"You stole my heart, Sveta, not my head. And you—what do you think your Little Father would say?"

"That isn't fair."

"It isn't fair to remind you of your oath to Russia? I ken I have one to Britain."

Svetlana looked down. Her whole body heaved with a sigh such as she had exhaled all the breath in her lungs. "Aye, it's fair. I guess it wasn't meant to be."

"So, I suppose this is fareweel."

She gave another coquettish smile. "Not quite yet. There's still time for us to participate in a little ritual I do after my successful missions, which is to say, all of them."

"What is it?"

"I'll explain later. First, we need to go to your favorite pub."

"The Breaches at Badajoz it is, then," MacKenzie said.

The somewhat ramshackle Breaches at Badajoz was, despite appearances, a very respectable establishment. That it maintained respectability seemed a marvel, for the story went that an English sergeant had founded it using his plunder from the infamous sack of Badajoz in Spain. The red brick exterior had sometimes haunted MacKenzie with memories of that day, but not this time. He opened the glass door for Svetlana and entered the pub with its atmosphere of smoke, chatter, and peppy tunes from performers in the corner.

"Is the private-saloon bar here worth the extra cost?" Svetlana asked.

"Can't afford it."

"Tonight, you can."

As she led him to the more expensive part of the pub, a second thought flashed across MacKenzie's mind. He knew where the funds to pay for the more exclusive service had come from. Still, he felt too curious about Svetlana's victory ritual to object.

A waiter in a white apron approached them. He was still wiping a wet glass with a towel.

"Your finest vodka, please," Svetlana said.

"Dewar's," MacKenzie said with a nod before turning back to Svetlana. "So this ritual isn't that complicated, is it? I must confess, I'm a little too tired still for anything terribly involved."

"Och, no. People do it every day. It's so easy, anyone can do it."

"Good."

The barman returned with the drinks.

"To the men at Magersfontein!" MacKenzie said as he lifted his glass.

"And confound the anarchists!" Svetlana added.

MacKenzie took a sip of his Scotch, but Svetlana quaffed her vodka. She immediately shuddered.

"This is terrible vodka!"

"You can try the Scotch instead."

"No, this will have to do. The second won't be as bad. Another, please."

MacKenzie had almost finished his Dewar's when Svetlana received and drained a second glass of vodka.

She cringed. "Dear me, this is going to be a long night if you fellows can't do any better than this," she said.

"We could skip to your ritual."

"Order another Dewar's."

For Svetlana's third round, and MacKenzie's second, MacKenzie determined to drink his as quickly as she downed hers. It seemed a shame not to savor the flavor of the whiskey, but honor demanded he not seem less manly than a woman.

"That's the style, Ranald," Svetlana said. "Another! You should get one too, Ranald. My father is paying…"

"You realize, I'm not going to get in a drinking contest with you."

"Fine—do it at your own pace."

MacKenzie returned to drinking half as quickly as Svetlana.

"Will you at least give me a hint as to what this ritual might be?" MacKenzie said after another round.

Svetlana held her index finger up as she upturned another glass of vodka.

Before much longer, MacKenzie felt the Scotch at work. He put his glass down. "Weel, that settles for me. I hate the feeling of alcohol. I only put up with it to the extent I have to."

Svetlana began weeping into her hands. "So much blood! Och, so much blood! If only these tears could wash it from my hands!"

"You… feel guilty?"

"Do you think I find it easy to kill? Did you see the look on that revolutionary's face when I shot him?"

"I saw it."

"Another memory seared into my brain!" she said through a sharp inhalation.

"If you feel that way, why don't you quit the Okhrana?"

"I gave my oath! And if I dinna do what makes me weep, they'll make countless millions in Russia, Ukraine, and the whole world weep instead. They *make* me kill them, Ranald. Their blood be upon their own heads."

"Then why do you want to wash it from your hands?"

Another vodka arrived for Svetlana. She snatched it up. "Thank heaven."

"In faith, Lana! I've had as much Scotch as I dare, and I ken you've had too much vodka. Now what is this ritual?"

"We've done it already," she said with her fox's grin, followed by a hiccup. "After every successful mission, I get dead drunk."

"Dead drunk? How is that a wise thing to do?"

"I didn't say it was *wise;* it's *necessary* for me to retain my sanity. I can't even remember the night after I got back from Siberia. For one night, at least, I can find some relief and peace of mind."

"By stupefying your conscience?"

"I have to silence it! It's wrong! It can't be moral to let them seize Russia!"

"*My* conscience is clear."

She swallowed her vodka, paused, and burped. "Perhaps guilt isn't the right word. I am preventing an unspeakable calamity from befalling the world, so I should have no reason to feel guilty. Let's call it uneasiness instead."

"It certainly seemed like guilt a second ago."

"Whatever it is, enough vodka can shut it up for one night."

"And what if you slip and let your identity be kent while you're drunk?"

"I dinna touch a drop until I have completely eliminated the enemy."

Another glass of vodka, and her "uneasiness" passed. She began singing from "The Polovtsian Dances." MacKenzie knew that it was originally an awe-inspiring vocal part, but she could do nothing but butcher it in her state. She slurred the lyrics and sloppily transitioned between notes.

She laughed. "I ken Scottish drinking songs. 'Garryowen,' perhaps?"

"That's Irish."

"Weren't your ancestors Irish at one point too, you Highlander?"

"Aye."

She thumped the table. "Come on! You could use a lighthearted song, I should think."

MacKenzie cocked his head in acquiescence.

Svetlana burst out:

> *Let Bacchus' sons be not dismayed,*
> *But join with me, each jovial blade.*
> *Come drink and sing and lend your aid,*
> *To help me with the chorus.*
>
> *For instead of spa, we'll drink down ale*
> *And pay the reckoning on the nail.*
> *No man for debt shall go to jail*
> *From Garryowen in glory.*

MacKenzie was impelled to join in. He never could resist the charm of that number.

Now *he* thumped the table. "Now for a Scottish one! 'Bonnie Dundee!'"

Svetlana hiccupped and sang along with MacKenzie:

> *To the Lords in Convention 'twas Claverhouse spoke:*
> *Ere the king's crown go down, there are crowns to be broke.*
> *So let each cavalier that loves honor and me,*
> *Let him follow the bonnets of Bonnie Dundee.*
>
> *Come fill up my cup; come fill up my can.*
> *Come saddle my horses, and call out my men.*
> *Unhook the west port, and let us go free,*
> *For it's up with the bonnets o' Bonnie Dundee!*

The two would not have appeared fit to sing at that moment to an objective observer, but to themselves, they sounded like mated nightingales delighting in each other's calls.

"Your knowledge of Scottish culture is impressive," MacKenzie said.

She hiccupped again. "Thank you."

"You almost convinced me you were Scottish. If you hadn't been angry about Tsushima or I hadn't seen the Cyrillic writing in your bag..."

"Och, I'm Ukrainian to the bone, but I do so admire your culture, Ranald. Those Jacobites trying to uphold a rightful, lawful king against upstart revolutionaries—no wonder it resonates with me. But I've been doing this Scottish act for so long, I'm practically Scottish as weel."

If only you were Scottish! If only you were.

***

MacKenzie fairly well staggered into headquarters the next day.

"Ow, Ranald, two hours late!" Audrey said. "That's summat you never do."

"Believe me, I wasn't fit for duty two hours ago. I'm still exhausted from all that."

Audrey grinned. "And celebrating your victory, I'd wager."

"Aye, with my Russian contact. She insisted."

Audrey's eyes narrowed suspiciously. "*She?*"

"Nothing happened!" MacKenzie said.

Just the same, Audrey seemed little settled by his response. "The colonel wants a report," she said formally.

Could she be jealous?

MacKenzie went to his desk and recounted in handwriting all the events from the meeting with Field. As he did, he could not believe he had survived everything he described. Every week, his life had been endangered by some new threat. Had he faced greater threats than he had on that day? One thing seemed certain: he could scarcely feel afraid again after all that.

Audrey delivered his report, and a few moments later, she summoned him to Connally's office. MacKenzie entered and jumped to a salute to find Connally beaming.

"That's my boy! I told you that you could do it, and bless my soul, you did. A Russian contact presenting the treaty to those who will oppose it? You exceeded my expectations. For our part, we have sent copies to His Majesty and the PM, who have arranged meetings with the French president. We'll torpedo this thing for sure. As for you, I doubt you'll ever find yourself behind a desk again. You spent the last three months scraping the moss off your bum, and I don't want it to ever accumulate there again."

"Sir?"

"I want you to be a field agent permanently, MacKenzie. I'm going to send you all over Europe. Seems to me, you're the best we've got."

MacKenzie thought back to his days as intelligence officer in South Africa. Until this moment, he hadn't realized how much he had missed those days. He had proven himself capable of shouldering this burden once again, and his heart glowed.

He would see to it there would never be another day like that day for the Royal Army. Now that he had conquered his fear, he was willing to go anywhere His Majesty sent him, as long as Providence went with him.

MacKenzie bowed his head. "I always kent God had preserved me through that day. Until this moment, I never kent why."

"That's a debt I'm going to see that you repay. You'll be jolly busy, my boy! There's no end of world saving for you to do!"

EPILOGUE

London
October 1, 1905

Nearly two months later, MacKenzie woke from a very pleasant dream in his flat to find an envelope below his mail slot. Picking it up, he saw a Russian postmark but no return address.

He scanned it and detected the so-called "fly," that inconspicuous mark of an Okhrana agent who had read the letter and was signaling to other Okhrana agents not to bother reading it again. He had no doubt as he opened the envelope that the same person who had written the letter had put the mark there. His hand trembling slightly with anticipation, he tore it open and withdrew the letter.

My dearest Ranald,

I ken that right now the horror haunts you and your superiors of confronting Russia, Germany, Italy, Austria-Hungary, and France together. I ken you all shiver at the thought of Russian armies pouring into India while French ships ferry hundreds of thousands of Hun soldiers over the North Sea into England. I realize it is not from lack of courage, for Britain has faced down the whole of Europe before, but simply from the reality that all Europe has become industrialized, and its conscripted armies are vastly superior in numbers to yours.

It is therefore my supreme pleasure to inform you that, according to my sources, we have together scored a great triumph in the name of global peace! Equipped with our forewarning, Grand Duke Nicholas and Count Lamsdorf have scuttled the whole unholy compact. They steel themselves with assurances from our ambassador in Paris that the French will sign no accord with Germany. They are hardened in that resolve, no doubt, by your prime minister's remonstrations and promises of support. Now the Russian cabinet has no intention of abiding by the Treaty of Bjorko. They have decided they would follow the most honorable course by adhering to their solemn oaths to France.

I pray that the frostiness between our two nations might soon thaw. With the French courting you, surely they will mediate a reconciliation and an end to this ridiculous, unnecessary, so-called Great Game between Russia and Britain. I am certain that the statesmen on both sides of the Baltic will realize that there are more important things to think of than who owns the steppes! Think—Russia, France, and Britain hemming Germany in on all sides! I long for this turn of events.

Doubtless, it would bring your people peace of mind after the chilling realization of loneliness when you fought the Boers in the face of all Europe's condemnation. And how better for my people to stem the bloody tide of revolution than to link arms with strong allies? Best of all, there would be no obstacles between us save distance, and technology is decreasing that all the time.

With fondest adoration,
Svetlana

MacKenzie donned his uniform to deliver the heartening news to Connally. His hand fluttered over the VC. For once, he gave no thought to the holes in his tunic. As he buttoned it, however, he paused.

"Russia, France, and Britain," he muttered to himself. "Is that the best way to win the war with Germany or the worst way to stay out of it?"

GLOSSARY

Ach: In German, "oh."

Aesir: The name of the Norse pantheon.

All Sir Garnet: A Victorian expression for, "Everything in order," a reference to the efficiency of General Garnet Wolseley.

Auld: In Scots, "old."

Awa': In Scots, "away."

Aye, fairly: In Scots, "yes, indeed."

Bedeen: In Scots, "quickly."

Bitte: In German, "please."

Bobby: British slang for a policeman.

Da: In Russian, "yes."

"Deutschland über Alles": A song on the theme of German unification, "Germany above All."

"Die Walküre": In German, "The Valkyrie," the second opera in Richard Wagner's Ring Cycle.

Dinna: In Scots, "do not."

DMO: Director of Military Operations.

Einherjar: The "valiant slain" who fight for the Norse gods.

Fareweel: In Scots, "farewell."

Fräulein: The German form of address for an unmarried woman.

Gang: In Scots, "go."

Gey and: In Scots, "very."

Götterdämmerung: In German, "Twilight of the Gods," the fourth and last opera in Richard Wagner's Ring Cycle.

Gut: In German, "good."

Hamelier fare: In Scots, "plainer food."

Hauptmann: In German, "Captain."

Ja: In German, "yes."

Jawohl: In German, "yes, sir."

Kameraden: In German, "Comrades."

Kelpie: A Scottish mythological water-horse.

Ken: In Scots, "know."

Kent: In Scots, "knew," or "known."

La Belle Dame sans Merci: In French, "The Beautiful Lady without Mercy."

Le Général Russe: In French, "The Russian General," a nickname of Peter Ivanovich Rachkovsky's.

Liebchen: In German, "dear."

Little Father: The Tsar's nickname among the Russian people.

Mein Herr, Meine Frau: In German, "Sir, Madam."

Meine Herren: In German, "Gentlemen."

Nark: A police informer.

Nein: In German, "no."

Neues Palais: Kaiser Wilhelm II's favorite palace. It means "New Palace" in French.

Nyet: In Russian, "no."

Oberst: In German, "Colonel."

Ower thrifty wee mannie: In Scots, "over-thrifty wee little man."

Peeler: British slang for a policeman.

Prost: The generic German toast, like, "cheers," in English.

Sae rantingly, sae wantonly, sae dauntingly gaed he: In Scots, "So rantingly, so wantonly, so dauntingly went he."

Soldat: In German, "Private."

Summat: British word for "something."

Tommy: A nickname for British soldiers.

Torch: British term for a flashlight.

Touche-à-tout: In French, "one who touches everything."

Tsaritsa: In Russian, "Empress," often called Tsarina in English.

Uitlanders: In Afrikaans, foreigners living in the Boer republics.

Untermenschen: In German, "the under-races."

Unteroffizier: In German, "Corporal."

"Up and Waur Them A', Willie": In Scots, "Up and Worst Them All, Willie," a folk song about the 1715 Battle of Sheriffmuir, also "Up and Warn A', Willie."

Verst: An old Russian unit of measurement, about two-thirds of a mile or a little over a kilometer.

Weaponshaw: In Scots, an inspection of soldiers.

Weel: In Scots, "well."

Weel than: In Scots, "very much."

Ye loons: In Scots, "you rogues."

Yobbo: British slang for an awkward brute.

Zakuska: Traditional Russian hors d'oeuvres.

HISTORICAL NOTE

The spies in this book are all fictional (other than the odd reference to Sydney Reilly), but the mystery they are trying to solve is real. During the Russo-Japanese War, Kaiser Wilhelm II paid court to his cousin Tsar Nicholas II in telegraphs and written correspondence. His messages subtly and, at times not so subtly, sought to create an alliance between Germany and Russia against Britain. He clearly desired to suck in France, Russia's ally, as well. With Germany already a member of the Triple Alliance with Italy and Austria-Hungary, this would create a Quintuple Alliance of every major power in Europe. In this way, he hoped to overpower his uncle, Britain's King Edward VII, whom he detested.

His ultimate motives are a little controversial. The splendid 1974 British miniseries *Fall of Eagles* tells of the demises of the Hohenzollern (German), Habsburg (Austrian), and Romanov (Russian) Dynasties. These families all used eagles as their family symbols, hence the name. Its rather sympathetic portrait of Wilhelm paints him as merely trying to insure Germany against the two-front war that eventually caused its downfall in both World Wars. Commentators closer to events, however, saw a conniving Kaiser cajoling a credulous Tsar into a compact that would make Germany overlord of Europe and could challenge the British Empire.

I personally think the truth about Wilhelm lies somewhere between the version in *Fall of Eagles* and the propaganda of World War I. The first makes him an overgrown child given a toy too big for him to handle in the German Empire, and in the second, he is a monster second only to Hitler. I am deeply indebted to the inspiration of *Fall of Eagles*, without which I would not have known about the secret treaty.

This novel came about after I dreamed a version of the events in Chapters 5 and 6 and adapted it to the story I had learned from the *Fall of Eagles* episode, "Dearest Nicky." The episode uses actual quotations from the Willy-Nicky correspondence.

Whatever Wilhelm's intentions, the leading Russian ministers torpedoed the alliance as a dishonorable betrayal of their eleven-year-old treaty with France. In reality, the British government had nothing to do with stopping the treaty. They knew the meeting at Bjorko had happened but did not know what the sovereigns had discussed there.

As he is credited with in the novel, Peter Rachkovsky of the Russian Okhrana really did help engineer the prior arrangement between Russia and France. He made republican France a palatable ally for autocratic Russia by arranging for it to publicly crack down on anarchists. Their mutual rivalry with Germany did the rest. When Wilhelm finally got his war with Britain, he had Russia against him instead of backing him up.

Since Britain went to war to protect Russia and France in World War I, it can be a little hard to conceive what bitter antagonists Britain and Russia had been just a few years before. The Great Game, as they called it, saw Britain and Russia competing over Central Asia (especially Afghanistan).

Britain ended its period of Splendid Isolation, in which it eschewed all foreign entanglements, by allying with Russia's rival, Japan, precisely to contain Russian influence in the Pacific. The British and Russians had not fought an actual war since the Crimean War in the 1850s, but countless scares had taken place. At one point, annoyed by Russian designs in the Balkans, the British sang in their dance halls, "We don't want to fight, but by jingo if we do, we've got the men, we've got the ships, and we've got the money too. The Russians shall not have Constantinople."

Wilhelm had his chance to ally with Russia precisely because Britain protested the assistance Germany gave Russia in its war with Japan. This included coaling Russia's Baltic Fleet as it sailed around the world to its doom at Tsushima. The fleet also fired on British fishermen at the Dogger Bank as it set out, which did nothing to improve Anglo-Russian relations. The Germans chose to roll the dice shortly after the Russo-Japanese War, hoping that Russia would not befriend Britain against them because they thought the two rivals hated each other too much to actually reconcile. It was a deadly miscalculation.

Regarding the use of the Mad Minute in the climax, I am aware that the particular drill and the colloquial name for it were not invented for another three or four years. The gun that could achieve this wonder, however, the bolt-action Lee-Enfield, did exist. MacKenzie only anticipates by a few years the crack marksmanship of the British Expeditionary Force at the onset of World War I. The BEF's consummate skill with bolt-action rifles made the Germans think they faced machine guns when they did not. When Ranald MacKenzie got in a scrape, I could not resist using a slight anachronism to get him out of it.

Regarding the espionage organizations used in the novel, I must confess to using a very free hand to make the novel suitable to a modern audience while retaining a historical setting. In fact, Britain and Germany did not care much for covert espionage before World War I. Most of their intelligence simply came from reading foreign publications. At this period, though, the British public devoured "invasion novels" with foreign spies and outside threats to Britain, the two most enduring of which are H.G. Wells's *War of the Worlds* and, arguably, Bram Stoker's *Dracula*. There were, it seems, far more enemy spies in British literature of the time than there were in Britain itself.

The Order of Siegfried is a complete fabrication, but a fitting foe bent on world domination for my hero to strive against. True to the novel, however, in 1905, British secret agents were actually overseen by the two officers in MO3. The famous MI5 and MI6 were still a few years down the road. The secret base at Vittoria House, as well as Archimedes and his technology, are also fictional. The Directorate of Military Operations was based at this time at Winchester House on St. James's Square.

The most realistically portrayed spy organization in the book is the Okhrana. Russia spent the most time and energy on covert espionage of any country before World War I. It may seem odd, given the current horrors wrought by Russia in Ukraine, for Svetlana to be Ukrainian and a fervent supporter of the Russian Tsar, but in a 1905 context, this makes much more sense. Ukrainian nationalism (which we see Svetlana shares) was just beginning to bloom, and the Tsar's Russification policies, while it may have irked the Ukrainian nationalists, were nowhere near as brutal as the persecution of Poles and Jews in the empire. Many Ukrainians still saw themselves as Little Russians and part of Russia's overall cultural heritage.

Svetlana is quite right to fear revolution more than Russification. The eventual beneficiary of the Russian Revolution, Josef Stalin, persecuted the

Ukrainians with bloody savagery costing millions of lives (such that many of them were willing to collaborate even with Hitler against him) and made a famine out of a grain-producing farmland so fertile that it had fed Ancient Greece. And we have all seen what the current beneficiary of the Russian Revolution (i.e., Putin) is capable of doing against Ukraine. His atrocities are in the vein of Tsar Ivan the Terrible, to be sure, but not Nicholas II or his immediate predecessors.

I would like to make clear that I do not share Svetlana's anti-Semitism. That remains a touch of realism, for though Rachkovsky's real best agent, Arkady Harting, was Jewish, the Okhrana could be viciously anti-Semitic. This was the time of violent anti-Jewish riots in Russia called pogroms. I hope you will take MacKenzie's remonstration with Svetlana when she insults the Jews and his missionary outreach to Tirzah as my own response to the Okhrana's irrational hatred. I usually agree with him rather than her.

A note on my sources. The Scripture quotations are taken from the exact wording of the 1611 King James Version, with my own updates to its spelling and punctuation. MacKenzie's Highland sayings all come from Donald MacIntosh's *A Collection of Gaelic Proverbs, and Familiar Phrases; Accompanied with an English Translation*, published in 1785.

The experience of a traumatic "that day" by each of my three main characters was inspired by the title of Rudyard Kipling's 1895 poem about the British disaster at Maiwand in Afghanistan. Svetlana and Tirpitz's "those days" are fictitious, but MacKenzie's "that day" at Magersfontein really happened and unfolded just as he narrates it when he bares his soul to Svetlana in Chapter 17.

The title of Chapter 20, "The Unforgiving Minute," is likewise borrowed from Kipling's poem, "If." MacKenzie's rallying cry at Magersfontein comes from my favorite Scottish number, "Up and Waur 'Em A', Willie." It is a "canty Highland song" from the 18th century about the Battle of Sheriffmuir. "Waur" is Scots for "to worst." The chorus from "MacPherson's Rant" comes from Robert Burns's version of the song. The tune and the lyrics, however, are traditionally traced back to the condemned outlaw Jamie MacPherson himself.

Two of my other favorite folk songs make an appearance at the end— the Irish "Garryowen" and the Scottish "Bonnie Dundee." Sir Walter Scott wrote "Bonnie Dundee," but I do not think anyone knows who originally wrote "Garryowen." Some readers will also have noticed a couple of lines from Shakespeare.

The quotations from the Willy-Nicky telegrams are, to the best of my knowledge, the original wording, since they were written in English. The text comes from *The Willy-Nicky Correspondence: Being the Secret and Intimate Telegrams Exchanged Between the Kaiser and the Tsar* by Herman Bernstein, which Theodore Roosevelt provided a foreword for, and was published by Alfred A. Knopf in 1918.

My paraphrase of the treaty (which was originally written in French) comes from *The Kaiser's Letters to the Tsar*, a collection copied by Isaac Don Levine, edited by N.F. Grant, and published by Hodder and Stoughton in 1920. Due to the publication dates, these works are all in the public domain in the United States.

ACKNOWLEDGMENTS

I am very grateful to those who have assisted me with turning this book into a reality. I would like to thank my beta readers: Len, Bridget, and my father. My great friend Will was an "unofficial" editor who has always provided good spiritual counsel in general and on my books in particular. He's usually the first to know when I have a new book idea. My developmental editor, Rachel Song, deserves much of the credit as well for her very helpful critique and her assistance with my Internet platform (for a Millennial, I'm not too handy with technology), and I am very grateful to my friend Claire for getting us in touch. Nathan Mallett, the editor of MilitaryHistoryNow, also helped me with the marketing for this book by editing and posting my listicles on his site, particularly the one on British Intelligence before MI6. Lyndsey Lewellen brought my characters to life on the front cover. I also thank Pam Gossiaux for being my book shepherd and playing a vital role in getting this novel published.

ABOUT THE AUTHOR

Douglas Brown has loved writing about history since the age of six, when he began composing stories about his toy soldier displays. He carried both passions into college, graduating with a major in History and a minor in English. He's proud of his ancestral heritage, with relations hailing from every nation in the British Isles—Scotland, England, Ireland, and Wales—and he often incorporates much of the culture into his work. He lives in Texas with his two West Highland White Terriers and continues to write historical novels as a witness to God's Glory. Visit his website at DouglasBrown-Author.com.

CPSIA information can be obtained
at www.ICGtesting.com
Printed in the USA
LVHW081520070722
722893LV00012B/210